TWO CAN PLAY AT THIS GAME

Fledgling PI Zachariah Davies's wealthy and eccentric client, toymaker Alton Beacher, wants to hire an investigator who can pose as his boyfriend while figuring out who is behind the recent attempts on his life. And Zach, struggling to save the business his father built, is just desperate enough to set aside his misgivings and take the job.

But it doesn't take long to realize all is not as it seems—and given that it all seems pretty weird, that's saying something. The only person Zach can turn to for help is equally struggling, equally desperate, but a whole lot more experienced rival PI Flint Carey.

Former Marine Flint has been waiting for Zach to throw in the towel and sell whatever's left of the Davies Detective Agency to him. But when the inexperienced accountant-turned-shamus turns to him for help, Flint finds himself unwilling—or maybe unable—to say no.

PUZZLE FOR TWO

Josh Lanyon

VELLICHOR BOOKS
An imprint of JustJoshin Publishing, Inc.

PUZZLE FOR TWO
June 2023
Copyright (c) 2023 by Josh Lanyon
Cover design by James at GoOnWrite
Book design by Kevin Burton Smith
Edited by Jennifer Jacobson
All rights reserved

No part of this book may be reproduced or transmitted in any form or by any means, electronic or mechanical, including photocopying, recording, or by any information storage and retrieval system, without written permission from JustJoshin Publishing, Inc.

Published in the United States of America

JustJoshin Publishing, Inc.
3053 Rancho Vista Blvd.
Suite 116
Palmdale, CA 93551
www.joshlanyon.com

This is a work of fiction. Sadly, any resemblance to persons living or dead is entirely coincidental.

To my Patrons —past and present.

I been openin' doors that I don't have keys to
Looking at the glass that Alice see through
The star to the north tryna find some peace too
The voice in my head says let it lead you

                                                          Carseuss

CHAPTER ONE

Was someone pranking him?

For the first four minutes of his interview with prospective client Alton Beacher, Zach couldn't quite decide.

It was the kind of elaborate joke Ben would find funny, but Ben was not about to invest energy (or money) in making Zach look foolish given that he *already* thought Zach looked like a fool for struggling to keep his dad's PI business afloat. Ben was probably right. Tactless, as usual, but probably right.

Nobody knew the dire financial situation of Davies Detective Agency better than Zachariah Davies, former accountant turned lead investigator.

Turned *only* investigator.

In the midst of these bleak reflections, Alton Beacher's light, slightly affected voice trailed off. The silence that followed was punctuated only by a faint chatter of Davies's receptionist (and Zach's kid sister) Brooke, coming from behind the office door. Judging by the giggles, Brooke was not speaking with another client.

Not least because they didn't *have* any other clients.

He'd spent the last month making new contacts in Monterey County, paying visits to insurance companies, lawyers, the risk-management directors of local municipalities, and anybody else he could think of who might need the services of a private investigator. Eventually, some of that footwork was bound to pay off, but so far *nada*.

Beacher's pale brows drew together in a frown as he waited for some sign of life from Zach.

Zach pulled himself together. He lifted his coffee mug, took a stalling-for-time swallow, said finally, "Let me get this straight. You're hiring me to pose as your boyfriend while I investigate a series of death threats you've received over the past couple of weeks?"

If he sounded skeptical—well, who *wouldn't* sound skeptical? For one thing, Beacher was wearing a gold wedding band. For another, well, this was as far-fetched as anything in those goofy PI novels Zach used to devour as a kid.

No, actually, it was more like something out of a screwball comedy movie from the 1940s. This could *not* be a serious job proposal.

Could it?

Beacher's "Correct," sounded stiff and a little defensive.

"*Really?*"

"Surely, you've run into this kind of situation before? You've been in business twenty years."

Right. Did Beacher actually think Zach had been working as a PI when he was ten years old? Cracking the case of Ms. Gordon's missing *Wall Street Journal* in between Little League practice and mastering common factors and multiples?

In fairness, Davies Detection Agency *had* been around for twenty years. Zach tried to imagine his bluff, gruff ex-cop dad being asked to pose as someone's boyfriend and nearly choked on his coffee.

No question Pop would have said *hard pass* to the Beacher case. Though less politely.

"What made you choose us?"

What Zach really meant was why pick a little indie operation rather than a large security firm with all the bells, whistles, and resources someone as rich as Alton Beacher would presumably expect. But Zach already knew the answer. A big, classy company would laugh Beacher right out of their expensively appointed lobby.

For one fleeting instant, Beacher looked uncomfortable. "To be honest, I was going to try that place at the other end of the shopping center."

Zach set his coffee cup down very carefully. "Carey Confidential?"

Beacher nodded curtly. "But I didn't like the look of the man. Those beady eyes. That sarcastic smile. No."

Oh my God. Zach would have given anything, ANYTHING, to see Alton Beacher ask Flint Carey to be his pretend boyfriend. And the beady-eyes comment? That was pure gold.

But Beacher was right about the sarcastic smile. Flint did have—could have—an unpleasant smile when he thought you were being a bigger ass than usual. His eyes weren't beady, though. They were hazel, that elusive combination of brown-green-gold, and disarmingly long-lashed. *Maybe* a little narrow, especially when he laughed, which admittedly, was rarely.

Zach said gravely, "He's a tough customer, that guy," ignoring the feeling that somewhere, somehow Pop was shaking his head at him.

"Then I saw your sign, and it seemed like a…a…"

"Sign?" Zach offered.

Beacher smiled. "Well, yes."

"The thing of it is, we don't really offer the kind of services you seem to req—"

As if to head him off, Beacher reached into the chest pocket of his abstract squares Patrick James sports shirt and pulled out a money order. He pulled out a second money order and laid it on top of the first. Then a third, a fourth, a fifth…a total of twelve money orders, which he slid across the desk.

Zach adjusted his glasses, glanced down at the amount of the top money order, and then could not look away. It was as if his eyes were magnetized by the figures written in that precise, angular hand.

$1,000.

Twelve money orders for one thousand dollars each.

Twelve. Thousand. Dollars.

He found his voice. "*Now* I'm worried."

Beacher laughed. "Why so? I did my homework. The going rate for a good PI in California is about two hundred dollars an hour. Five hundred if special skills are involved, and I think we can both agree special skills are required for this job. So, for two-plus days' work…I'm sure you can do the math."

Oh yes. If there was one thing Zach was good at, it was doing the math.

"Just to be sure we're on the same page. I'm not a bodyguard."

"I already have a bodyguard."

Really? Where? But Zach wasn't going to argue. "That's probably a good idea."

"I need someone to figure out where these threats are coming from as soon as possible. I don't want to jump to the wrong conclusion."

"I'm flattered you think I can figure out who's behind this in two days, but—"

"I don't think that for a moment. This is simply an advance to cover the weekend at Pebble Beach."

"Right," Zach said blankly. It was possible he'd missed a few details during the initial minutes of their interview, but he was damn sure he hadn't missed *that* detail.

But it was true what they said, money *did* change everything, and it was with renewed attention that he studied his client, sitting unblinking in the blinding glare of California's autumn sun streaming through the tinted office windows.

From the oversize rubber soles of his Alexander McQueen leather sneakers to the snipped tips of his blond classic side sweep, Alton Beacher, the handsome, aggressively Nordic-looking fortysomething owner and CEO of the Beacher Toy Company, exuded money and privilege.

Which was exactly what Zach needed right now.

Money, that is.

Even with the sky-high prices of Ensenada del Sello's commercial real estate, the short stack of money orders lying on his desk would cover their lease for the next three months *and* the tuition of Brooke's junior year of college.

It wasn't the answer to all Zach's problems, but it was the answer to the most pressing.

If it seemed too good to be true, it probably was.

Still. That money

Zach picked up the Cross-Townsend pen he'd bought Pop last Christmas, drew the yellow legal pad his way. "Okay, Mr. Beacher. Let's start with the threats."

"Alton, please." Beacher gave Zach an odd smile. "I imagine we'll have to get used to addressing each other by our first names if our little ruse is going to work."

Zach cleared his throat. "Right." He was no actor, but how hard could it be to feign interest in a guy you weren't all that interested in? Hadn't he managed to do it with Ben for those last six months while he struggled to steel himself to end things? Beacher was not his type, but he was handsome and rich, and maybe Zach would get a couple of nice meals out of their…dates. Pebble Beach for the weekend might even be fun. Maybe?

Nothing he could ever talk about, of course, because the first thing Alton Beacher had done when he walked into Zach's office was have him sign an NDA. That had probably been the point at which Flint's sarcastic smile had appeared.

Anyway, everything was contingent upon how far this *ruse* was supposed to go. If it was supposed to continue into the bedroom, then no.

As hard as it would be to pass up all those thousands of beautiful dollars. No. No way. Like Pop always said, a guy had to be able to face himself in the mirror every morning.

Zach repeated firmly, "About those threats?"

"They started two weeks ago. At first, I didn't make too much of it. Silly jokes or hate mail aren't unknown to a man in my position."

Zach's brows rose as he jotted down this information. It was hard to imagine what hate mail the owner of a toy company would receive. Still, given the current social climate, anyone whose circle of acquaintanceship stretched wider than their immediate family could probably expect to receive hate mail eventually. He'd received a couple of doozies from Ben, though Ben had never threatened him with bodily harm.

"Email or snail mail?" Both could be prosecuted as state or federal crimes. As could threatening phone calls. Funny how many people didn't know that.

"Mail. Post. They always came by post to my home address in the shape of toys."

"Toys?"

"Correct."

"Did you—"

Zach didn't have to complete the question. Beacher opened his leather messenger bag and produced a small gold box, no more than six inches tall, which he set on the desk.

Casting Zach a grim look, Beacher pressed a button, and a flimsy plastic clown sprang from the box, bouncing gently back and forth on springs. The clown held a business card in its tiny mitts. Printed in block letters were the words: YOU ARE DEAD.

Tiny clowns bearing death threats. Because this case wasn't weird enough already.

"Cute." Zach tossed his pen aside, pulled a pair of plastic gloves from the desk drawer—undoubtedly pointless, given that Beacher had handled the toy barehanded how many times? He picked up the little box. "This is how it started?"

The jack-in-the-box was a cheap, mass-produced novelty item manufactured by Old Timey Fun Ltd.

"No." For the first time, Beacher seemed uncomfortable. "The first one was a crossword puzzle. The answer cells were filled in with words like *murder, blood, pain, death, payback*, etc. It was clumsy, lazy. Not a true crossword puzzle. The entries were unkeyed."

"Unkeyed?"

"Unchecked. Uncrossed. The answers didn't intersect."

"Gotcha."

Beacher sighed. "As I said, I get my share of hate mail. I simply assumed someone was being more creative than usual, and tossed both the crossword and the envelope it arrived in."

Zach grimaced, but in fairness, he'd have probably done the same.

"A week later I received a doll's severed head with the eyes gouged out and the hair burned." Beacher propped Exhibit B on Zach's desk. The doll's ripped eye holes seemed to gaze accusingly at Zach. "Then two days ago, the jack-in-the-box arrived. I decided that level of...commitment should perhaps be taken seriously."

"I think you're right about taking this seriously. But why hire a private investigator? Why not go to the police?"

Beacher shook his head. "The police are better at prosecuting than preventing. Wouldn't you agree?"

"Well, not n—"

"I'm a businessman, Zach. I can't afford the scandal of a police investigation. I need someone to handle this quietly, discreetly."

"Sure, but—"

"Besides, there's still the other thing." Beacher raised his eyebrows meaningfully, reminding Zach of the part of this job he was least thrilled about. The part that took the case from weird to wacko.

"Right. The, er, dating game. I couldn't help noticing that you're wearing a wedding ring, Alton."

For the first time Beacher's smile reached his pale-blue eyes, briefly warming them. "Thank you for noticing."

"Um, my pleasure?"

Beacher laughed. "I admit, the idea of hiring an investigator who could also pose as my companion only occurred to me a little while ago."

Zach asked warily, "How little a while ago?"

Beacher shrugged. "When I was sitting in your waiting room, listening to you argue with your former boyfriend."

Zach winced. Their Del Sello Center office space was not just small, the walls were practically see-through. They were definitely hear-through, and had he realized they had a prospective client waiting, he'd have declined to take Ben's call.

"Of course, it's rude to eavesdrop, and I apologize, but I do think our little…charade will work to both our advantages."

Zach opened his mouth, but his gaze fell upon the mutilated face of the severed doll head. He pressed his lips together.

"Granted, I could only hear your side of the conversation, but that was enough to persuade me that you're a patient and...empathetic young man. Too much so, I imagine. I'm neither of those things."

"Good to know."

"It's difficult to explain without making myself sound worse than I am."

Yeah, probably not. It wasn't just about what Zach wanted. He had to think of what was best for Brooke and for his mom as well. This scheme sounded shadier by the second.

He reached to push that little stack of temporary solutions back toward Beacher, but Beacher covered his hand with his own.

He said quietly, "Please hear me out."

Zach stared down at the well-shaped hand gripping his own with surprising strength. Beacher's nails were trimmed and buffed, his palm soft and well-cared for. A platinum Rolex gleamed on his tanned wrist.

Zach withdrew his hand, sitting back in his chair. "I'm listening."

Beacher's pale gaze bored into him. "I want desperately, *desperately* to divorce my wife. But it's complicated."

It always was, as Zach, working in an industry where more than fifty percent of the business had to do with divorce and marital discord, could have told him.

"Zora is truly...unstable. For years she's accused me of having affairs with other women and done her best to punish me accordingly."

"Have you had affairs?" Zach wasn't judging. He just needed to know the score.

"No. I've never been unfaithful. Frankly, I wouldn't dare. I *have* been *miserably* unhappy. As has Zora. That's the most ridiculous part of this. She's an unhappy as I am. I honestly believe she hates me. But anytime I try to bring up the topic of divorce, she threatens to destroy me. Destroy me personally and financially."

"Does she have the power to do that? Destroy you financially, I mean."

"Unfortunately, yes. When I first started out, I was broke. I had no capital. Zora's family invested heavily in my company. And profited accordingly, I might add. I've tried many times through the years to buy Zora out, but she won't sell. She wants that hold over me. I think she'd prefer to bankrupt us both rather than allow me my freedom."

"I see."

Beacher's sigh spoke volumes. "That's not even the worst of it. She's also threatened numerous times to kill herself if I leave her. Kill herself in such a way that I'm framed for her murder."

Zach blinked. "That's…pretty extreme."

"Zora is the definition of extreme. And no wonder. The whole family, the Kaschak clan, are certifiable. Believe me when I say this is no idle threat on Zora's part. You'll understand when—if—you read the dossier I've compiled. Anyway, when I was sitting in your lobby, it suddenly came to me. If I were to come out as gay, everything would be different."

"Would it, though?"

Beacher leaned forward in his eagerness, and Zach had to stop himself from rolling his chair backward. It wasn't that Beacher was unattractive, but something about the guy...

Possibly the whole pretend-to-be-my-boyfriend-to-decoy my maybe-suicidal-wife thing?

"*Yes*. Yes. Zora is very insecure and competitive. She can't bear the idea of losing me to another woman. But losing to a man? That's not about *her*. That's about me."

"She's still short a husband."

"Yes. But it's a loss her ego can survive."

Zach nodded, though he wasn't convinced by Beacher's reasoning. Granted, Beacher knew Mrs. Beacher and Zach did not.

He had to ask. "*Are* you gay?"

Beacher got a funny expression. He licked his lips as though his mouth was suddenly dry.

"I..."

"Forgive me if this feels intrusive, but what I mean is, would there be any truth to this...scenario? Have you had gay relationships in the past?"

A tiny, barely perceptible wince from Beacher. "No. Not yet, at any rate. As I said, I wouldn't have dreamed of being unfaithful. But that doesn't mean..."

Zach waited, but Beacher didn't finish his thought.

Finally, Zach said, "Of course not. I really only bring it up because, well, if your plan is to succeed, we'd—*you'd*—have to be convincing in your role."

Beacher smiled a slow, strange smile that sent a little frisson of unease rippling down Zach's spine. Beacher's light gaze studied Zach's face, dropped as if to assess the width of his shoulders, the breadth of his chest, and though Zach was seated behind a very sturdy desk, he had the uncomfortable sensation of being stripped naked and assessed from head to foot.

He was not shy nor insecure about his looks, but that kind of auction-block appraisal wasn't a pleasant feeling.

Beacher continued to smirk in that troubling way, saying lightly, "No need to worry. *That* won't be a problem."

CHAPTER TWO

"What was *that* about?" Brooke stared at Zach as the heavy glass door swung shut behind Alton Beacher.

Zach watched Beacher lope across the parking lot and climb into a black Porsche Boxster parked diagonally across two spaces. Two seconds later, the Porsche glided silently away on its ultra-high-performance radials, cutting off both an SUV and a minivan as it progressed out of the parking lot.

"That's our new client."

"Alton Beacher hired *us*?"

Zach, smiling ruefully, glanced at Brooke. It wasn't like looking into a mirror or anything, but there was a strong family resemblance. They were both tall and lanky. Both had their mom's wavy, chestnut hair and lousy eyesight, their dad's blue eyes and stubborn chin, and a smattering of Grandpa Lake's freckles across the bridge of their noses. The freckles were adorable on Brooke. On Zach? Nobody took a boyish accountant seriously. Let alone a PI who could have passed for one of the Hardy Boys.

"I'm on my way to deposit the twelve grand he just paid us for a weekend's work."

Brooke's eyes widened. "Who do we have to kill?"

"Nobody. We have to keep someone from killing *him*."

"Uh, that might be a little above our pay grade."

"Not anymore." Zach waved the short but satisfyingly thick stack of money orders.

Brooke's brows shot up. "Money orders? Who's he worried about snooping through his check book?"

Zach grinned. "Very good."

"I know. I'm wasted behind this desk."

"Well, you won't be behind the desk much longer. These guarantee you can head back to school this fall."

Brooke looked pained. "Yeah, Zee, about that."

Zach shook his head. "You're going back to school. That's what Pop wanted."

"What about what I want? I wasn't sold on being a business major when Pop was still here to disappoint. Now that he's gone—will you *please* stop shaking your head at me?"

Zach stopped shaking his head, but his expression must have said it all.

Brooke muttered, "Never mind. How long will you be gone? I'm supposed to meet Pepper for lunch."

"I'm going to deposit this and be right back. Ten minutes at most."

She nodded, then turned back to her computer monitor.

Zach pushed open the door, then stopped. He let the door fall back into place, glanced back at his sister, who was tapping the antiquated keyboard with short, sharp *clicks* like an under-siege telegraph operator sending out an SOS.

He sighed inwardly.

Twenty-three was *so* young. Too young to realize just how young you were. Too young to know what you really wanted. Let alone what you really needed. But technically, *legally*, Brooke was an adult. He couldn't force her to do anything she didn't want to do. He didn't *want* to force her to do anything she didn't want to do. He especially didn't want to browbeat her into training for a career that bored her even before she'd accepted her first job offer.

He spoke to the irrepressible bounce of her ponytail. "Hey."

"Hey."

"Beacher compiled a dossier on the people he thinks are most likely to have a grudge against him. I left it sitting on my desk."

Brooke continued to stare at the screen of her monitor. She said shortly, "Don't worry. I'll put it away for you."

"Actually, would you want to read through it? We can compare notes."

His reward was the bright smile she gave him as she swiveled her chair around. "I can do that!"

"Back in ten," Zach promised, and pushed out into the bright autumn morning.

While there were obvious disadvantages to being a private eye located in a shopping center—and worse, sharing the limited possibilities of that real estate with another PI—there were advantages, too.

For example, the large, chain grocery store that anchored the smaller shops and businesses of the Del Sello Center made it very convenient to pick up a carton of half-and-half for the office fridge. Or grab a frozen dinner on the way home. There was a dry cleaner and a Starbucks inside the grocery store, as well as a mini-branch of Del Sello Savings and Loan.

Zach strode through the market's sliding glass doors and headed straight for the short queue at the bank desk.

If there was any problem with depositing those money orders, he needed to know ASAP. But also, having that amount of (essentially) cash lying around the office made him very nervous.

It was a relief when he stepped up to the counter and handed the stack of money orders to pert, pretty Mary Anne Spenser.

Mary Anne took the bills, flicked through them, and her eyes nearly popped out of her head. "I guess you finally sold the business?"

"Ha-ha."

Mary Anne giggled. She had gone to high school with Brooke, and once upon a time had quite the crush on Zach. "How did you want this? Unmarked dollar bills in a paper sack?"

"Remind me when you're playing the comedy club again?"

Another giggle. "I'm just teasing you, Zee. Business must be looking up. That's great."

"Yeah. Well." The news of their windfall would be all over the valley before the end of the day, but as gossip went, it wasn't the worst that could be spread about them. It might even do some good. With Pop gone, even longtime clients were leery about placing their confidential business in the hands of the firm's accountant and his kid sister.

Mr. Martinez, the bank manager, wandered up to say hello, and Mary Anne was instantly all business. Zach and Mr. Martinez chatted briefly. Mary Anne asked Zach if he wanted any cash, Zach asked for one hundred dollars in twenties and, tucking the crisp bills in his wallet, left the queue.

He was hugely relieved to have safely disposed of—er, deposited those funds. Granted, now Davies Detective Agency had to *earn* that generous fee. He was a little vague on some of the details there. Not least because he was pretty sure he did not have all the details or even *half* the details.

Still. Eleven thousand nine hundred dollars in their business checking account went a long way toward soothing his doubts.

He'd been heading for the market exit, but since he was right there, why not grab a sandwich from the deli counter? Zach wheeled around—and walked straight into a briskly moving grocery cart.

"*OOF.*"

He staggered back a step or two, and the glass doors shot open and then noisily closed. He was more embarrassed than hurt. The collision seemed unreasonably noisy—the cart rattling like a train coming off the rails, the bottles and cans in the cart clinking and clanking alarmingly, and the conductor, well, driver of the cart, saying in a loud, exasperated voice, "What the hell do you call that maneuver?"

Zach's wince had nothing to do with the bumper of the cart's lower tray hitting his lower shins.

Flint Carey. Carey Confidential himself.

In the flesh.

Well, no. Thank God not in the flesh. In Levi's, a black-and-white floral Hawaiian shirt, and white PUMA Easy Riders. Because he'd apparently learned how to dress for success by watching reruns of the original *Magnum PI*.

Rubbing his shins, Zach muttered, "Second thoughts."

Flint leaned on the handlebar of the cart, seeming to enjoy the moment. "You're supposed to signal when you change lanes."

"I know. Sorry. I was…"

"Fleeing?"

Zach straightened and glared. It was true that over the past week he'd been trying to avoid running into Flint, but he'd figured his efforts were more subtle than that.

"Of course not. I didn't even know you were in here"—he glanced at the beer bottles in the cart— "buying your lunch."

Flint's thin mouth curled into what Alton Beacher had called his "sarcastic smile."

"I thought you accountant types lived for your three-martini lunches."

Well, there was another *OOF*. Only that one struck home. Flint knew Zach had worked his ass off to get his PI license. And Flint knew how much Pop had been against that very thing.

Zach summoned an equally sarcastic smile. "See? You're not as good a detective as you imagine."

Flint's eyes narrowed. He drawled, "L-O-L," actually spelling it out in a dry, derisive tone. "At least I can recognize a lost cause when I see one."

Was that supposed to be funny? Or were they really going to do this here and now?

Judging by Flint's unrelenting expression, it seemed they were.

Zach retorted, "Good, because we're not selling."

"It's my last offer." Flint was no longer making a pretense at joking, and neither was Zach.

Zach repeated, "Good, because we're not selling." He hadn't wanted to have this conversation at all, let alone in the middle of what amounted to the town center, but leave it to Flint, who had all the tact and finesse of a blunt instrument.

But as he answered, Zach realized he was not being held at gunpoint. He could simply escape this awkward situation by walking away. Sure, it was rude, but rude was Flint's native language. Accordingly, Zach nodded curtly on what he figured was a pretty good exit line, turned, and went out through the sliding glass doors.

Unfortunately, Flint was also not being held at gunpoint. He abandoned his cart and followed Zach onto the sidewalk outside the market.

"I don't understand you. I'm making you a good offer."

"It's a decent offer." Zach wasn't going to deny it.

"It's more than decent. More than I can afford, frankly."

Zach couldn't help a snide, "I believe it."

Flint's eyes narrowed again, like he was lining up a sniper's scope. "It's also more than that business is worth."

Maybe Zach deserved that one. "It's not about the money."

Flint sputtered, "It-it's not about the money? This is business. What the hell else would it be about?"

"It's our *family* business. It's..." Hard to explain. Hard to explain to someone like Flint, who didn't look like he had a sentimental bone in his body.

His lean, muscular body that always made Zach feel like he needed to work out more. A lot more. Like his clothes were too big for him or too small for him or something. Flint was actually a hair shorter, yet Zach always felt like Flint towered over him with his irritatingly broad shoulders and pronounced biceps.

"I don't follow you," Flint said. "You know as well as I do that Fred didn't want you to be a field op. He spent a fortune sending you to college so you could be an accountant."

"I don't *want* to be an accountant!"

Okay. *That* was embarrassing. That was a—loud—call back to when he'd been Brooke's age. Of course, the circumstances were different. Zach cast a quick, sheepish look around, but the people rolling their carts in and out of the market paid them no attention. The drivers in the cars flashing past in their never-ending circles of the parking lot had eyes for nothing but potential empty spaces.

"But that's what you are." Flint was inexorable. "That's what you trained for. You can't just...just pick up and become a PI on a whim."

"It's not a whim! I've wanted this for years." He stopped himself right there because A—it was none of Flint's business, and B—this was painful territory.

"It's not what Fred wanted. Fred planned on selling me the business when he retired."

Maybe. Probably.

"Well, he didn't retire," Zach clipped out.

Flint's hard expression changed almost imperceptibly. "I know, and I'm sorry. I really am. Your dad and I were rivals, but it was a friendly rivalry. I had a lot of respect for the guy."

Zach nodded tersely. Every single thing Flint said was true. He knew it. Flint knew it. It didn't make it hurt any less. But more to the point, his dad was gone, and as painful as that was—too painful to stand here casually discussing with Flint—it changed everything.

"Here's what's going to happen," Flint said. "In your enthusiastic inexperience, you're going to run what's left of Fred's business into the ground. And then you'll end up going back to being an accountant for some high-powered firm, just like your dad wanted. Only instead of having a nice little nest egg for your mother and sister, you'll be shit out of luck because this is *my last offer.*"

"You already said that."

Flint looked genuinely baffled. "I don't get it. You're a smart guy. An educated guy. No one's going to offer you more. No one's going to offer you *anything.*"

Zach struggled with himself. Maybe he *was* being too impulsive, too sentimental about this. Flint was right about no one offering more. In fact, the real question was why did Flint want their client list so badly when his was the more successful firm?

He let out a long breath, straightened his shoulders. "Okay. Listen. Our new client advanced us enough to see us through the next couple of months. I want my shot at running this business. I got my PI license *before* Pop died. It's something I've been thinking of for a long time. So if in three months, you're still interested—"

"What new client?"

"What does it matter? We have a client."

Flint stared at him. *"Alton Beacher?"*

"I'm not at liberty—"

Flint gave a disbelieving laugh. "Are you *nuts*?"

Zach's heart sank. Flint's tone was not the tone of someone regretting he hadn't landed a lucrative contract. And so much for Beacher's story of coming up with his preposterous scenario while eavesdropping in the front lobby. It was pretty clear from the expression on Flint's face that Beacher had tried to run the same crazy idea past him.

He said defensively, "It's twelve grand in the bank."

Flint's lip curled. "Yeah? Well, you come cheap."

Zach felt himself turning red and then white. He was not about to violate his NDA *or* explain himself to Flint. Not least because that sardonic gleam in Flint's eyes made it clear he wasn't buying it. Any of it. And maybe Flint's reaction was the right one. The normal one. The reaction of someone who wasn't so desperate they'd do almost anything, even if it was something that went against their own best instincts.

He pulled himself together, said tersely, "Go to hell."

As he turned and walked away, he could hear Flint laughing behind him.

CHAPTER THREE

"**I**'d almost forgotten what that stuff looked like," Brooke joked as Zach replaced the long gone fifty dollars in the petty-cash drawer. "It's so green when it's freshly picked!"

Zach grunted acknowledgment, handed twenty-five of the remaining cash to her. "For the mailing supplies you paid for last week."

"Thanks!" Brooke tucked the bills into her magician's bag of a purse. Despite the fact that her purse didn't look like it had room for more than a credit card and her phone, she was constantly shoving things inside or whipping things out with Felix The Cat alacrity. She glanced at him, glanced at him again. "Are you okay?"

"Hm?" Zach threw her a distracted glance.

"You look a little…rattled."

"Rattled?" Zach shook his head. "Nope. Not me." He picked up the dossier from her desk, flipping through it. "What do you think?"

"That you ran into Flint." Her tone was sympathetic.

"Huh? *No.* I mean, yes. But it has nothing to do with Flint."

"What does? Doesn't?"

Zach gazed at her, baffled. "What are we talking about?"

Brooke shrugged. "Beats me."

"Did anything jump out at you when you looked through the file?"

"Literally? No."

Zach gave her a long, steady look, and Brooke grinned. "I do wonder what kind of person puts together a dossier on his friends and family."

"The kind of person friends and family want to kill?"

"Maybe. He has a reputation for being eccentric."

"Nothing that's happened so far makes me think that rep isn't justified."

Brooke cooed, "And yet you still fell in love with him!" At Zach's glare, she admitted, "Okay, yes. I did hear more than I let on. You know how thin these walls are. You'll be lucky if Mr. Yen next door didn't hear the whole scheme over the dumpling steamers."

"That was *very* unprofessional," Zach said crushingly.

Brooke was uncrushed. "I don't see how. We're in the snooper business. You have to assume everyone in this office is practicing their tradecraft at all times."

"Everyone meaning *you*?"

"Until we're in position to hire another operative." She kept talking as he opened his mouth to object. "*Anyway*, it's not like you could keep that part secret from me."

Probably not, but he'd sure planned on trying. Especially after Flint's scathing reaction. He still felt hot with embarrassment at the memory.

Brooke's thoughts were running in a different direction. "My money's on the wife. *Cherchez la femme.*"

"Yeah, well, that's not much of a leap, given her threats to destroy him personally and professionally *and/or* kill herself and frame him for her murder."

"It's a little extra," Brooke agreed. "But you know who she is, right?"

Zach admitted, "At this point, you probably know more about our suspects than I do."

"Zora *Kaschak*-Beacher. Zora *Kaschak*."

"Is that someone from *People* magazine?" Brooke was an inveterate *People* magazine reader. She also claimed to be Army, whatever the hell that was, and seemed to communicate with her comrades almost solely through hashtags and gifs. Which was just one reason why Zach was secretly dubious about Pop's plans for her to become a human-resources manager. He wasn't convinced she was entirely human. Surely somewhere in outer space an alien civilization was scouring the volcanic plains for one of their Army?

"The Kaschak family owns the Haunted Hollow Theme Park chain. Zora's the sole heir to a multimillion-dollar empire."

"With inflation, that doesn't mean what it used to." But Zach flipped back to the file pages on Zora. The photo at the top of the page (Alton was nothing if not thorough) showed a pale, washed-out-looking woman with fair hair and light-brown eyes. Her face was round and colorless. Nondescript. Someone who could easily blend into a crowd. Except, according to the file, she was an independently wealthy fifty-seven-year-old agoraphobe, so blending into crowds was probably not her thing. Supposedly, she had not left the family estate in over a decade.

Could staring at the same four walls for ten years drive you to suicide?

Brooke was saying, "Didn't you ever go to Haunted Hollow with your friends?"

"Sure. High school grad night."

"I didn't know they were around back then!"

There were only six years between them, but sometimes it did feel like he was of a different generation. Zach sighed. "What it is to have a straight man."

"Sidekick," Brooke corrected.

Zach ignored that, continuing to read over Zora's details. She was about a decade older than her husband. And a lot wealthier.

At one time, the Kaschak amusement park empire had been worth nearly a billion dollars, but the family fortunes had fallen—all things being relative—to a mere three hundred million-ish. Was that somehow a factor in Alton's decision to, er, uncouple? Zora was still worth a lot more money than her husband.

He said slowly, "Honestly, on paper at least, it looks like if anyone's life is really in danger, Zora's the more likely victim."

Brooke's brows drew together. "You mean, Alton might be setting up—"

She broke off as the door flew open and Pepper Martini breezed in.

"Ready to go?"

"Am I ever!"

Pepper was a short, curvy blonde: the Jeff to Brooke's Mutt. The pair of them had been BFFs since second grade, meaning she viewed Zach—when she noticed him at all—as a necessary evil. "Hey, Zee."

"Hey." Zach nodded hello.

Brooke, postage-stamp-bag in hand, was already out from behind the desk and heading for the door.

"Have a nice—"

The glass door *voomped* shut on the rest of his comment, Brooke and Pepper talking animatedly and laughing as they passed the front windows and crossed the parking lot, where Pepper's red Kia Stinger was parked.

Zach sighed, watching them. Then he poured himself a cup of coffee and carried the Beacher dossier into his office.

His stomach was growling as he settled at his desk, and he regretted letting Flint chase him off before he'd grabbed something to eat from the deli counter. Ben had his faults, but he had packed a mean brown bag lunch. However, just as man could not live on love alone, neither could he live on lunch alone. Or even three-square meals alone.

Anyway.

Zach flipped open the file and resumed reading.

There was a lot of information to absorb.

And a lot of information missing. For example, no financials on the Beacher Toy Company or the Beacher family. No information on insurance policies or prenuptial agreements. No employment records for those working on the Beacher estate or at Beacher's company. No family background on Alton and very little on Zora. Did they have children? Siblings? Parents? Did they have friends? Did they know anyone outside this skinny file folder? It sure didn't look like it.

Was that because Alton was convinced he'd already identified the culprit?

Probably. You couldn't—shouldn't—make assumptions based on first impressions, but Alton did not seem like someone prone to second-guessing himself. He'd painted a portrait of a mentally and emotionally unstable woman capable of just about anything. If that was an accurate picture of the situation, he was right to be concerned. There was clearly animosity on both sides—and maybe it was justified on both sides. According to Pop, who probably knew better than most, the most difficult relationship to understand from the outside was marriage.

However, either in an attempt to appear objective or because Alton was a stickler for details, he had supplied one alternate suspect: Ronald (Rusty) Jordan. Jordan was listed as a friend, but he was also clearly a competitor. He owned Old Timey Fun Ltd.

Zach's gaze zeroed automatically on the jack-in-the-box sitting on the edge of his desk.

He considered the tiny black bead eyes and the miniature felt hands glued to the card printed with the words YOU ARE DEAD. Not subtle, for sure. But would Jordan really send death threats via his own merchandise?

Pretty unlikely, unless the whole point was for Alton to know the threats were from his rival. Even then, wouldn't there be a less incriminating way for Jordan to get his point across?

It seemed most likely that using toys produced by Old Timey Fun Ltd. was more about throwing dust. Or maybe it was just about expediency.

Unless Jordan was using his own merchandise to create the illusion that someone else was trying to make him look guilty?

Sure. But were Jordan and Alton *really* competitors? Beacher's Toy Company crafted beautiful handmade retro-style toys. Whereas Old Timey Fun Ltd. specialized in drowning the market with cheap, mass-produced junk not intended to give more than a few minutes' amusement. These captains of industry had to be targeting two completely separate market shares.

There was a third suspect, though Alton had not included his younger brother, Ransford, in his dossier. Ransford was only mentioned in passing as Alton built his somewhat halfhearted case against Rusty Jordan. According to Alton, Ransford had accused Jordan of dissolving his company, Pacific Playhouse, after a bankruptcy acquisition.

From Alton's perspective, this accusation strengthened the case against Jordan. From Zach's perspective, Ransford was financially pressed, inclined to blame others for his problems, and, very possibly, in Alton's will.

So, three potential suspects to start with—and a whole lot of legwork ahead. Zach smiled contentedly, glancing at the signed contract still lying on his desk. His first real case. And already profitable before he'd even put in his first day's work.

There was just one little cloud on the sunny horizon, and that was the fake-boyfriend charade. His face burned again at the recollection of Flint's derisive *you come cheap.*

Not that he really gave a damn what Flint thought. Well, he *already* knew what Flint thought: that it was amateur hour over at Davies Detective Agency. That Zach needed to wake up and sell whatever was left of the business's assets while there were assets left to sell.

It wasn't as if Carey Confidential was in such great financial shape either. But at least Flint knew what he was doing.

Okay. Stop.

Zach had been working alongside Pop in various capacities for nearly a decade. He had experience, knew how the business worked. He had his PI license. He wasn't a complete novice, regardless of what Flint believed.

Regardless of what Flint, Pop, his mother, Ben…

Frankly, everyone but Brooke believed he was out of his mind. And the fact that Brooke was behind him one hundred percent should probably be the most discouraging reflection.

Whatever. When he thought of that beautiful eleven thousand nine hundred dollars sitting in Davies Detective Agency's business checking account, he felt calm and confident in a way he hadn't since…since that terrible Sunday afternoon when Pop, who'd never taken a sick day in his life (not including getting shot in the line of duty) had dropped dead mowing the front yard.

Something he really, *truly* did not want to think about.

Besides, that money was just the *advance* on the weekend at Pebble Beach. Let's say the case took a week—which was pretty optimistic, but still. Seven days at five hundred bucks an hour?

Granted, first he had to get through that weekend, and that was where his stomach knotted up and his doubts set in.

Thank God he didn't have to try and explain any of this to Ben.

Ben had been against pretty much every professional decision Zach had made ever since he'd left his first accounting job with Kaufman & Cohen, CPA, APC, to work for Pop, and Zach's decision to try to keep the agency going after Pop had passed had been the final straw for Ben. Ben had given Zach an ultimatum, which Zach had, frankly, been secretly relieved to reject.

Yes, it had been a *relief* to have a legitimate reason to end things. To not have to be the bad guy in anyone's eyes but Ben's.

Ben had tried to back down, but no way was Zach willingly stepping back into what had increasingly felt less like a relationship and more like a cage. That bird had flown.

However, there were still potential problems.

Ben had the troubling habit of showing up in unexpected (and inevitably public) places to try and "win" Zach back. Meaning, coerce, coax, debate and, when all that failed, berate Zach into resuming their relationship.

Alton Beacher would probably not take kindly to public scenes.

And previously quiet, mild-mannered Ben had become better and better at making scenes in public.

But then, for a control freak like Ben, this situation had to be hell, and as exasperated as Zach was, he couldn't help feeling a little sorry for his ex. He had no wish to hurt Ben any more than he already had by walking out, and seeing Zach in a "relationship" with Alton Beacher would certainly hurt.

Luckily, Ben wasn't any more into golf than Zach was, so the chances of him showing up at Pebble Beach were slim.

A noise from the lobby interrupted Zach's thoughts.

Had he locked the front door after Brooke and Pepper left for lunch? He suspected he hadn't. Had Ben decided to drop by for another chat?

God.

He set the file aside, half rose—stopping as a familiar voice called with a trace of impatience, "Anyone here?"

Flint.

That was a surprise, and a welcome surprise at that. He much preferred arguing with Flint to bickering with Ben.

"In here." Zach headed for the lobby and walked straight into Flint, who apparently took *in here* as an invitation.

"*OWW*," said Flint. More noisily than strictly necessary.

Zach's, "Ouch," was pointedly dignified.

They hastily backed up like dueling Roombas encountering unexpected obstacles.

"*This* is what I'm talking about!" Flint's tone was accusatory. His hazel eyes were narrowed and his cheeks a little red. He did not like being caught off-balance, literally or metaphorically.

"What is?"

"Are you open or not?"

"You didn't have to pick the lock, did you? So, we're open." What was it about Flint that automatically brought out the smart-ass in Zach? He was usually a very amiable guy.

Predictably, Flint retorted, "The problem is, running a business is about more than door hardware. If you're closed for lunch, you need a sign on the door."

Oh, right. Zach was just responding in kind. He said with strained courtesy, "We're not. Did you have some reason for dropping by? I know how busy you are." He couldn't help adding, "Turning down lucrative cases."

Flint's eyes grew slitty, but then, surprisingly, he said, "I wanted to apologize for that…for the crack earlier."

The crack?

"*Oh*." That took the wind out of Zach's sails. He had been trying to convince himself that the *you-come-cheap* comment hadn't bothered him, but the realization that Flint, of all people, felt it warranted an apology almost made it worse.

He shrugged. "You're entitled to your opinion."

"Yep. I am. And I think taking on Alton Beacher as a client is a big mistake. But…that was out of line. I'm sorry."

"It's fine. Apology accepted."

Flint continued to gaze at him in that half irritated, half troubled way. Zach, already made uncomfortable by Flint's apology, felt even more uneasy.

Flint began, "I know it's none of my business—"

"No, it's not," Zach interrupted. "Besides, what's left to say? You think I shouldn't have taken the case. Well, I'm not crazy about this situation either. But I don't have a choice. I can't pick and choose our clients. If I can get this resolved, we'll have enough capital to see us through the next few months. Plus, if Beacher's satisfied, it could mean more clients and more business."

Flint shook his head. "Fred would not be okay with this. You know that, Zachariah."

Flint must have addressed him by his first name before, but Zach couldn't remember it, and he felt an odd flicker of…something…at hearing Flint pronounce *Zachariah*. As if Flint too found those four syllables unexpectedly difficult, tricky, foreign.

"Really? You're going to drag my dad into this? Do you even *know* the full details of the case?" When Flint hesitated, Zach said hotly, "No, you don't. You're making assumptions. You're jumping to conclusions. You don't have all the facts."

"Neither do you, I bet. Anyway, I heard enough. When you've been doing this as long as I have, you get an instinct."

"Oh my God." Zach stared ceilingward. "Spare me the Sam Spade routine."

Flint stopped talking, pressed his lips together. His eyes had narrowed to slits again.

"Look, I think you mean well. I really do," Zach said. "But I also think you're overestimating the complexities of the case. And you're *under*estimating me."

That was equal parts defiance, worry, and bravado because with every terse word out of Flint's mouth, he was undermining Zach's confidence. Zach too had an instinct that he might have taken a wrong turn somewhere, and if he was ignoring his *own* instincts, he sure as hell wasn't going to rely on Flint's.

Flint studied him for a long moment. He smiled a smile guaranteed to frost sunflowers on the hottest summer's day, and said gently, "Well, you know best."

CHAPTER FOUR

Ben was waiting when Zach got home that night.

Waiting *inside* the house, to be precise. And to be *more* precise, sitting on Zach's recently purchased black plaid sofa, stroking Mr. Bigglesworth.

Ben was Zach's age. Slim, medium height, with curly, dark hair and wide green eyes and dimples—although it had been a long time since Zach had seen Ben's dimples. There were no dimples in sight that evening, though Ben was smiling smugly.

"Well, this is a little creepy," Zach replied in answer to that smile.

He was trying to play it cool, but he was genuinely shocked. Ben was the most law-abiding person he knew, so this foray into criminal trespass was as out-of-character as it was unwelcome.

Ben's smile faded, and he flushed. "It's not creepy when it's *me*."

That's what all the creeps think. Zach didn't say that, though. Ben's flushed face did not match his defiant words. Besides, Ben wasn't a creep, really. He was just…

"I'm not a creep," Ben said. "Your mom suggested I drop by. If you won't talk to me, what am I supposed to do?"

That was equal parts reassuring and upsetting. Because, yes, Zach's mother probably had given Ben this idea. She was Team Ben all the way and believed Zach was making yet another major life mistake in letting Ben go.

"How did you get in?"

There was a hint of criticism in Ben's, "Spare key in the barbecue grill. Same place you always hide your spare key."

Not after this. But Zach didn't say that either. Instead, despite the fact that it was late and he was tired and still had to pack for tomorrow's trip to Pebble Beach, he strained to be reasonable, to remember that once upon a time he'd envisioned spending the rest of his life with Ben.

"I'm not sure what the point of this is, Ben. We *have* been talking. We were talking this morning when you hung up on me. Every conversation ends in an argument."

"Because you're not listening!" Mr. Bigglesworth began to wriggle, and Ben released him. The lavender sphynx leaped away, coming to greet Zach with plaintive meows.

Zach picked Mr. Bigglesworth up, and the cat bumped his funny little triangular face to Zach's chin, rubbing back and forth in noisy greeting. Zach smiled. He gently nose-bumped Mr. B. in return.

Everybody needed a little unconditional love in their life.

"Hey, Mr. B. I missed you, too." He sighed inwardly and said to Ben, "Let me feed Mr. B. and then we can—"

"I already fed him," Ben said.

"Oh."

That was very thoughtful. Very...Ben. It was unreasonable for Zach to be instantly irritated by Ben's thoughtfulness. Right? Why should Mr. Bigglesworth have to go hungry when Ben was right there, lurking in Zach's house, ready and willing to dish up the Smalls fresh cat food on demand?

He swallowed his annoyance, moved to the room's only chair, and sank into it, still cuddling Mr. Bigglesworth. "Okay. I'm listening. You have my full and undivided attention."

Ben frowned. "You're not going to pour yourself a drink or anything?"

"Ben—"

"I feel like you're holding a stopwatch on me!"

Zach closed his eyes. For one really weird second, he actually struggled with tears.

He was trying so hard. He really was. Trying to do the right thing. Trying not to hurt anyone. Trying not to disappoint anyone. It was overwhelming to know he was failing at all of it. He was hurting Ben. He was disappointing Ben, his mother, probably his father, Mr. Bigglesworth... Hell, he was probably disappointing the rival PI on the other side of the shopping center. He had taken on a job he was uneasy about and which he probably wasn't equipped for, a job which involved another person's health and safety. He had ended a stable relationship with someone who loved him. He was going against his dad's wishes; he *missed* his dad—

Buck up, kid. Tough times make tough people.

Zach drew in a sharp breath. He could hear Pop's gruff voice as clearly as if his father stood over him. He pulled himself together and opened his eyes.

"I'm not timing you. I'm listening to everything you have to say without any distractions."

"Because your mind's already made up," Ben said bitterly.

Zach began to regret not having that drink. "If you think that, why are you here?"

Ben jumped to his feet as if he couldn't contain himself a moment longer. "Because I don't understand! *I gave in to you*. I was willing to go along with everything you wanted, even though everything you wanted wasn't the plan. Wasn't what we planned for our life *together*."

Zach rose too, dislodging Mr. Bigglesworth, who scrambled away to crouch in the corner of the chair, watching them warily. There had been a time they never raised their voices with each other. But that time had passed.

"*This* is the problem, right here. You haven't been listening. From the time we were in college, I said I wanted to go into business with my dad."

"Your dad didn't *want* you to go into business with him!"

"*It's* my *life. I get some say in it!*" Zach shouted.

The volume, and the emotion fueling it, startled them both into silence.

It wasn't even true, what Ben had said. Zach's father hadn't wanted him to throw away better job opportunities, sure, but he'd been delighted when Zach had come onboard to manage Davies Detective Agency's finances. Had he wanted his son working as an investigator? No. He'd firmly believed Zach was meant for bigger and better things. Like a CFA or a CMA.

Ben recovered first. "Which is why I've agreed. To everything."

"*Grudgingly.*"

"Yes. Grudgingly. Because you're making a mistake. *I* think you're making a mistake. This was not the plan. This was not *our* plan. What am I supposed to do? Keep quiet when I think you're wrong?"

"Maybe? I don't know. What I do know is I don't want—I don't want to feel like I'm in the wrong all the time, which is how you make me feel. I don't want to feel like you're waiting—hoping—I'm going to fail. And I don't want to keep having to hear *I told you so* every time something goes wrong."

Ben's green eyes were bright with anger. "That's on you, Zach. I'm already bending over backward to accommodate you. You can't also expect stoic silence when you're trampling over everything we were working toward."

This was how all his attempts to talk to Ben went. No matter how determined they both were to keep their conversations low key and reasonable, they went from zero to sixty within the first five comments. There was just so much pent-up resentment on both sides. So much frustration with each other. And, on Ben's side, so much anger.

Zach sighed wearily. "I don't want my parents' marriage."

"That's a shitty thing to say! Your mom is a saint. The things she had to put up with!"

Ben did not have a great relationship with his own parents. In fact, he pretty much had no relationship. Understandably, he had grown attached to Zach's family, and that was great. That was fine with Zach. Especially since his mom said she was choosing Ben in the custody battle. He was pretty sure she wasn't kidding either.

Zach said patiently, "What I mean is, my parents weren't happy together. They stayed together for me and Brooke. Because they believed that was the right thing to do. They felt they didn't have a choice. We *have* a choice. And I'm choosing happiness."

"We were perfectly happy together until your dad died and you got this idi—idea that you would run the agency on your own. So if that's what you're trying to tell yourself now, it's just an excuse for bailing on *us*."

This was why it was pointless, if not an actual mistake, to keep trying to talk this out with Ben. There was no talking out *I don't love you anymore. I don't want to be with you anymore.* There was no good way to tell someone that. And with each conversation, the animosity and hard feelings grew, solidified.

But Zach kept trying, saying earnestly, "People change. That's all I'm saying. I think we *both* deserve to be happy. And I think we—"

Ben broke in, "Is there someone else? Is that what this is about? You keep saying no, but I have to wonder."

"No, of course not." As the words left his mouth, Zach remembered he was about to spend the next few days, if not weeks, pretending to be Alton Beacher's boyfriend.

If he and Ben had still been together, he would have had to explain what was going on. It went through his mind that, even though they weren't together, it might be a good idea to warn Ben. Except he wasn't sure he could trust Ben to keep that information to himself. Ben was so angry and emotional these days. But if he didn't warn Ben, and Ben somehow caught wind of Zach's supposed relationship...

His expression must have revealed some of his uncertainty because Ben's eyes narrowed. He demanded, "Wait. *Are* you seeing someone?"

"*No.* Ben. Come on."

Ben's expression only grew harder and more suspicious. "But you're *interested* in someone? That's it. Who? Is it Flint Carey?"

"*Flint?*" Zach goggled with genuine amazement. "Flint Carey? That-that wannabe Magnum PI? Are you serious?"

"I notice you're not answering."

"I'm not interested in Flint Carey. No way. I can't think of anyone I'm *less* interested in. Or who would be less interested in *me*."

Ben didn't reply. He continued to study Zach as though waiting for the moment when he could jab his finger and burst out, "AH-HA!"

But it seemed the moment never came, so maybe he did, unwillingly, believe Zach's protestations.

Zach said, "Ben, I don't want to argue. It's late. I've still got to pack. Can we—"

Mistake.

"Pack for what? Where are you going?" Ben questioned, his gaze boring into Zach's.

The temptation to yell, *None of your goddamned business!* was powerful, but Zach managed a relatively mild, "It's work-related. I'm sorry, but I can't go into it with you."

"Since when? You're not a secret agent, you know!"

"Ben."

"Are you going for the weekend?"

"Ben, will you stop?"

Ben was unfazed. "Who's going to take care of Mr. Bigglesworth?"

"Mr. B. is staying with Mom and Brooke for the weekend."

"He can stay with me."

"It's already arranged. He's staying with—"

"Why can't he stay with me?" Ben interrupted. "I love him. He loves me. He's lived most of his life in the condo."

"*No.*" Zach didn't mean it to sound so harsh, but he'd hit his breaking point. "No. It's already arranged."

Ben shook his head as though once again Zach was fulfilling his worst expectations. "As usual, it's just about what's convenient for you. What *you* want. Nobody else's feelings matter. Mr. B.'s feelings don't matter to you."

"Mr. B. loves Brooke and my mom, too." Zach bit back the rest of it. Was he really going to stand here arguing about who the cat—*his* cat, for the record—loved more? No. He wasn't. This whole exchange simply underlined why he and Ben no longer worked.

He'd hoped at one point they could stay friends, but that looked less and less likely.

He moved toward the front door, saying, "Maybe another time, okay?"

"Sure." The word was terse and unfriendly.

Ben followed him to the door, which Zach opened onto a chilly October night.

Not looking at him, not speaking, Ben brushed past Zach, going down the three little steps and cutting a diagonal across the straggly square of lawn.

"Good night, Ben," Zach said quietly.

He didn't expect, nor receive, a reply.

CHAPTER FIVE

"**W**hat made you decide to become a PI?"

It was Sunday morning, and Zach and Alton were having a lazy, luxurious breakfast on the mostly empty patio of Roy's at Pebble Beach. The off-season chill was dispersed by strategically placed heat lamps and firepit tables. Over country omelets and Keoke coffee (a decadent concoction of Kahlúa, brandy, crème de cacao, and coffee), Alton read the *Wall Street Journal* and Zach played Wordle and enjoyed the breathtaking view of ocean and golf links—or at least what could be seen of them through the mist.

Glancing up from his phone, Zach smiled ruefully. "Too much TV at an early age?"

Alton snorted, but returned the smile.

"Forgive me, but you seem a little…refined to be a PI."

"Is *refined* code for gay?" Zach inquired.

Alton looked momentarily self-conscious. "No. Not at all. I meant you seem…educated."

Zach shrugged. "I finished college with a degree in accounting. I have my CPA license."

"*A CPA?* Now I *am* surprised." Actually, Alton looked more thoughtful than surprised.

This was the first glimmer of personal interest he'd shown since he'd arrived in his chauffeured Bentley Mulsanne to pick Zach up on Friday evening. That wasn't to say that Alton hadn't been polite and pleasant over the course of the weekend. He had been unfailingly polite and indifferently pleasant. But it was clear to Zach he'd been relegated to the role of background actor from the minute he slid into the back seat of that Bentley.

Which probably made sense. From Alton's viewpoint, Zach was largely there for show. From Zach's viewpoint, spending the weekend at Pebble Beach was mostly slowing his investigation into who might want Alton out of the way. He'd tried bringing this point up to Alton on the drive from Ensenada del Sello, but Alton had dismissed Zach's concerns. Alton's immediate priority was to create the illusion that he and Zach were romantically involved.

Given that Alton believed Zora was behind the death threats, maybe he imagined that convincing her he was actually gay was the fastest way to diffuse her anger and desire to see him punished? Zach could understand and sympathize where Alton was coming from, but he thought the hope for a quick and painless resolution was misplaced. Not least because it was hard to imagine that anyone watching them together over the past thirty-six hours would be fooled into thinking they were intimate, let alone in love.

Alton was a little bit of what Pop would have called a *cold fish*.

Not that Zach wanted anything else from his employer—*yeesh!*—but this charade wasn't going to fool anyone, especially someone who presumably knew Alton as well as his wife did. Of course, this was only a practice run, and the few people they had run into so far were business acquaintances of Alton's, like the trio of potential investors he'd spent most of Saturday with on the links.

To Zach's bafflement—and frustration—he had not been included in the day's golfing. Alton had explained that his chauffeur, Chico Martinez, was also his bodyguard, so it made more sense for Chico, in the guise of caddy, to accompany him. Zach had been handed a roll of bills and told to amuse himself for the afternoon. He had also received instructions to mention *my boyfriend Alton* as much as possible.

Which was idiotic. If he and Alton were really having an illicit affair, the last thing Zach would be doing was name-dropping his sugar daddy everywhere. Alton had bad instincts, which was something to keep in mind moving forward.

Then again, who was Zach to talk, given that he had gone against his own instincts by taking the job to begin with?

Not that the job didn't have considerable perks.

For one thing, the accommodations were world class. Half hidden by gardens and majestic Monterey pines, the Inn at Spanish Bay was bordered by wild coastline on one side and miles of manicured Scottish-style links on the other. The charming two-bedroom suite Alton had booked included a fireplace, a private patio, and a ridiculously spacious bathroom with a double shower and free-standing deep soaking tub. From the fresh flowers to the paintings on the wall, no detail had been overlooked. The meals, the cocktails—so *many* cocktails—the Scottish piper at sunset, everything about the hotel was perfect.

Excluding the company.

Alton interrupted Zach's rueful reflections with one of his light, ironic laughs. "It seems you have hidden facets, Zach. Once again, I'm reassured I made the right choice by not hiring that lout on the other side of the shopping center."

Lout. Zach repressed a grin. It wasn't easy. Flint certainly seemed to have gotten under Alton's skin during what sounded like a pretty brief encounter. Zach couldn't help thinking that it was more likely Flint who had turned down Alton than the other way around. But maybe not. Alton usually got what he wanted.

He asked, curious, "What about you? Did you always want to be a toymaker?"

Alton grimaced. "I don't think the Beacher Toy Company makes *toys* so much as works of art. Our creations are for the parents of children as much as the children."

"Ah."

Maybe Zach sounded unconvinced because Alton said, "We design beautiful playthings intended to evoke a sense of nostalgia and tradition. The expectation is that our work will be handed down through each generation, treasured more with each generation."

Zach nodded, said peaceably, "Sure."

The Beacher Toy Company was a multimillion-dollar enterprise, so presumably Alton understood his target market. Making toys for parents rather than children seemed counterintuitive to Zach. But his family wasn't the hand-down-the-treasures-through-each-generation kind. He'd hung onto a few of his favorite comic books and a couple of Hot Wheel cars, and that was about it for the mementos of his childhood. Nor did he plan on having offspring to pass those items on to. Maybe if he ever had any nieces and nephews? But Brooke had already proclaimed she was never having kids.

Alton began, "You're not alone in your thinking. My brother Ran—"

"This time you've gone too far, Beacher!"

The man who had materialized out of the mist to loom over their table was maybe in his mid-forties. He was squat and heavyset with slightly protuberant gray eyes and salt-and-pepper hair cut in the style of Julius Caesar. His voice was deep and croaky, like a frog's—in fact, he kind of looked like a toad. A well-dressed toad. His baggy brown golf pants were not the kind of thing you picked up at Target or Walmart, and his green lambswool sweater looked straight off the loom of a croft in the Hebrides.

Alton put his coffee cup down and offered a tight little smile. "Hello, Rusty. I didn't realize you were staying here this weekend."

Zach studied the newcomer. This would be Ronald (Rusty) Jordan, owner and CEO of Old Timey Fun Ltd. and Alton's oldest friend and business rival. While Alton didn't look thrilled to see Rusty, he also didn't seem unduly alarmed, despite Rusty's aggressive posture. But Zach was alarmed. He was alarmed that Chico Martinez, Alton's supposed bodyguard, was nowhere in sight.

Jordan was saying, "You could at least have the decency not to rub Zora's nose in it."

Alton smiled apologetically at Zach. "I'm afraid by *it*, Rusty means you, Zach."

Jordan glanced dismissively at Zach. "I mean *you*, Alton. This is about you. And only you. You're going out of your way to humiliate Zora. She doesn't deserve this. There's no reason for it."

"How do you know there's no reason for it?" Alton demanded with sudden hostility. "You have no idea what goes on behind closed doors. But if you're concerned for *my* wife's feelings, keep your mouth shut about this."

Jordan's flushed face grew even redder. He seemed to waver—Zach half rose, anticipating a swing at Alton—but then, without another word, Jordan abruptly turned and made his way through the mostly empty tables and firepits. Heart still thumping with that rush of adrenaline, Zach watched until Jordan disappeared inside the restaurant.

Zach subsided in his chair, staring at Alton. Alton gave a short, dry laugh, and finished his coffee. His cheeks were dotted pink, and there was the slightest tremor in his hand. That wasn't fear, though. Alton didn't like scenes in public.

"No going back now."

Probably not. But really, from the point you hired a PI to investigate the people close to you, was there any going back?

Zach said, "Well, no. But that was the idea, right?"

Alton thought it over, said, "I suspect the news of our affair will reach Zora before too much longer. Rusty Jordan's an old friend of mine. Well, more Zora's friend than mine, as you saw. But at one time we even considered going into business together."

"I recognize him from his file."

"Of course." For the first time since Rusty Jordan had accosted them, Alton met Zach's gaze directly. "I hope you won't find it all too upsetting."

"Find what too upsetting?" Zach couldn't help a flicker of disquiet.

"The inevitable fallout. Rusty has never been what one would call closemouthed. I'm sure he'll tell Zora. And Zora..."

"Great." What did *fallout* mean exactly? Angry phone calls from Mrs. Beacher? Zach's photo in the *Ensenada Signal*'s gossip column? A PI trailing *him* around?

At Zach's tone, Alton's pale brows rose. "After all, for the plan to succeed, our relationship has to be common knowledge."

"Yep." Zach did know that, of course, but he kept hoping Alton's circle of common knowledge would not overlap his own. Not least because no one who knew Zach would believe for one minute he was romantically involved with Alton Beacher.

Well, maybe Ben. But that was more about Ben than Zach.

Alton patted his lips with the linen napkin. "We should probably be on our way. I think we'll take the coast route home. The view is spectacular. How does that sound?"

As with Friday evening's chauffeured drive, Alton spent most of the trip on his phone, haranguing the minions back at the Beacher Toy Company. Given that it was Sunday afternoon, Zach wouldn't have expected a lot of doing business to take place, but maybe working weekends was how someone got to be a multimillionaire.

While Alton worked the phone, Zach took in the yes, spectacular views of dramatic coastal cliffs, white and rocky beaches, old-growth cypress and oak forests and, sure, plenty of golf courses, while he tried to sort through his impressions of the weekend.

Uppermost was his troubled conviction that his employer did not seem like a man in fear of his life. The unexpected encounter with Rusty Jordan had solidified his feelings. At times Alton appeared worried, nervous, agitated, but he didn't seem—at least to Zach—like someone afraid of physical harm. He hadn't seemed so in their first meeting, and he'd seemed even less so over the course of the weekend.

Equally troubling was the behavior of Alton's chauffeur and so-called bodyguard. Chico Martinez was young, wiry, and fit, and he did wear a shoulder holster (along with what seemed to be full body tats) beneath his immaculate uniform. But where the hell had he been when Alton had been approached by Rusty Jordan that morning? Chico had not behaved like any bodyguard Zach had ever seen. He had not inspected their hotel room when Alton and Zach checked into the inn. He had not been present—or seemingly even within shouting distance—at any of their meals. Yes, he had been there for Alton's golf games, but Zach couldn't help feeling that was more about Chico's usefulness as a caddy than Alton's need for a bodyguard.

Nor had Chico seemed open to discussing Alton's safety with Zach on the two occasions Zach had tried to broach the subject. He hadn't pretended not to know what Zach was talking about, but he'd brushed Zach's concerns aside and assured him that everything was under control.

Another thing—and kind of a big thing, in Zach's opinion—why had Alton largely discouraged Zach from discussing the case that weekend? It wasn't concern with being overheard because they'd been alone most of the time.

Time that had been spent watching television, drinking—Alton was a Scotch drinker, but he also liked brandy and a cigar after dinner—and wandering the inn's garden and grounds.

They had not done a lot of talking, and the talking they had done did not have anything to do with threats on Alton's life.

Maybe Alton really did just need a break from his problems, but the whole setup made Zach uncomfortable. Or at least, as uncomfortable as you could be when everything possible was being done to ensure your comfort.

The drive from Pebble Beach to Zach's home in Salinas was fairly short—at least in physical miles. As they reached the well-worn suburbs, he had the sensation of leaving one world and reentering another. When the Bentley was about a mile from Pine Street, Alton put his phone away, leaned forward to reach into the front seat, and removed a flat, rectangular box. He handed the box, which was wrapped in silver foil paper and fastened shut with violet and silver ribbons, to Zach.

"What's this?" It came out sounding a little more wary than Zach intended, but he wondered if Alton was terminating his contract. Had he secretly only been hired to pose as Alton's boyfriend for the weekend?

Alton offered that odd, smirky smile that always made Zach uneasy. "Open it and see."

Zach gave Alton another dubious look, opened the box and...didn't understand what he was looking at.

Lying in the folds of creamy tissue paper were three pairs of women's panties. Two pairs of white lace and one pair of black satin.

"Uhhhh..." Zach glanced up in alarm and caught Chico's brown gaze in the Bentley's rearview mirror. He blanked that image out, and looked at Alton.

Alton said in a perfectly ordinary tone, "I'd like you to wear these whenever we're together or speaking on the phone."

"You'd... No."

"No?" Alton looked startled.

"Nope." Zach handed the box back to Alton. Tried to, anyway, but Alton put his hands up as though Zach were offering him a ticking bomb. "Thank you? I guess. But no." Zach pushed the box at Alton again, and again Alton put his hands up.

"But... Why?"

"*Why?*"

"Are you offended?" Alton seemed genuinely confused.

"You're my employer. Of course I'm offended!"

"But...Zach."

"Alton."

"Hear me out, if you will," Alton urged. "These will go a long way to making our little charade seem real."

"To *whom*?" Zach asked. "Who the hell do you think would know?"

"*I* would know." Alton licked his lips. All at once his face was pale, his eyes fever-bright. Zach's disquiet shot up another few degrees. "I would know you were wearing them, and it would help me stay in character."

"Yeah, you're already enough of a character, Alton."

Alton gave a shaky laugh. "But you can't be this naive. You're a-a man of the world."

If by *man of the world* Alton meant Zach must be aware that some men liked to wear women's panties, sure. He was a man of the world. Or at least, a man who occasionally read a magazine.

Zach said, "I'm not telling you—I'm not judging. I'm just saying…whatever, but *I'm* strictly Fruit of the Loom."

Alton blinked, said quickly, "You don't even have to really wear them. Just let me *think* you're wearing them. It would help—"

"*Help?*"

"—if I knew these little bits of lace and satin and elastic were caressing you, clinging to your body. If I could picture this soft cotton cradling your testicles, imagine delicate lace rubbing, straining against your penis."

Zach's jaw dropped. He made a strangled sound that was somewhere between a hysterical laugh and protest. Alton put his ice-cold fingers against Zach's lips.

"Wait. Don't say anything else. Yet. If you *should* decide that perhaps you want more from me, just tell me you're wearing the black panties."

What in the hell was happening?

It wasn't like Zach felt under assault or threatened. Embarrassed, yes. Discomfited, yes. But with each passing moment, he was less offended and more, well, sorry for Alton, who was clearly getting worked up about the idea of Zach in ladies' undies. A fetish for women's underwear wasn't a sign of anything except an interest Zach didn't share. That wasn't the point. The point was his employer was making an unwanted sexual advance. And trying to gaslight him into thinking there wasn't anything wrong with it. That was not okay.

Zach lightly batted Alton's hand away. "Don't take this personally, but I prefer we keep things strictly professional."

Alton stared for a moment, as if digesting this, then said, "I'll pay you an extra one hundred dollars an hour to wear these any time we speak, whether in person or on the phone."

Seriously?

Zach managed to control his exasperation. "That's generous. But no."

"Two hundred dollars."

Zach barely registered those husky words.

"Stop. It's not about the money. I would find that—I find this—very…um…distracting. From the job I agreed to do."

Alton frowned. "I didn't imagine someone your age would be so closed-minded."

"No? Well. Sorry." Zach set the box on the seat between himself and Alton.

Alton leaned back in his seat and glared out the window.

Zach regarded him, his heart pounding in a mixture of disbelief and alarm. Alarm because two hundred dollars an hour on top of the five Alton was already paying him was one hell of a lot of money, which he could very much use, and the fact he was even *thinking* this way was…alarming.

Not another word was spoken until they reached Zach's house.

Alton continued to stare pointedly out the window. Zach hopped out of the car and waited for Chico to get his luggage from the trunk of the Bentley.

Chico, Zach's bag in hand, nodded with his chin for Zach to proceed him up the little cement walk.

Was he fired? Zach had no idea. He did not want to lose this very lucrative job; however, things had definitely taken a turn for the weird, and he wasn't sure what to do about that. There had probably been a more graceful, tactful way to decline Alton's wishes, but he'd been caught off-guard and, well, maybe he *was* closed-minded. But no way.

No. Way.

Not least because he was starting to realize he didn't trust Alton as far as he could throw him.

They reached Zach's screen door, and Zach felt for his keys. Chico put down Zach's suitcase and handed him the silver box, which he must have grabbed from Alton after Zach started for the house. Zach tried to hand the box back. Chico pushed the box back. Were they going to brawl over possession of the goddamned box?

Ignoring Zach's scowl, Chico said, "Consider it a compliment, GQ."

"That would be a backhanded compliment. At best."

"Nah. He's harmless. You don't even have to wear 'em. Just let him think you've got them on."

"I'm not going to lie."

"Don't worry. He loses interest fast."

"Speaking from personal experience?"

"Fuck no." Chico seemed genuinely amused. "I'm not his type."

"And he's not mine."

He was talking to Chico's uniformed back. But as Chico marched down the steps, he threw back, "Rich guys are everyone's type."

CHAPTER SIX

"**M**orning!" Brooke called cheerily when she breezed into the office ten minutes after nine on Monday morning. "You're here early."

"Uh, no. You're fifteen minutes late." Zach finished pouring water into the coffee maker and flipped shut the lid. He turned on the machine.

Brooke cast a dismissing look at the clock on the wall, set Mr. Bigglesworth's cat carrier on the reception desk, and slipped out of her rain-spotted trench coat. She dropped into the chair behind the reception desk and turned on her desktop. "How was your weekend?" Before Zach could respond, she added slyly, "How was your date?"

Zach, flipping open the door of the cat carrier, lifted Mr. B. out. Mr. B. meowed a tuna-breathed complaint about the weather. Zach bumped his nose against the cat's suede-soft face. "It was a job. Not a date."

"*Awwww*," Brooke sympathized. "But you know, the course of true love ne'er did run true."

"Maybe college isn't the answer. Maybe a nice high-security prison?"

Mr. B. concurred. Brooke chuckled. "Maybe. Anyway, how did it go?"

Zach restrained himself to a mild, "It could have been worse. We're still employed, at least. I just got a call from Alton's secretary asking me to have dinner with him tonight."

Brooke glanced away from her monitor screen—apparently the Sephora site was her homepage? "His secretary asked you out?"

Zach sighed. "No. His secretary contacted me to arrange my having dinner with Alton tonight."

"Okay, that's even weirder."

"I think that's how people like Alton do it."

"You mean weird people?"

"Rich people."

Brooke snorted. "No wonder his marriage is in trouble."

Zach opened his mouth, remembered the box with the lace panties, and swallowed his reply.

"Where are you having dinner?" Brooke clicked away from Sephora's website and gave Davies Detective Agency's empty inbox a disapproving look.

"I can't remember the name. It's in Carmel. American Fusion Tuscan... Whatever that means." Besides expensive. Where Alton was concerned, expensive seemed to be the default.

"Pinch?"

"That's it."

"Nice! Seems a little trendy for Alton, but I guess the idea is for lots of people to see you together."

"Yee...ah." Zach considered that for an unenthusiastic moment. "Anyway, after this weekend, I was thinking maybe it would be a good idea to have some backup." Zach filled Brooke in on the puzzling case of a client unfazed by death threats and a bodyguard seemingly uninterested in guarding any particular body.

Brooke's expression was thoughtful as she heard him out. "Maybe Martinez knows something we don't?"

Once again, Zach couldn't help remembering those panties—currently lying, silver box, lavender ribbons and all—in his bedroom wastepaper basket. "I'm sure he knows plenty we don't. But after the encounter with Rusty Jordan, I'm not ready to dismiss the idea that the threat is real. Maybe Alton is paranoid. But he's also kind of..."

"Arrogant?"

Zach nodded. "I had plenty of opportunity to watch him this weekend, and he puts people's backs up. He's not deliberately, consciously rude, but that's almost worse. It's like everyone else is just there to serve him."

"Including you?"

No way was Brooke ever hearing the details of the drive home from Pebble Beach. Zach said, "Sure. But he's also very generous. He gave me five hundred bucks to just amuse myself while he was busy golfing. He can be considerate and thoughtful. But I can also imagine him doing things that enrage people—and not having a clue."

"I want to hear what happened to those five hundred dollars."

"I ordered room service."

Brooke's expression was a study. Zach laughed. "I deposited it into the business account this morning. My point is, I'm not so sure that, if someone came after Alton, Martinez would show up in time. Or at all."

"You want me to double-team you tonight?"

"What?" Zach scowled. "No. I sure don't."

Brooke wiggled her brows. "Planning on getting lucky?"

"Brooke, I'm serious."

Brooke sighed. "Well, okay. But I'm perfectly capable of sitting in a restaurant and keeping an eye out for trouble. I'm a better photographer than you, that's for sure."

"We're not snapping school portraits."

"You have no idea what we're doing," Brooke retorted. "Besides, it's not like we have a lot of choice."

This was depressingly true. After Pop had passed and the jobs had dried up, Zach had been forced to let their only other experienced operative go. In fairness, Hank had been trying to retire for the last two years, so it had been more of an act of mercy to decline his reluctant offer to *hang on till you kids get on your feet*.

"What I was thinking was maybe we could hire Flint to provide some backup."

"*Flint?*" Brooke looked surprised—and then thoughtful.

"It doesn't seem like he's a lot busier than we are."

"True. And he's a lot more experienced."

Zach opened his mouth to object to that, but it was true. Irritating, but true. He settled on, "At field work, yes."

"I didn't think you planned to have him go over our books. Speaking of which, how would we pay him?"

"We have the spending money Alton gave me. Not to mention the advance he paid. We only need Flint for a couple of hours here and there. I think we could swing it." It would be worth it to have some kind of reinforcements—preferably someone not on Alton's payroll.

"That's actually a good idea." Brooke's tone seemed to hint this was an unexpected first.

"Can you phone him and ask him to come in for a meeting?"

"Why don't you just go over and talk to him now?"

"Because that's going to look like I'm asking for a favor. We're going to—try to—*hire* him."

Brooke rolled her eyes. "Oh my God. I get it. It's a power-play thing."

"Yes. *No.* But he doesn't take anything seriously. He doesn't take *us* seriously. We have to be professional about this."

Brooke uttered a much put-upon sigh. "Fine." She reached for the phone, and Zach started for his office, Mr. Bigglesworth draped around his neck.

Brooke called, "By the way, Ben stopped by this weekend."

Zach stopped in his tracks, his heart sinking. "Ben stopped by Mom's?"

"Mm-hm."

"Why?"

Brooke's grim expression didn't match her casual tone. "Because, per Mom, Ben will always be welcome because he'll always be part of our family. They had a nice couple of hours commiserating with each other over you."

Zach absorbed this intelligence unhappily. Despite, probably sincere, efforts on both sides, he and his mother had never been close. And relations had not improved following what Mom considered the twin disastrous decisions to keep the detective agency open and break up with Ben.

"So long as everybody's happy," he said with a lightness he didn't feel.

Brooke started to reply, but her expression changed and she said in her best official business voice, "Hi, Arlisse; it's Brooke. Is Flint available to take a meeting this afternoon?"

Maybe Flint had read the same *How to Succeed in Business* articles as Zach because it turned out he had but one available time slot in his busy, busy day, and that was four minutes after Brooke phoned. Whether this was gamesmanship or he really did have more clients than Zach and Brooke calculated, he arrived in their lobby, damp and slightly disheveled, wearing blue jeans and a gray hoodie. He smelled of rain and mouthwash, and did not appear to have shaved for the last three days. He was also slightly out of breath from his jog across the parking lot, dodging numerous cars driven by maniacs desperately seeking spaces closer to the shops.

Even so, even damp, disheveled, and disapproving, there was something about Flint. Something that made it hard to dismiss him however much Zach tried. Flint had presence; a raw, vaguely disturbing virility that seemed to charge the air around him.

"Hi, Flint!" Brooke greeted him brightly as he dripped on their welcome mat. She liked Flint.

"Hey, kiddo." Flint pushed back his soaked hood. His sun-streaked brown hair was a mass of wet ringlets, giving him a slightly crazed look. "Zachariah."

It took Zach a moment to process that look of hungry anticipation on Flint's lean face.

Hell.

As Flint's bright hazel gaze held his own, Zach realized Flint was thinking he'd changed his mind about selling the agency. There was no reason to feel guilty about that misunderstanding, but somehow, he did.

"Did you want to step into my office?" he asked.

Flint shrugged. "Sure."

"Would you like a coffee, Flint?" Brooke piped up.

"No thanks."

Zach stepped into his office, closing the door behind Flint.

"I think there *might* be a slight misunderstanding," Zach began.

He was interrupted by Mr. Bigglesworth, who—never a fan of anyone or anything that might steal Zach's attention—made a big production of leaping from the chair in front of the desk across the room and onto the narrow bookshelf, where he proceeded, secret-agent style, to blend into the tidy row of houseplants. His giant sea-glass gaze peered through the foliage.

Flint looked taken aback. "What the hell was that?"

"That's my cat."

"That's not a cat."

"He certainly is."

"Nope."

"Yep. In fact, he's purebred."

"*That?* Purebred? No way."

"He has the papers to prove it."

Flint snorted. "Then he forged them."

Against his will, Zach laughed.

This seemed to encourage Flint, who said, "Admit it. You found him going through garbage cans in a back alley, and he sold you some sob story about a pair of bulldogs mugging him for his fur coat."

Who knew Flint had a sense of humor? Zach said gravely, "He's not a client. He's an associate."

"Of course he is." Flint sighed and dropped into the chair vacated by Mr. Bigglesworth. "Okay. What's the big misunderstanding? Or should I guess?"

"Sorry, but this isn't about selling the business." Zach squeezed in behind the desk and sat down. "It's about hiring you."

Flint's obvious disappointment gave way to surprise. His brows shot up. "Hiring *me*? For what?"

"For surveillance work. The Beacher case is...well, to do it properly, we need more manpower."

Flint's smile was sardonic. His large hands fastened on the arms of the chair, and he started to rise. "Sorry. I've got my own caseload."

Zach blurted, "I'll pay you two hundred dollars an hour—and it's not that many hours."

Flint lowered himself to the chair again. He eyed Zach skeptically. "Go on."

"You already know it's a complicated situation."

"Are you asking me or telling me?"

Flint had the kind of face that was really hard to read. Maybe behind that cool, glinting gaze beat a sympathetic heart, but Zach wouldn't bet on it. Then again, he hadn't realized Flint had a goofy sense of humor either. So maybe a more accurate reading of Flint's emotional temperature was his smile: that faint, ever-present crease in his cheek, like Flint was secretly laughing at everyone and everything. What had Alton called it? *Sarcastic.* For sure, it wasn't an all's-right-with-the-world smile.

"Well, what did Al—Beacher tell you?" Zach asked.

Flint stared at him for a long moment, then gave a little shake of his head, like *I give up.* "I don't like domestic cases. I make it a rule not to get in between spouses. Also, Alton Beacher's reputation precedes him. So he didn't get a chance to tell me much of anything."

"What's his reputation?"

"Are you telling me you took on a messy divorce case without knowing anything about your principals?"

"I'm not being paid to investigate my client. Sometimes people in terrible marriages need help, too."

Flint considered that, grimaced. "Okay. Fair enough. Your client has a reputation for involving others in sticky situations."

"I don't know what that means."

"It means you're out of your league, junior."

Zach said shortly, "Do you mind? I'm thirty. I've been earning my living since I was twenty-three." He bit his lip, considered. "Alton's been receiving death threats. He thinks his wife is behind them, but of course he's not sure, which is why he hired me."

"I'm sure it's not the only reason he hired you." Flint's tone was dry. Meeting Zach's gaze, he added, "Like I said, his reputation precedes him."

What *exactly* did that mean? Zach didn't know Flint well enough to judge whether Flint's opinion of messy divorces and sticky situations was to be taken seriously.

Frankly, Flint was already displaying an unexpected streak of, well, squeamishness Zach wouldn't have expected.

At least, he thought it was squeamishness. They were both so busy fencing, it was difficult to know if they were even talking about the same thing.

"Okay, well, I can't discuss the details unless you're willing to sign an NDA as an independent contractor for Davies Detective Agency."

Flint's eyes narrowed, but he seemed to be looking inward rather than at Zach. He said finally, "Two hundred bucks an hour?"

"Yes."

"What's the gig?"

"I'm supposed to have dinner with Alton tonight. I feel like I need another pair of eyes on the scene just in case, well, something happens."

Flint said nothing. Rain ticked against the windows.

As the silence stretched between them, Zach realized something. He'd been thinking he was just being extra conscientious in making sure he could provide the level of service Alton had paid for and rightfully expected. But as he waited for Flint to come to a decision, he recognized he was genuinely uneasy, and that at least some of that unease was for himself.

He could probably count on one hand the things he knew about Flint: that he was an ex-Marine, that he was thirty-five, unmarried and had no children, that he was firearms certified, that he had started his PI business five years earlier (which, ironically, meant he'd been Zach's age), and that he was a fan of OG *Magnum PI*.

Not a whole hell of a lot. And yet, somehow, Zach knew that if he did really end up in a jam, Flint would be the guy he could trust to have his back.

The guy in question drew in a long, weary breath. "I've got to be honest. I'm already stretched too thin. I spent the weekend on stakeout. I can't—"

Zach said quickly, "Two, maybe three hours. No more. I wouldn't ask, Flint, but there's something weird going on with this case. I can't put my finger on it, but I can feel it in my gut. Something's wrong..."

Zach trailed off. He knew exactly what Flint was thinking. *How is this my problem?*

Fair enough. Flint and Pop had been friendly, but they hadn't been *friends*. Zach and Flint barely qualified as friendly. There was always some awkwardness, some odd tension underlying their exchanges. Yet here he was asking Flint for a favor. A well-paid favor, yes, but still a favor.

Flint opened his mouth, and Zach gulped, "Sorry. You're right. Not your problem. I'll figure something out."

Flint directed a look of exasperation at Zach. He said tersely, "When and where?"

CHAPTER SEVEN

"**D**id I even bother to mention how wonderful you look tonight?"

Zach, preoccupied with casing the crowded restaurant patio, glanced across the table at Alton—and then took another look. In the shadowy firelight, Alton's pale eyes held a predatory gleam. His smile—and the glimpse of his canine teeth—was a little unsettling.

"Your hair looks almost red in this light. And your eyes are as blue as the sea at Spanish Bay."

Zach said hastily, "I'm wearing gray and blue plaid boxers." For good measure, he added, "And blue retro stripe socks."

Alton blinked, then laughed and sat back in his chair. "I should probably warn you that for me, the chase is ninety-nine percent of the fun."

"I should probably warn you I made the national HSSA Boys Cross Country—" The waiter arrived then, and Zach stopped there.

While Alton took his time grilling the waiter on how every entrée on the menu was prepared, Zach looked again for Flint on the crowded patio. He was relieved when he finally spotted him tucked away by one of the small waterfalls. For some reason, he'd pictured Flint in one of his

Hawaiian shirts, ball cap, and shades, but in fact, Flint was soberly, unobtrusively dressed in a tailored white shirt and gray slacks. He was sipping a glass of wine and staring meditatively up at the tall, rain-glittered olive trees, and Zach had to give it to him, few people looked as comfortable dining alone.

"Zach, dear," Alton prompted, and Zach snapped back to awareness. He realized it was his turn to order.

He also realized when Alton said *dear*, he said it in the same tone as Zach's mother when she was about to explain to him why he was wrong again.

Zach chose the charred broccolini with Romesco sauce and Marcona almonds, and the grilled lobster tails in coconut cream, Scotch bonnet, and thyme with honey nut squash, scallions, and toasted coconut rice. He figured after the stunt with the lace panties, Alton owed him a lobster dinner at the least.

The waiter departed. Zach said, "I spent the day looking into the threats you've received so far. The Old Timey Fun jack-in-the-boxes were discontinued two years ago due to a potential choking hazard. They weren't actually recalled, though. The company voluntarily stopped production. Vendors still had the option of selling old stock. That makes it a little harder to track—"

Alton looked ever so slightly pained. "Let's save the business discussion for after our meal."

Zach's brows drew together. "Okay, but—"

The sommelier appeared beside their table. Once again Zach had to bite his tongue while Alton went through the wine list, exhaustively considering pairings and vintages and bouquets. Zach didn't care for wine. Ben had been the wine expert in their household. Zach preferred craft beers, ideally IPAs, but Alton seemed to be anti-ale. He liked wine with his meals, brandy after, and scotch in between—and plenty of all, though so far Zach had never seen him noticeably inebriated.

While Alton put the sommelier through her paces, Zach considered the crowded patio. It was pretty busy for a Monday, and a rainy Monday at that, but the greenery and waterfall absorbed a lot noise—or maybe a lot of people were enjoying quiet, intimate dinners. Beyond the restaurant staff, nobody seemed to be paying them attention.

After Pebble Beach, he'd been expecting something very different from the elegantly rustic, graciously casual eatery located right there in the middle of Lincoln Street. The attention to detail was the same, though: a quaint cottage vibe of dark wood, marble, slate, and tile. Accordion windows opened onto the rain-wet garden with its mysterious lights, waterfall, and firepits.

If he ever went on a real date again, this was where he'd bring the guy. He glanced automatically at Flint, and happened to catch Flint's gaze. Flint winked.

Zach hastily looked away.

"What do you think of this marvelous cheese board?"

"Uh...nice." It was very nice. But honestly? Zach thought Alton had ordered way more food than they could possibly eat. He wasn't a big fan of food waste. That was no doubt the accountant in him.

"Have you tried this brie? It's tremendous." Alton smothered a toasted cracker with a creamy chunk of cheese and held it up so Zach could take a bite—which he did, uncomfortably aware of *beady-eyed* Flint sitting a few tables away.

"Mm." He licked his lips, trying to catch the crumbs.

Alton seemed preoccupied by every flick of his tongue. "Do you have to wear glasses? You have such pretty eyes. Had you considered contacts?"

"I've considered them, yeah. I don't find them comfortable."

"I wear them."

Zach said politely, "That's nice."

"You get used to them."

The mood—whatever mood this was—was abruptly broken.

"Well, isn't this cozy!" Ben's indignant voice floated overhead.

Zach looked up and then around—his fellow diners looked equally startled—and finally he located Ben's disembodied head poking through a short wall of black bamboo dividing the upper-level patio from the lower level where he and Alton were seated.

"*Ben?*"

"*Now* it all makes sense." Ben turned his glare on Alton. Alton looked taken aback, though not particularly alarmed.

Zach said calmly, as though jealous boyfriends popping out of shrubbery was a normal occurrence, "This isn't the time or the place."

"I disagree," Ben said. "I think the moment I catch my boyfriend cheating is *exactly* the time and place."

Zach, hoping Ben might follow his lead, kept his voice down. "Ben, we're not together. We split up four months ago."

Ben had no interest in keeping his voice down. He said more loudly still, "You know there's a courtesy no dating period!"

"*What?*"

Alton cut in with a chilly, "Perhaps you two should discuss this outside."

"We *are* outside," Ben informed him. Ben was not a surly guy, but he sounded downright pugnacious for a man with leaves in his hair.

"I'm sorry, Alton." Zach was already on his feet. "Come on," he said to Ben, who withdrew, noisily rustling the wall of bamboo. A quick glance toward Flint's table offered a glimpse of Flint calmly retaking his seat. That was both reassuring—Flint had been ready to spring into action—and embarrassing.

But then, what was one more embarrassment on a night which was now in contention for the most embarrassing of his life?

Zach made his way through the gauntlet of curious gazes and murmured comments. He couldn't help noticing that, once again, Chico Martinez was nowhere to be seen.

Was that really just a coincidence? But what was the alternative? It's not like Chico could have known Zach was about to be accosted by his ex.

Ben waited impatiently in the wide doorway as Zach reached the entrance leading into the restaurant.

"I don't know what the hell you think the point of this is," Zach said tersely, quietly.

"The point is to let you know how I feel. The point is to ruin your evening." Ben turned his back and led the way through the crowded and much noisier restaurant, out the front door, and into the small chef's garden.

"Where are we going?"

Ben did not reply.

Zach tried again. "Ben, what are we doing?"

They were literally standing in a large planter, rutabaga and tomatoes to their knees, and not that far out of earshot of the diners seated just inside that huge front operable window. The smell of damp earth and pungent herbs hung in the moist night air. Misty rain whispered down around them.

A couple passing on the cobblestone street threw them puzzled looks, went up the steps on the side, and entered the restaurant.

"Ben, is there some reason we have to do this in a lettuce patch?"

Ben turned, and his face was hard and unfamiliar in the gloom. "You told me there wasn't anyone else."

"There isn't! But I didn't say I wasn't going to date! Sooner or later, I'm going to go out with someone. Sooner or later, I hope there *is* someone else. But tonight, it's work. There's nothing going on."

Ben turned his face skyward and gave a sound that was half-groan, half-outrage. "Give me a fucking break! He was hand-feeding you like you were his pet parakeet."

Zach swallowed his anger, tried to remember that he really did care for Ben, really did hope they could one day be friends again. "Ben, this *has* to stop. It's been four months. You *have* to move on."

"I guess my feelings run deeper than yours."

That hit home. Because Zach *did* feel guilty about falling out of love, about jettisoning all the plans they had made. Or at least, the plans Ben had made and that Zach had gone along with. But guilt wasn't love, and it wasn't a good enough reason to stay in a relationship. And despite his best intentions, he was losing his temper.

"I thought that, too," Zach said. "But now I'm wondering if this is more about you being a control freak and having to deal with things not going to plan. Because you really don't seem to care at all about what *I* want or what would make me happy."

"You seem concerned enough about that for both of us."

"Ben, how many times can we go through this? I'm really, *truly* sorry. It's not like I planned this. It's not my fault."

"So it's *my* fault? You left *me*," Ben burst out. "How is *any* of this *my* fault?"

"I didn't say it was your fault. It's not about fault. I left after you gave me an ultimatum."

"Which I *retracted*."

"It doesn't work like that!"

"Why wouldn't it work like that?"

Once again, they were arguing in circles.

Zach didn't want to keep saying these things. He didn't want to keep hurting Ben. Not for the first time, he wished he could have somehow figured out how to be happy without actually being happy because it would have been so much easier to stay with Ben.

Except…would it *really* have been easier?

Once again, he tried to explain the inexplicable. "Because. Because once I went through the process of realizing there were things I wanted more than our relationship, that I could be happy without you, there wasn't any going back."

Ben was silent for a long moment. He said huskily, "Everything I ever did, every choice I ever made, was for *us*, for *our* relationship, for *our* future."

Zach absorbed that and said equally huskily, "I'm sorry. I am. But I don't know that that's true. Or at least, if it's true, then I still think you were doing what made you happy."

Ben was stone silent. He said finally, bitterly, "Your mother's right. You're completely selfish. Completely self-centered. You don't deserve love. I hope you're lonely and alone for the rest of your life."

It took Zach a moment to be able to say steadily, "Okay. If that makes you feel better."

"What will make me feel better is to never see you again. I wish you were dead."

There were any number of things to say to that. Zach choked all of it down. What were his hurt feelings compared to Ben's?

Maybe his silence said it anyway because after a moment, Ben turned, forging through the vegetables and herbs, climbed out of the planter, and strode down the cobbled walkway into the night.

Zach took a moment to gather himself before also wading through the lavender and lettuce. He stepped over the short stone wall and returned inside.

It seemed very loud, jarringly loud, and muted though the lights were, they dazzled his eyes. He walked right into someone, startled at the strong grip that closed on his arms, steadying him.

"That was awkward," Flint remarked.

Zach wiped the rain from his face and focused on Flynn's face. "It could have been worse."

Flynn's expression was genuinely curious. "How so?"

"He could have brought my mom."

Flint's brows shot up. He laughed, glanced past Zach, and said in carrying tones. "We worked the Gunderson case together."

It took Zach a moment. He too amplified for the back row. "I remember. How've you been?"

"Can I buy you a drink?"

Zach gave a brief shake of his head. "I should get back to my table."

Flint said quietly, "Your client is making business calls at the moment. Let's confab."

As they made their way to the bar, Flint remarked, "You didn't think to mention the situation to your boyfriend?"

"We're not together anymore."

"Does he know that?"

Zach grimaced.

When they reached a pair of empty seats at the bar, Flint said, "The bodyguard left in the Bentley right before your cheese plate arrived."

Zach forgot his own woes. "*Left?*"

"What'll you have to drink?" the bartender asked.

"Whisky highball." Flynn added to Zach, "I've got this."

Zach told the bartender, "Dirty martini."

Flint's mouth twitched as though this confirmed something. His three-martini-lunch jibe?

Zach said, "Alton finds beer *disappointing*, and I don't want to mix my drinks."

"Very prudent. So yeah, Martinez took off like a bat out of hell in the Bentley not long after you arrived."

"That seems weird."

"Not for a chauffeur. For a bodyguard, yeah. But tell me something about this gig that *isn't* weird."

"I'll have to rack my brain."

"No sign of Rusty Jordan. No sign that anyone followed you or is watching you."

That was a relief. Well, twin reliefs. Flint had actually memorized the photos Zach had provided. "Okay. Thanks."

Their drinks arrived, and Zach took a bracing swallow of chilled gin, vermouth, and olive juice.

Flint sipped his highball, cocked an eyebrow. "You know, it's really unlikely anyone's going to try to take Beacher out in a crowded restaurant with over sixty witnesses."

Zach made a face. "I know. It's not like I think we're going to come under siege over the main course. But I can't get rid of this nagging feeling that something's wrong."

"Something's wrong, yeah." Flint shrugged. "Something's usually wrong when people feel they have to hire a PI."

He was a little surprised at Flint's casual acknowledgment—and acceptance—of his unease. Zach had fully expected his doubts to be dismissed as inexperience and nerves. Which, for the record, wasn't necessarily untrue.

He admitted, "It turns out I don't like being responsible for someone else's life."

"You're not his bodyguard."

Zach nodded, swallowed the rest of his drink. "I should get back to our table."

"Right." Flint added casually, "I'm going to hang out here. Beacher *might* have made me."

"Oh *hell*."

Flint shrugged. "Be cool. Even if he did, it doesn't mean I'm here for him. Besides, PIs have to eat, too."

"Somehow I don't think this would be your kind of place to grab a meal."

Flint tilted his head, studying him. He said quite seriously, "You don't know anything about me, Zachariah. I don't need to be a millionaire to know my way around a cheese plate."

Which…yeah. He probably deserved the smackdown. Zach admitted, "True."

"We should debrief this evening."

God only knew why, but for a crazy instant the image of Flint holding those white, lacy panties in his large capable hand flashed into Zach's brain. He blinked. "*Tonight?*"

Flint looked slightly exasperated. "You do know the PI biz is not nine to five? You *had* to have picked that much up."

"Of course I know that! I just… I'll phone you as soon as I get back to the office."

Flint sighed, gave a slight shake of his head, and took another swallow of his highball.

Zach groaned inwardly and returned to the patio. Alton was putting his phone away as he reached their table and slid into his seat.

Alton frowned, opened his mouth, and Zach beat him to the punch. "Everything okay?"

"Hm? Yes. That was Ran. He's flying in tomorrow morning and wanted to be sure someone would be at the airport to pick him up."

Ran would be Ransford. Alton's younger brother. The guy who blamed his financial struggles on Rusty Jordan, for reasons that were so far unclear to Zach.

"Business or pleasure?"

"Both." Alton was still frowning. "Were you able to calm your friend?"

"Maybe." Zach's smile was apologetic. "I'm sorry for that little scene, but you did hear me on the phone with him before you hired me."

"I had no idea he was following you around town."

"Neither did I. Hopefully, tonight will be the end of it. I think seeing me with someone else may have finally made the end of our relationship real for him."

Alton relaxed, said lightly, "Well, I'm sorry for him. But Happy Ever After is for fairytales."

"Yeah." No doubt true, but Zach still found that a depressing thought.

Alton offered one of those distant, chilly smiles. Zach waited for him to mention seeing Flint, but their meals arrived, fragrant and as beautifully plated as something out of a magazine. By the time their server departed, Alton had moved on to other topics.

As he savored a bite of his short ribs, he remarked, "I need something to look forward to. What do you do for fun, Zach? What should we do this weekend?"

Were they spending another weekend together? This was something Zach hadn't anticipated—and frankly, wasn't thrilled to hear. As welcome as the money would be—

His thoughts were interrupted by a high, brittle voice behind him. An unfamiliar voice. A woman's voice.

"Yes, Alton," the woman said. "What *are* we doing this weekend?"

CHAPTER EIGHT

"**Z**-Zora!"

This was the first time Alton sounded truly rattled, and Zach felt a flash of alarm. He swiveled in his seat and stared up—and up.

The woman towering over their table reminded him a bit of a Tim Burton character. She had a pale moon of a face set on a long, stick-thin body draped in sheer, flowy black...curtains? Probably not. But flowy black garments suitable for prowling the sea cliffs at midnight or rising from the family crypt as required. Her hair was colorless and lank. She wore no makeup, and her pallid face was oddly featureless—not counting her scary, blazing eyes.

"What are you doing out?" Alton demanded.

Which definitely sounded peculiar until Zach remembered that Zora was supposed to be an agoraphobe who hadn't left the family estate in more than a decade.

Actually, even after that recollection, it *still* sounded peculiar—and so did Zora's response.

"I thought I'd see how the other half lives." So far, she had not even glanced at Zach, which he wasn't entirely sorry about. Her burning gaze was laser-focused on Alton, who was almost literally shrinking in his chair. "Anyway, I'm not your prisoner yet. However much you wish I was."

Alton's laugh sounded cartoonishly guilty, which was not reassuring. Nor was the uneasy glance he threw around the patio. Unsurprisingly, their fellow diners were as rapt as if watching dinner theater.

Alton half rose. "Zora, you're not well. This is a-a business dinner. Let me have Chico drive you home."

Zora raised her hand, and Alton subsided in his chair. Zach couldn't help wondering if the former Miss Kaschak hadn't served as inspiration, if not the actual model, for some of the more disturbing animatronics at the Haunted Hollow theme park.

He glanced around instinctively for Flint and spotted him lounging casually in the open door leading into the restaurant. He was sipping his drink as he took in the evening's entertainment.

"You're not the first, whatever he told you. And you won't be the last."

Zach realized he was being addressed. He glanced back at Zora and found her withering gaze trained on him.

"Mrs. Beacher, this really is a business dinner." It *was* a business dinner, although that's what he'd say in any case, but also he couldn't help his instinctive rejection of the idea that he was fooling around with a married man.

Zora smiled a scary smile. "Whatever he told you about my not giving him a divorce is a lie. He knows he can have his freedom whenever he wants. But it comes with a price." She turned her smile on Alton. "He doesn't want to pay the price, do you, Alton?"

Alton said faintly, "Zora…"

Zora's, "Don't say you weren't warned," could have been directed at Alton or Zach or both of them.

In any case, that was her final word. Zora turned and walked—well, with all the black shrouds it was more like wafted—away.

Waitstaff scurried out of her path. As she passed Flint in the wide doorway, he raised his glass in salute. She never turned her head, never blinked.

After a moment or two, Zach and Alton's fellow diners returned to their meals, although Zach could feel the weight of surreptitious gazes, hear the murmur of delightfully scandalized discussion.

Alton let out a long shaky breath. "Well...that was an unpleasant surprise."

"Yep."

Alton opened his mouth in response to Zach's terse comment, but the waiter arrived to see if they needed anything.

A cloak of invisibility? Police assistance? A time machine? Zach kept his mouth shut, of course.

"Shall we get this to go?" Alton asked of him, and Zach nodded. His stomach was too full of knots to have room for food. He couldn't have faked his way through the meal if his life had depended on it.

Alton handed his credit card over, and the waiter departed with their plates. Alton leaned forward, saying quietly, "Zach, I'm sorry. I never expected Zora to show up. She only ever leaves the house to visit her mother or to see her doctor."

Conscious of the surrounding ears straining to hear their conversation, Zach restrained himself to a mild, "Sure."

It wasn't like he blamed Alton. But the point of all this pretend dating was for word to get back to Zora, and once that end was achieved, Alton had to have anticipated *some* reaction. Zach had hoped any drama would be held behind closed doors—that had been naive on his part—but Alton had to know his wife well enough to more accurately gauge her response.

Alton finished his drink in a gulp. "She must have discovered where I was dining from Mrs. Honeybun."

"Mrs....?" Zach tried to remember if there had been a Mrs. Honeybun in Alton's dossier.

"Honeybun. Our housekeeper. Or perhaps she pried it out of Topper. Our butler."

The butler did it!

Zach swallowed an unseemly laugh. "Maybe. But isn't it more likely Rusty Jordan filled her in after the weekend at Pebble Beach?"

Alton frowned. He said thoughtfully, "He'll have certainly told her by now that I'm involved with a very handsome young man, but Rusty couldn't know where I was dining tonight."

True.

"Maybe she's having you followed."

Alton's eyes widened. For a moment, he looked truly alarmed. "You mean, *Zora* could have hired a PI?"

"It's been known to happen."

Alton's jaw dropped. He looked automatically toward the wide doorway where Flint had previously positioned himself to enjoy the festivities. "My God. I think you're right! In fact, I know you are. I think she hired that thug who operates across the parking lot from you."

"*Flint?*"

"Yes! You had to have seen him. He was sitting here on the patio. He went inside right after you and your friend left to talk."

For one startled instant, Zach wondered if Flint was indeed playing double agent.

How ironic if Zach was paying him to do what Flint had already been hired for. Was it possible?

Second by horrified second, he relived every word of every conversation he'd had with Flint over the past twenty-four hours.

But no. That was too hard to swallow.

Flint really *hadn't* wanted to take this job. He really had seemed tired and out of sorts. Whereas, if he'd already been hired by Zora, he'd surely have jumped at the opportunity.

Flint was not devious.

At least...Zach didn't think so. In all honesty, he didn't know Flint well enough to know if he was devious or not. If he was, he was really good at concealing it—and what could be more devious than that?

"Are you all right? Your eyes are glazed," Alton observed.

"Hm? Oh. No. I just... Yes, I saw Flint earlier. But is he the kind of person Zora would hire?"

"I suppose he has a certain animal magnetism." Alton's tone was grudging.

Yes. Flint definitely had a certain...something.

Zach remembered that little silent toast Flint had made as Zora passed him in the doorway.

Was it possible?

His heart sank.

Yes. It was possible.

The waiter arrived with their elegantly packaged meals. Alton scrawled his signature on the check. "Ready?" he asked Zach.

Zach was already on his feet, shrugging into his coat.

They moved toward the restaurant entryway, Alton's hand resting possessively on Zach's back.

"Why don't we drive to the beach house," Alton was saying. "We can finish our meal in private and consider our next move."

"*Is* there a next move?" Zach scanned the crowded interior of the restaurant, but there was no sign of Flint.

Was he in the gents? Had he left to follow Zora? The job was to keep an eye on Alton. Zach tried unsuccessfully to smother his rising anxiety.

"Of course there's a next move. What do you mean?" Alton ushered Zach through the front doors.

The crisp night had that vaguely melancholy, earthy autumn scent. A smell of sugary decay, as though all the pumpkin-spice candles in the world had been pinched out in one fell heartless swoop. The Bentley, rain-glittered in the lamplight, sat idling on the cobbled street. Chico stood at attention beside the car.

Had Flint been wrong about Chico speeding away earlier? Would there be any advantage in lying about such a thing? Hard to imagine. More likely Chico had just been in a hurry to have his dinner and return before Alton was ready to leave the restaurant.

Trails of exhaust wound ghostlike through the herb garden and around their ankles as they walked down the steps.

Chico held the door as Alton—his hand still plastered to Zach's back—guided him in.

"We're going to the beach house," Alton informed Chico.

"Yessir."

"After you drop me off at my office," Zach said quickly.

"What? No," Alton protested. "We're still having dinner." He ineffectually pawed at Zach's back.

"We're going back to the office," Zach told Chico, and Chico shook his head. Not in refusal, but like Zach was a bigger fool than he'd imagined.

"But we haven't eaten." Alton was still patting Zach. Like… What the hell? "*You* haven't eaten."

"Thanks, but I had all the dinner I need." Zach crawled to the relative safety of the farthest corner of wide ostrich-leather seat. He felt tired and disgusted, mostly with himself. His goal was to get home safely, without any further fireworks.

The idea that Flint might be playing both sides had left him feeling unexpectedly, uncharacteristically depressed and full of self-doubt.

And Alton…

He was getting very tired of Alton's efforts to corner him.

I hope to hell he didn't spike my drink when I left the table…

It was not a good feeling to realize you couldn't trust your colleagues, let alone your client. He could just imagine what Pop would think about all—or any—of this.

Alton climbed into the luxurious back seat next to Zach. Chico slammed the door shut. Mere seconds later, the car glided soundlessly away as though on velvet-covered tires.

"I don't understand you, Zach. What's wrong?" There was a small rattle as Alton popped a breath mint.

"Why did you lie to me?" Zach asked. "I specifically asked when you hired me whether you'd had affairs in the past, and you said no."

It was hard to see clearly in the gloom, but he heard the little *smack* of Alton licking his lips. He didn't answer Zach.

"I asked whether you'd had gay relationships, and again, you said no. Both those things are clearly a lie."

That seemed to sting Alton to a response. "Zach, you can't go by anything Zora says. She's not well. She's not *sane*."

"I'm not going by what Zora said. I'm going by what Rusty said yesterday morning at the hotel. Zora just confirmed it. You've done this before."

"Never." Alton sounded adamant.

"Okay. Maybe not the hiring-a-PI part. Maybe you didn't go out of your way to *publicize* these relationships, but you've definitely engaged in—"

"They were *not* relationships." After a pause, Alton added reluctantly, "They were, at most, sexual liaisons."

"Okay, well, talk about splitting hairs. Obviously, these encounters were something I needed to be aware of."

Alton said huffily, "I don't see why."

"*Alton.*"

"You don't need to be jealous."

"*Jealous?* Are you serious? Alton, the main reason—or at least, I *thought* the main reason you hired me was to find out who's threatening your life."

"We already know who's threatening my life!"

"Zora." Zach's tone was flat.

"Yes! Zora. *Of course,* Zora. I told you that at the outset."

Well, in fairness, he *had* told Zach that at the outset. Which, in retrospect, made this entire job all the more baffling.

"I thought there was more of a question about it. If there was no question about who was sending those threats, then was I really only hired to play escort?"

Alton patted his knee. "Of *course* not. I wanted—needed—to have my suspicions confirmed by a professional. But the *most* important aspect of the job was this. Yes. I'm sure I made that very clear."

Zach pointedly moved Alton's hand off his knee, twisting his wrist away when Alton tried to clasp his hand. He did not want to get rough. Not least because he was afraid Alton might enjoy that.

"What isn't clear—please don't do that—is how this helps anything."

Alton made a sound of impatience and, to Zach's relief, scooted an inch or two away. He stared pointedly out the window.

Zach had a younger sister prone to dishing out the silent treatment. He was a master at ignoring being ignored. He said, "It's obvious Zora already knows you're bisexual. She already knows you've had affairs with men. It's pretty clear she doesn't feel any more kindly about giving you a divorce now than when you first showed up on Thursday morning. So what's the point of all this?"

"Because now it's real," Alton snapped. "Now others know about it, too. *Now* the threats won't be enough. Zora will certainly try to kill me."

As Zach gazed in disbelief at what he could see of Alton's shadowy features, Alton added unemotionally, "And probably you as well."

CHAPTER NINE

What a god-awful evening.

Between Ben's unexpected appearance, Zora's unexpected appearance, and Flint's unexpected *dis*appearance…

Would Flint even show up for their "debriefing"?

There had been no response to Zach's text, and Zach had his doubts, though this late-night meet had been Flint's idea.

He stared out at the empty shopping center parking lot. The night sky was starless. Tall silhouettes of palm trees swayed in the wind. Rain peppered the windows and glass door. The other businesses were shuttered and closed.

No question, the world felt like a dark and unfriendly place.

The odd part was, the thing most bothering him was his fear that Flint was working against him. That he had so misread Flint, so misjudged the situation. It wasn't as if he didn't know Flint was his business rival. Hell, not just his rival. Flint actively, openly wanted to take over his business.

Zach knew that. Yet he had somehow thought asking Flint for help, sharing the confidential details of his biggest and most important case with a competitor, was a good idea. *Brooke* thought it was a good idea. That alone should have clued him in to what a bad idea it was. So really, if he was upset with anyone, he was upset with himself. Flint was just being Flint.

You couldn't fault a tiger for preferring gazelle over the salad bar.

Zach smothered a yawn, wiped the fogged glass of the front door. He really needed to get some sleep. How long was he planning to wait here under the glaring fluorescent lights when Flint was probably tucked up in bed dreaming of…whatever Flint dreamed of. Hot chicks in red Ferraris?

Yeah, a good night's sleep, a good breakfast, a million cups of coffee, and he'd be back to his normal optimistic, confident—delusional, in Ben's opinion—self. And then he could figure out what the heck he was going to do about Alton. Because he really, really, *really* hated to lose this gig. But he'd already earned that advance on the weekend, and maybe he needed to be satisfied with that. Alton was a handful, and while Zach felt fully capable of fending off his awkward advances, the unsettling suspicion that Alton just might be off enough to eventually try drugging him persisted.

Alton did increasingly seem like the drug-your-drink-when-you-weren't-looking type.

Not that Zach had experience with that type, but the more time he spent with Alton, the more he suspected Alton was a genuine, bona fide creep.

In fact, he was starting to wonder if there had ever actually been any real death threats. Alton himself could easily have manufactured those toys bearing ominous messages.

Who better? Maybe this was a stunt Alton pulled on a regular basis.

Although to what end? It seemed a little elaborate if the goal was just to find guys to hook up with.

The twin dots of headlights appeared at the shopping center entrance, and Zach's heart sprang awake. He watched as the white beams swept down the drive. A silver Ford Explorer cut across the empty lot, speeding toward Davies Detective Agency.

Flint.

He was startled at the rush of relief that washed over him. Was he really that afraid Flint might be working against him?

Come to think of it, did Flint's showing up prove that he wasn't in cahoots with Angelique—er, Zora?

The SUV came to a stop catty-corner across two empty parking spaces. The lights blinked off. The car door opened, and Flint, in a hooded parka, got out and loped across the oil puddles and gleaming asphalt to the sidewalk.

Zach unlocked the door and held it open.

"Hey," Flint said, pushing back the hood of his coat. His expression was unexpectedly bleak.

"What happened to you?"

"I followed the wife back to her lair."

"Why? The job is Beacher." Zach was frowning, and Flint frowned right back.

"Because I wanted to make sure she actually made it home."

"Why wouldn't she?"

"Are you serious?"

Here was a new and startling idea. Zach said slowly, "You thought Zora might have been lying in wait to ambush Alton?"

"Huh?" Flint did a double take. "What? *No.* Are you kidding?"

"Isn't that what you—"

Flint laughed. It was unexpectedly and even sort of boyishly attractive the way his eyes crinkled and his nose wrinkled just a smidge—or at least would have been attractive if the laughter hadn't been directed at Zach. "You think she's going to jump out of the bushes or roll a gigantic mirror across the road?"

Zach flushed hotly. "I'm asking what *you* think!" But yeah, something like that had flitted through his brain—and then *kept* flitting, because *of course* either of those scenarios was bonkers, but that had seemed to be what Flint was suggesting.

Jeez. It was *late*. He was *tired*. Okay?

He managed not to make that protest, though.

Flint was saying, "I didn't like the fact that clearly someone tipped her off about your date or that Beacher's bodyguard suddenly took off after dropping you two at the restaurant."

"It wasn't a date," Zach said automatically.

Flint snorted. "Really? Well, you could have fooled me and everyone else at that restaurant."

"My relationship with Alton Beacher is completely professional."

"I'm not arguing. I just think you may be confusing professions."

Zach turned red again. "Ha. Ha. HA. Look, I already had to hear it all from Ben. There's *nothing* going on between me and Alton. It was a job. Not a date."

"Beacher thinks it was a date, and that's all that matters from his wife's point of view."

"Whatever. I still don't understand why you—" Zach recoiled as Flint snapped his fingers in front of his nose.

"*Wake up, Zachariah!* Did you even bother to read that file you copied for me?"

"Stop it. Of course I read it!"

"Then how the hell do you not see that the intended victim here is *her*, not him."

"Her?" Zach blinked. "Her who? *Zora?*"

"Is there another woman in this case I'm unaware of? Yes. Zora. *Of course,* Zora. And, possibly, probably, eventually *you*."

"*Me?*"

Flint shook his head. "Yes, *you*. Wake up! You're a born patsy if there ever was one."

"Well, thanks a lot. And you're a born asshole."

"Possibly," Flint said evenly. "Which doesn't change the fact that I think your client is trying to kill his wife."

"I need to know the truth. Are you working for Zora?"

There was no mistaking the astonishment on Flint's face. "Huh?"

"Is that why you agreed to this job? Had you already been hired by Zora?"

Flint repeated almost wonderingly, "Already hired by *Zora*?"

"Were you?"

"Hell, no. Are you kidding? Where in the hell did you—I don't have to be working for someone to be concerned for their safety. Or to see what's in front of my nose. You can believe everything Beacher told you, but take it from me, there are always a couple of different outcomes for any given set of circumstances."

Combinatorics, that's what Flint was talking about. The branch of mathematics concerned with problems of selection, arrangement, and operation within a finite or discrete system. Flint was perfectly right.

Zach opened his mouth, but no words came to him. A series of unwelcome and unsettling inklings flashed through his memory.

Flint's eyes narrowed. "You think so, too."

"No," Zach protested. "Of course I don't think that. But..."

"But?"

"But *something* weird is going on. I told you earlier I felt something was off. You said yourself you thought something was off when Alton first approached you. That's why I wanted some backup."

"Something's off all right. You're helping this creep commit murder."

Zach's dismay—in particular, dismay that Flint might be right—grew. "The hell! How can you be so sure that's what's going on? You've been working this case less than twenty-four hours."

Flint slapped his forehead, which, until that moment, was a move Zach had only seen in cartoons. "Forget all the *he said, she said*. Just look at the setup on paper. Who has an actual motive for murder? The wife's the one with the real money."

"Wealth is relative."

"Spoken like someone who's broke. Multimillions are not relative. The Kaschak Corporation brings in over a quarter of a billion annually—and Zora's the sole heir to that fortune. Beacher's company brings in not quite three million a year. And he's still paying off her initial investment in his company. I thought you were an accountant. Do the math."

That smarted on multiple levels. Zach said, "Money's not the only motive in the world. People commit murder for plenty of other reasons. In fact, more murders are committed out of anger or the need to exert control or assume power over the victim than for money."

"Says you."

"Yes, says me. Because it's true."

"Not in my experience."

"But you won't handle anything to do with divorce or adultery or infidelity, so your experience is limited."

Flint spluttered, "*M-my* experience is limited?" But then, surprisingly, he fell silent, seeming to consider. He said grudgingly, "Okay, maybe you've got a point. But I don't have to be an accountant to know there are huge financial incentives for your client getting rid of his wife. That's not even calculating in the fact that they live on *her* family estate. And those are just the *nothing-personal-honey* reasons for getting her out of the way."

"All of that was true when they married, though. If he was just going to knock her off for the money, why would he wait so long? They've been married over twenty years."

Flint said, "Because things change. Maybe they did love each other at one time. People fall out of love. Sadly. Sometimes they even end up hating each other. There's a reason husbands and wives are always the first suspects when the other is knocked off."

Zach was thinking about that *sadly* of Flint's. Flint didn't seem like the sentimental type, but yeah, it was sad that love didn't always last forever. He was sad about how things had ended with Ben. Speaking of ending up hating each other, Ben was well on the way to hating him. Zach's mom and pop were another case of two people who started out in love and ended up not even liking the other person. They had stayed together, though. They hadn't hated each other. Mom's tears had been real when Pop passed.

"I didn't see any love lost tonight, that's for sure," Flint said.

"No."

Alton wasn't easy to read, but Zach hadn't seen anything but guilt, discomfort, and a nervousness that bordered on actual fear. Alton had showed no real concern or sympathy for anyone but himself.

In fairness, who knew what he put up with at home? Maybe Zora made his life a living hell. Maybe he had good reason to be afraid of rather than concerned for her. Just because there were solid financial reasons (at least on paper) for wanting Zora out of the way didn't mean Alton was actually planning to kill her.

Alton was the one receiving death threats. And if looks could kill—Zora's expression that night had been murderous.

Zora hated Alton. Of that, Zach had no doubt.

Zach protested, "This isn't even circumstantial. It's entirely speculative. I mean, why would Alton hire a PI if he's planning to murder his wife? The last thing he'd want is to draw the attention of another investigator."

Flint sighed. It was a very weary sound. "Have you really never stopped to wonder why Alton Beacher, with his money and his resources, tried to hire two small independent PIs rather than a big, high-powered firm? I can guarantee you that when Beacher's got a problem with employee theft or insurance fraud or industrial espionage, he hires the Pinkertons or somebody like that. He doesn't drive to the local shopping center and play eeny, meeny, miny, moe."

"Maybe he's never had those kinds of problems at his company. Maybe this is the first time he's ever needed a private investigator." Before Flint could respond, Zach added, "Plus, hiring someone to pose as his boyfriend might not fly with one of those companies."

"In my experience, money—enough money—will buy you anything you want. But okay, let that go. What's the advantage of making sure that not just Zora, but lots of people know he's got a young and very pretty new boyfriend?"

Zach did a double take at that *very-pretty* descriptor, but he let it go. "Alton said that if Zora believed he was actually gay, she would give him his divorce without trying to ruin him."

Flint nodded. "Okay. You saw Zora in action tonight. How do you think Alton's plan is working out?"

"It's not."

Flint gave another of those encouraging—and slightly exasperating—nods. "Good. Because?"

Zach said reluctantly, "Because, for one thing, she already knows he's bisexual. Alton being involved with me doesn't change anything as far as she's concerned. And also, Zora is already willing to give him a divorce."

"I mean, right there. What does *that* tell you?"

"Okay, but she did say in a very sinister tone that there was a price to be paid. It's just that I'm not sure the price is what Alton led me to believe. He said she'd threatened to kill herself and frame him for her murder."

Flint's mouth twitched at Zach's very-sinister-tone comment. But all he said was, "How convenient if she subsequently turns up dead under possibly suspicious circumstances. He's got a ready-made witness to the fact that she'd threatened to frame him for her suicide."

"It's hearsay. But yeah."

"*I* think your client is going out of his way to make his wife look crazy."

Zach couldn't really argue. He thought it over, said, "In fairness, she didn't exactly seem the model of stability."

"The model of stability wouldn't have married that guy in the first place."

Maybe? Probably? Was there anything more mysterious than what drew dissimilar people together?

All at once Zach was very tired. The evening had gone from peculiar to surreal. Was he really standing here under these too bright fluorescent lights, trying to make sense of that little glimmer of something like sympathy in Flint Carey's hard, hazel eyes?

He let out a long, shaky breath. "I was already thinking I should probably terminate my contract with Alton."

"I think that's a very good idea." Flint was crisp. "I don't trust Alton not to have some backup plan to turn you into the fall guy if there happened to be some suspicion in his wife's death."

Zach absorbed that dully. He wasn't as shocked as he would have been twenty-four hours earlier. In fact, he thought Flint was probably right.

"If Alton really is planning to murder Zora, I can't just leave it at that. I can't just quit and walk away. I *have* to go to the police."

He was expecting Flint to approve of this idea, but Flint looked noncommittal.

"You don't think so?"

"I think we don't have any proof. I think Alton Beacher has a lot of clout around these parts. We can go to the police, but they might not believe us. Either way, we'll have tipped our hand to Alton."

"But then... We can't just stand by and do nothing!"

"We could be wrong."

Zach said, "We could be right! In which case, an innocent woman dies because we—*I*— was afraid of looking stupid."

Flint's brows rose. "*Are* you afraid of looking stupid?"

Zach said bitterly, "Not particularly. It seems like I have plenty of experience at it."

"There's another possibility," Flint said.

"Which is what?"

"We go to Mrs. Kaschak-Beacher, share our suspicions of her husband, and see if she wants to hire us to stop him."

CHAPTER TEN

Zach didn't enjoy sleeping alone.

He liked the warmth of another body sharing his bed. He liked sharing a quiet late-night chat or waking up to smiling eyes or—whatever. Hell, he liked cuddling, although that was probably not something a PI should admit to. So sue him. He just liked having someone there—even if that someone was sound asleep—when he woke from a bad dream. He'd been having *a lot* of bad dreams lately. And Monday night was no exception.

Mr. Bigglesworth, however, did his best to fill the void, and Zach woke on Tuesday morning to Mr. B. batting at his hand, as he did when trying to get some reaction from his mouse toys.

"*Hey!*" Zach snatched his nipped finger back. "Not so hard!"

Mr. B. objected—or maybe he was simply pointing out the lateness of the hour. Zach peered at clock on the bed stand, pushed his hair out of his face, and peered closer.

"*Hell.*" He kicked the blankets off, then stumbled into the kitchen to turn on the coffee maker and feed Mr. B. He retrieved the soggy morning paper from the bottom front step, dropped it off in the kitchen, and headed to the bathroom for a hot and steamy shower.

Despite the bracing combination of eucalyptus mist and green-tea soap, his memory of the night before felt slightly out of focus. He agreed with Flint, in principle, about speaking to Zora Kaschak-Beacher about the potential threat to her safety. But he also felt it was only right to talk to Alton as well and give him a chance to further explain his position. After all, Alton was his client. Alton had come to him for help. And, while his doubts about and distaste for Alton grew daily, it didn't change the fact that he had an obligation to, at the very least, treat him fairly.

Flint had not seen it that way. Which wasn't exactly a surprise.

What *was* maybe a surprise was that Flint, having stated his position, didn't try to push or pressure Zach into making a decision then and there.

"Sleep on it," he'd said. "We'll talk more tomorrow."

That's where they'd left it.

Zach was grateful for the breathing room, but a few hours of uneasy sleep had not helped him reach a decision. Or at least, did not leave him feeling better about what he viewed as his only real choice.

Plus, in the cold light of day—well, dawn—the dramatic turns of the night before felt distant and dreamlike. Starting with Ben popping out of the bamboo hedge and ending with Alton informing Zach he too might be a target.

Well, no, the final moment of surreality—was that a word?—had been when Flint shared his theory that Zach's client was actually plotting to murder his wife.

Not that Zach dismissed Flint's concerns. When he'd first flipped through Alton's dossier, it had occurred to him that, on paper at least, Zora looked like the more likely candidate for murder.

Even so... It was just so *bizarre*.

Then again, this case had been bizzarro from day one.

He had to admire Flint's clarity of vision and straightforward approach to problem-solving. Not that that would work in all circumstances—Zach wasn't even sure Flint's approach was the right one in *these* circumstances—but there was something relaxing about someone who didn't constantly second-guess himself. Something refreshing about someone so...unblinkingly pragmatic.

Zach turned off the shower tap, shook the water from his hair, and climbed out of the tub.

He went mechanically through his morning routine of tooth brushing and shaving and blow-drying his hair.

Alton was already not happy with him. Was there a way to ask if his hiring Davies Detective Agency had actually been a cover for plans to murder his wife that *wouldn't* end with the termination of their contract? Probably not.

That wasn't even Zach's first concern. Alton was wealthy and, in this part of the state at least, influential. Not someone Zach could afford to have as an enemy. Not because he was personally afraid—although he wasn't thrilled at the idea of mayhem or murder—but because of the damage that could be done to Davies Detective Agency and, by extension, Brooke and his mother.

Last night, Flint hadn't seemed to share those fears, but he too had had a few hours to reflect and consider. Maybe he would feel differently about approaching Zora directly. Maybe they could come up with a Plan B. Or even a Plan

C that did not leave them in such a strategically precarious position.

"Maybe," Zach told his reflection, slowly emerging from the steamy mists fogging the bathroom mirror. "We'll see."

He headed for the bedroom, dressed, and returned to the kitchen, where he popped his frittatas in the microwave, poured his coffee, spread out the drying pages of the *Ensenada Signal*—and nearly sprayed the cupboards with caffeine.

TOYMAKER ALTON BEACHER DEAD IN CAR ACCIDENT

Zach's breath stuck in his throat. His horrified gaze was fixed to each dire letter of the stark banner headline.

ALTON. BEACHER. DEAD.

No. No. No. This is a mistake.

His heart was pounding so hard, little black spots danced before his eyes. He could barely make out the words of the newspaper article. It did not sound like there was much chance of a mistake.

Wealthy toymaker Alton Beacher died early Tuesday morning in a fiery car crash on Paradise Road on Mount del Sello in Monterey, California. Beacher appears to have been behind the wheel when his Porsche Boxster swerved on the winding road and went off the embankment. The vehicle's second occupant, identified as Marcus Topper, an employee and member of Beacher's household, was thrown clear and has been taken to Monterey Memorial Hospital. His condition is listed as critical.

Marcus Topper? Who was Marcus Topper? Was that the butler? Why had Alton been on that road at that time of day with his butler? Where was Chico? Why wasn't Chico driving?

Monterey County Sheriff's Office has not yet identified the cause of the accident.

"She killed him," Zach whispered.

But it was so much worse than that—as bad as that was. *He* was to blame for this. *He* had failed to protect his client.

Not only that, he had begun to believe his client was out to get the woman who had just murdered him.

His cell phone rang, the sound shrill in the tiny kitchen, and Zach jumped. He looked around wildly. It took him a moment to locate his phone on the table. A glance at the screen showed a local number he didn't recognize.

He pressed Accept, answering with a cautious, "Zach speaking."

Flint said, "Have you seen the news this morning?"

Zach gulped out, "Just now."

"We need to talk."

Zach said huskily, "Yes." But really, did they? Flint had got it about as wrong as you could—and Zach hadn't done much better. Zach needed to go to the police and share everything he knew about the case.

"When can you get here?"

"I—I'm about to leave now."

"I'll see you at my office."

"Okay. I guess?"

"Zachariah?"

"I'm here."

"Stay sharp."

"Stay…"

Flint snapped, "Watch your driving!"

"Of course. Right. Yes." Zach spoke automatically. He was wondering if Flint thought he was a target as well. No, more likely, Flint recognized that Zach was deeply shocked and maybe not at his…well, sharpest.

Not at his sharpest? That defined his performance on this case from the beginning.

"I'll see you when I get there." Zach disconnected.

"**O**h my God," Brooke greeted Zach when he pushed through the glass doors of Davies Detective Agency thirty minutes later. "I can't believe it!"

That wasn't Brooke's latent sleuthing skills surfacing; that was one sibling recognizing the reason for the shock and distress on the face of another. Brooke herself was looking a little green around the gills.

Zach said gruffly. "Me neither."

"The news really didn't say anything. Could it have been an accident?"

"I don't know. That would be pretty coincidental."

"Coincidences *do* happen."

Zach said tersely, "I don't buy it."

"It's so *awful*."

Understatement of the century.

"I'm supposed to meet with Flint. Can you…" He met Brooke's stricken gaze. What? Hold his calls? What calls? Their best and only client was dead. They would probably never have a call—or client—again. Which was not nearly as bad as what had happened to poor Alton.

God. He couldn't stand to think about it.

You had one fucking job...

Brooke nodded. Zach opened the door again—he was just fumbling through the motions, in honesty—and Brooke said quickly, "Zee, it's not your fault."

He turned to face her. "Really? Whose fault is it? Alton hired us—*me*—to prevent this. I've had nearly a week to figure out who was behind those threats, and I haven't figured out a damn thing. And now he's dead!"

"It wasn't a week! It's been barely...not even really five full days!"

Zach closed his eyes, pinched the bridge of his nose hard.

"Zee. You always do this. You always take the blame for other people's bad choices."

He shook his head. Opened his eyes. "I blew it. It's that simple." He appreciated Brooke's loyalty, but come on. He'd made *zero* progress in finding out who had wanted Alton dead. In fact, he'd gone so far off the rails, he'd started imagining Alton was the real bad guy!

He stepped outside, letting the door fall shut on Brooke's protests.

Arlisse Smith, Flint's smartly dressed, sixtysomething office manager, was briskly typing away at her desktop when Zach pushed through the glass door, and the mood in the tiny office was so utterly calm, so utterly *normal*, he felt as if he'd accidentally wandered into another dimension.

"Good morning, Zach." Arlisse's smile seemed eerily untroubled, but once upon a time she'd worked as the administrative assistant to Portola Elementary School's principal, so the transition to PI's Girl Friday was probably a cakewalk.

Zach resisted the temptation to offer a bitter *Is it?* and instead mumbled a subdued, "Good morning."

"You can go straight through," Arlisse informed him as she had informed generations of six graders.

Zach stepped past the desk—Flint's front office was even tinier than theirs—and knocked once on the closed door.

The door swung open. Flint, wearing jeans and a dark hoodie—perhaps forgoing his usual Hawaiian shirt out of respect for the departed—seemed to be blocking the doorway. For a second Zach thought it was standing room only in the closet, but no. It turned out Flint was throwing darts at the dartboard behind his desk.

"Hey." Flint was even more laconic than usual, his expression bleak and uncharacteristically weary. He leaned past Zach, their chests brushing in a way Zach found startlingly distracting, and requested, "Coffee, Arlisse?"

Surely Arlisse's cheery, "You got it, Chief!" was ironic?

"Sit." Flint backed up, pointed to the room's second chair, which had been pushed to the far—far, being relative—wall.

Zach dropped into the small club style chair—had Arlisse liberated kindergarten furniture from Portola Elementary School when she departed?—and Flint took the chair behind his cluttered desk.

He folded his arms across his broad chest and brooded at Zach for a long moment. "I hate to cut short the all-expenses-paid guilt trip, but we've got work to do."

Zach's head snapped up. He glared. "Guilt trip? I *am* guilty. I was hired to protect—"

The office door opened, and Arlisse appeared, bearing a small wooden tray with two coffee mugs and miniature-sized accoutrements.

She set the tray on Flint's desk and said to no one in particular, "Just a reminder that these walls are thinner than the bargain brand toilet tissue in the restroom."

Flint growled, "Is there anyone in the waiting room?"

"I continue to hope."

"I continue to pay your salary," Flint retorted.

"Is that what you call it?"

Having had the last word, Arlisse let the door fall closed behind her.

Flint reached into his desk drawer and removed a small silver flask. He uncapped the flask and splashed…well, going by the standard tropes, rye whisky? in his mug.

Zach said, "Now there's a cliché." Adding hastily, "None for—"

Flint had already splashed amber liquid into the second mug. "Relax. It's a vitamin B wellness tonic."

"*Is* it?"

Flint laughed. "Hell no." He sipped from the first mug. "Drink your coffee, Zachariah."

"Thanks, but I don't need to be hammered at nine in the morning."

Flint spluttered into his coffee. "You'd have to be six years old to get hammered on half a shot of Bushmills." Zach opened his mouth, and Flint sighed. "Listen, you're in shock, understandably, so just this one single, solitary time will you please forgo the chance to argue?"

Lips compressed, Zach leaned over, tore open a packet of sugar and emptied it into his coffee, splashed in a tiny capsule of half-and-half, ripped open the stir stick and briskly stirred, then sat back with his mug. He sipped the whisky-laced brew and said shortly, "I don't always argue about everything."

Flint's mouth twitched, but he preserved his all-business-all-the-time expression. "If it helps, I didn't see this coming either."

"It doesn't help," Zach replied.

Flint sighed. "I know."

"I failed my client in the worst possible way."

Flint's eyes narrowed. "Then you *were* his bodyguard?"

"No, but—"

"Then you *weren't* his bodyguard?"

Zach stared at Flint's hard, impassive face. "No, I wasn't, but..." Maybe it was the whisky. Maybe it was the unexpected understanding in Flint's gaze. But some of the tightness eased in Zach's chest. He felt like he could finally take a full breath again.

He said, more shakily than he'd have liked, "I know what you're trying to do, Flint, and I...but Alton expected me to find out who was behind the threats. He was relying on *me* to figure that out so he could take the steps to protect himself."

"Okay." Flint nodded in acknowledgment. "You spent plenty of time with him, so you can answer this better than I can. My impression, watching you two together last night, was Alton was not in fear of his life. In fact, if anything, he was going out of his way to provoke a response from his wife."

Zach continued to regard Flint, but he was looking inward, reviewing the long, weird weekend with Alton, remembering the way Alton kept brushing him off every time he tried to bring up the investigation. That had become a pattern early on. He turned his thoughts to the evening before.

He said slowly, "He was nervous, uneasy, after Zora showed up at dinner. I think he was a little afraid. Then."

"Maybe because the missus was acting out of character? She's supposed to be chained to the estate by acrophobia, right?"

"Agoraphobia. Acrophobia is fear of heights."

"Regardless."

"He was surprised for sure. I think it was clear there was no going back."

"Be careful what you wish for," Flint commented. "Do you think your client was honest with you?"

"No." That time Zach didn't have to think about it.

"Do you think your client's failure to tell you the truth about what was going on limited your ability to investigate?"

Zach wrestled with it. Certainly, to some extent, his investigation had been hampered by misinformation and misunderstanding of the overall situation. But the real roadblock had been the fact that Alton seemed more interested in seducing Zach than allowing him to investigate. He'd actually seemed a bit impatient, even bored with Zach's attempts to figure out what was going on.

When he didn't answer, Flint said, "I don't know how much, if any, responsibility you have in Beacher's death. We all have to own up to our actions, so for damn sure your client also bears responsibility. And if he failed to be honest with you, if he hamstrung your investigation by lying to you, that's definitely on him."

"I still—"

"I know you still," Flint cut in. "And I'm not saying it was okay for Mrs. Alton Beacher to cut Mr. Beacher's brake line, but I still stand by my theory that your client was planning to get rid of his wife."

Zach stared. "Is that what happened? Was a brake line cut?"

"I have no idea. Yet. I'm going with the obvious scenario for now. I have a call in to a friend at the sheriff's office."

Zach turned that over in his mind for a moment. "You don't think there was any chance it was an accident?"

"You're joking."

Zach frowned. "But then…"

Flint's dark brows rose in inquiry.

Zach said doubtfully, "Does that mean you're investigating this?"

"Hell yes, I'm investigating this," Flint said. "*We're* investigating this."

CHAPTER ELEVEN

Zach's initial flash of hope faded. "I appreciate the offer, but I think this is now a matter for the police."

Flint gave a slight shake of his head. "I'm not asking your permission; I'm telling you I'm going to investigate. I assume we're combining forces, but that's your call."

"But..."

Flint's brows drew together. "But what?"

"We can't—the police won't want or need outside interference."

"Spoken like the kid of an ex-cop."

Zach flushed. "It happens to be the truth. Not to mention, we don't have a client. Who's going to *pay* for this investigation?"

Flint drawled, "I see. You're too busy with all your other cases to do a pro bono?"

Zach could feel the flush receding from his cheeks. "No. You know I don't—I'm not. That doesn't explain why it makes sense for you—for either of us—to interfere in a police investigation."

"Who said interfere? I'm not planning on interfering."

"That's how our involvement will be viewed. I can guarantee it."

"Well, I won't argue. You're the expert on that angle. But you're sitting here chewed up with guilt over Beacher's death. Wouldn't you like to know whether you've got anything to be guilty about?"

"I already know the answer," Zach said shortly. "What I don't know is what you think's in it for you? What's *your* angle?"

"You want the truth? I still plan on acquiring Davies Detective Agency."

Zach blinked. "You…"

"That's right. And I don't want my soon-to-be acquisition sued into bankruptcy before I can even take control."

There was a lot there to unpack—and later set on fire—but the word that really stood out, in fact branded itself on Zach's frontal lobe, was *sued*. He tried to read Flint's impassive face for any sign he was kidding.

He did not appear to be kidding.

"Why would we be sued?"

"Is that a serious question?" Flint studied Zach for a moment. He said gruffly, "Just because *I* don't think you're to blame for what happened to Beacher doesn't mean his wife will agree."

"But if Zora killed him…"

"That's one theory. Beacher's theory, and he wasn't exactly batting a thousand. But let's say Zora *is* this Machiavellian mastermind Beacher feared. If he dies under suspicious circumstances, she knows she's going to be suspect number one. She's going to need a patsy. A fall guy."

Zach said doubtfully, "Right."

"She may have been confused about the role you played in her husband's life, but that's going to be cleared up in a day or so—if it hasn't been already. She's going to know you were hired to investigate the threats on Beacher *and* she's bound to realize he shared his suspicions and fears regarding her with you. That makes you a double threat."

"*Does* it, though? I mean, it's not like I have any proof of anything."

"If I'm Zora, I know I have a very short amount of time to redirect the inevitable suspicion. I have to move fast, and I have to sow a lot of confusion. The first thing I'd do is sue Davies Detective Agency for negligence, wrongful death, and everything else I can think of. That's what an innocent, grieving wife would do, so that's what I do. But it can't stop there."

"Why can't it?" That seemed plenty to Zach. More than he was ready to deal with, frankly.

"Because you know too much. You're a threat to me, so putting you out of business is just the first phase. The second phase of the attack is to implicate *you* in Beacher's death."

Zach had the very weird sensation that his glass lenses were fogging over. They weren't, of course; he could still see perfectly well Flint's glinting eyes boring right into him. But he definitely had the sense of wandering through a misty dreamscape.

He'd always thought of himself as overimaginative, but Flint turned out to be even more imaginative. Or maybe the word was *delusional*?

Or was the word *devious*?

Flint was saying, "Unfortunately, your pervy pal Alton set you up for that one with the fake-boyfriend idiocy.

Anybody who saw you two together last night would have trouble believing that was a strictly-business meeting."

Did that mean Flint still had trouble believing it? The idea bothered Zach probably more than it should have.

"I have a signed contract to prove that's all it was."

"I'm glad to hear it. But that doesn't mean your relationship with Beacher didn't become increasingly personal once the ink dried."

The memory of those lacy panties, now at the very bottom of his trash barrel, made his blood run cold.

"Anyway, she doesn't have to believe it. She just has to make sure enough *other* people do."

This was all getting a little evil-mastermindy. But wasn't that how Alton had described Zora? As some kind of Machiavellian princess willing to kill herself if she could also destroy her husband.

He said slowly, "And you think we should what? Go to the police? I was already going to do that."

"Obviously we go to the police, but not to do the whole mea-culpa, throw-yourself-on-your-sword thing you're clearly planning."

Jesus Christ. This guy!

Zach bristled. "For the record, I'm *never* selling Davies Detective Agency to you!"

Which was a little off-subject, but he had reached the boiling point with Flint's digs.

And Flint. Flint had the gall to smirk. "Yes, you will, Zachariah. Because it's the logical thing to do and, mostly, you try to do the logical thing. Notwithstanding the occasional blip."

"What blip?"

"For starters, the baby-blue vintage Mustang you've been trying to rebuild since you were eighteen."

"How do you…"

Jeez, did he have to sound like a thunderstruck ten-year-old at a magic show? But how the hell did Flint know about Zach's prized, er, hobby, or as Ben liked to refer to it: *the rolling money pit in the garage.*

"Once a year you haul the 'Stang out of mothballs and drive it over here, where you inevitably have to phone a tow truck to get it home. If you think everyone in the shopping center doesn't notice a pristine, baby-blue Mustang on fire—"

"It *never* caught on fire!"

Flint's grin was slightly malicious. "No? My point is, even if that vehicle ran properly, it's totally wrong for an investigator. You can't park that on a street, let alone tail someone, without being instantly made. You know that, but you can't quite let go."

"I don't plan on driving it while I'm tailing someone!"

Flint offered—and his tone really was that of someone who thought he was making a great concession, "I could keep you on as bookkeeper. Arlisse has threatened to quit if she has to spend one more tax season wading through my box of tax receipts."

"Buddy, you couldn't *afford* me as your bookkeeper," Zach said shortly. His sympathies were entirely with Arlisse. *My box of tax receipts* indeed! He could imagine only too well.

Flint shrugged. "It was just a thought."

"Well, keep thinking."

"I will. Anyway, we're probably not going to be able to get into the hospital to talk to the car's passenger yet. There's no point trying. He's still unconscious."

"Get into the hospital?" Hopefully, Flint intended to follow the usual protocol for interviewing a hospitalized witness, and yet Zach could uneasily picture a scenario that included stolen scrubs and one of them—guess who—crouched in a laundry cart.

"So after we touch base with the cops, we pay a visit to the widow."

"And why would we do that?"

"Because it's what we'd do if we didn't believe she'd knocked off her old man. We—you—would offer your sympathies and explain what you'd been working on and see if she wanted to continue the investigation. And while we're trying to throw her off our track, we'd be interrogating her and everyone else we could lay our hands on at that estate."

"That's…not bad."

Flint said gravely, "I'm honored you think so."

"No, you're not. You think I'm stupid and inexperienced and I just got my client killed. And I agree. Which is why I think maybe we should try to do this your way."

Flint frowned. "We need to be clear on something. I don't think you're stupid, and I don't think you got your client killed. Furthermore, I get why you want to hang on to the business your dad built. Okay? I didn't have that relationship with my old man, but I get it."

Zach wasn't sure what to say.

Flint wasn't waiting for his input, in any case. "Believe it or not, you can trust me. I've put it all out there. I'm not hiding anything. I don't have an ulterior motive. I'm helping you because I intend to take over your business—I plan on paying you a fair price—and that's all there is to it. If you want to try to do this on your own, have at it. But that *would* be stupid."

Given current events, yeah, it probably would. Anyway, just because he was working with Flint—accepting Flint's help—didn't mean he had to sell his agency to Flint. Surely, Flint recognized that if they *were* successful, it would help Zach avoid selling? At least for a while longer.

Not that Zach was quite as enthusiastic about the agency or his ability to run it as he'd been twenty-four hours earlier. The idea that he was at least partially responsible for Alton's demise was about as demoralizing as it got. He couldn't help feeling he should maybe shutter the shop before anyone else got hurt.

Flint snapped his fingers a couple of times. "Hello? Zachariah? Still on the line?"

"Still here," Zach clipped, and Flint gave another of those evil grins.

"Just checking. You have that glassy-eyed look again."

"Maybe because I'm wearing glasses."

"Very stylish, too. You're definitely in the running for *GQ*'s PI of the Year Award."

Zach's mouth popped open to ask why the fuck Flint had to be such a nonstop A-hole at such a time, when it dawned on him that all this poking and prodding was Flint's idiosyncratic way of keeping him from slipping back into that shocked, numb state of near inertia in which he'd arrived on the welcome mat of Carey Confidential.

So instead of responding as Flint no doubt anticipated, Zach said calmly, "Bill Cameron with EDS police department is my godfather. I'll give him a call."

Flint picked up his coffee cup—and put it down again. "Lt. Cameron is your godfather?"

Zach nodded.

"That's news."

Zach shrugged.

Flint said, "Yeah, talking to Cameron would be a very good idea. And I'll touch base with my guy at the sheriff's office. We can compare notes on our way to talk to Elvira."

"Who?"

"Elvira. Queen of the Night. Never mind. You wouldn—"

Zach interrupted, "Do you mean Elvira, Mistress of the Dark?"

Flint blinked, then said mildly, "I stand corrected."

Zach rose. "If we're working together, it won't be the last time."

Flint gave a funny laugh. "Oh-kay, then."

"When did you want to meet up?"

Flint threw a distracted look at his watch. "Not counting last night, the missus is supposed to always be home. Let's see if we can catch her at lunch."

"Sure. Why not?"

As if Zach had objected, Flint said, "I can be very charming when I have to be."

"I'll believe it when I see it." Zach reached for the doorknob, but then stopped. He turned back to Flint.

"You know, being gay doesn't automatically make you pervy."

"Huh?" Flint sounded genuinely taken aback.

"Alton wasn't pervy because he was gay."

"Are you for real?"

"Yes. I'm for real. Alton obviously had some...I don't know. Quirks. But the fact that he was maybe struggling with his sexuality is a whole different issue. Being gay doesn't make you a pervert."

Flint's laugh was disbelieving.

"Go to hell." Zach opened the door, only to have it slammed shut. He turned to find Flint right behind him—so close that Zach had to lean against the door to avoid bumping noses.

Flint was speaking, but for a moment or two, Zach was distracted by this unexpected proximity to another man's hard, muscular body. Flint's breath, laced with coffee and a hint of whisky, warmed his face. Flint's eyes, that unusual green-gold—electrum? Was that what it was called?—stared intently, unblinkingly, into his own.

"What are you— What do you think I'm saying?"

It took Zach a moment to process Flint's words. And then... Good question. Because in Zach's—okay, somewhat limited experience—straight guys did not typically invade your personal space while gazing deeply into your eyes and almost, *almost*, brushing mouths.

"I..."

As usual, Flint cut straight to the chase. "How do you not know I'm gay?"

CHAPTER TWELVE

"*G*AY?"

Zach's tone was so flabbergasted that Flint actually laughed. "It happens in the best of families."

Well, yeah. The truth was, he'd never seen Flint with *any* potential romantic partner, male *or* female. In fact, beyond a vague from-a-distance admiration for Flint's, er, physical charms, Zach hadn't given a whole lot of thought to the owner of Carey Confidential. Not until Flint had proposed buying him out.

Zach said defensively, "How should I know? You sounded—"

"I sounded like someone who thinks—given things I've heard over the years—that Alton Beacher is—was—a weirdo with some alarming tendencies."

"Like what?"

Flint opened his mouth, hesitated, and then shook his head. Meaning?

The funny thing was Flint didn't draw back. He was still leaning into the door, eyes locked on Zach's, his firm mouth hovering within kissing distance. And Zach? Zach couldn't seem to stop staring right back into Flint's eyes, noticing things he'd never noticed before: the little smile lines, the gold flecks in those green irises, the unexpected length of Flint's lashes—you couldn't tell from a distance because the tips of his eyelashes were blond.

"Did you really not know?" Flint's voice was so soft, so…something that sent a funny little shivery sensation down Zach's spine. A sensation that was awfully like anticipation.

Zach whispered, "I do now."

He was so sure Flint was going to kiss him that it was an almost physical shock when Flint abruptly straightened, took a step back, and leaned against his desk. He folded his arms, studying Zach skeptically.

"I find that hard to believe, Zachariah. What did you think I was doing at the Jack of Hearts? Working undercover?"

"The what?"

"Jack of Hearts."

The Jack of Hearts was Ensenada del Sello's most popular LGBTQ-friendly nightclub. Once upon a time, Zach and Ben had been regulars, but gradually life—work—had altered their feelings about how and where to spend their Friday nights. Which could have been fun, if working overtime hadn't ended up being their default.

That didn't change the fact that Zach had zero recollection of ever running into Flint at the Jack of Hearts.

"When was this?"

"A few years back."

"No way. I'd have remembered *that*."

Flint's scowl was one of disbelief. "You don't remember me saying hello to you and what's his name?"

"You said hello to us?"

"Well, more like waved."

"Waved?"

"Nodded," amended Flint. "On a couple of different occasions. Your boyfriend sure saw me. You're saying you didn't notice?"

No way was Flint lying, and it didn't seem likely he could be mistaken. Zach stared at him in bafflement, but then, thanks to Flint's *GQ* quip, it dawned on him what must have happened.

"I used to wear contacts."

Flint's brows shot up. "Were they painted over?"

Zach laughed—sort of—and admitted, "They might as well have been. My eyes watered so much, I'd pop them out, and then I couldn't really see much beyond arm's length."

"You can't be serious."

"I know. It's... I was self-conscious back then. I couldn't seem to find a pair of glasses that didn't make me look like Poindexter. So I kept trying to wear the contacts."

He was about to add that it was funny Ben had never mentioned seeing Flint, but on reflection, no, it wasn't really. Ben had always considered Flint a shady character. He wouldn't have encouraged any social interaction, particularly between Zach and Flint.

Flint's scowl turned scornful. "That's the most—"

"Why would I lie?" Zach interrupted, and Flint fell silent. "There's no reason I wouldn't have said hi. Or nodded hello."

Flint said a little grudgingly, "I kind of wondered why you seemed so stuck on yourself."

Zach snorted. He found it amusing that Flint's idea of *saying hi* was a curt nod from a distance.

Flint seemed to decide to let bygones be bygones. He changed the subject with a brisk, "Okay, well, let's meet back here at eleven thirty."

"Synchronizing my watch," Zach assured him gravely.

Flint shook his head, murmured, "Smart-ass," but it seemed to be a compliment, and abruptly, unreasonably, Zach began to feel better. Certainly better than he had when he'd walked into Carey Confidential half an hour earlier.

Flint moved away from the desk, and Zach instinctively braced, but Flint was merely squeezing past as he retook his chair. Zach opened the door and slipped out into the cell-sized lobby. Arlisse nodded pleasantly. He nodded in return.

As he pushed out through the glass door into the damp morning air, he was uncomfortably aware of the tiniest sense of disappointment.

"How are you doing, kid?" Lt. Bill Cameron briskly ushered Zach into his office, nodding toward the hardback wooden chairs in front of his desk. "Hold my calls, Mona," he called, then shut the door to his office.

"Coffee?" Cameron asked Zach.

"No. Thanks."

At sixty, Cameron was a tall, lean, broad-shouldered man with iron-gray hair and piercing green eyes. He had been a smart and capable officer. He had also been charming and personable, and those traits had aided his rise through the ranks.

"How's your mom doing? I've been meaning to give her a call." Cameron took his seat behind the neatly organized desk.

"She's okay." Zach said, "She's taking it one day at a time."

"Sure," Cameron said. "That's all anybody can do. Well, give her my best when you see her."

"I'll do that." Zach knew he would not, just as he knew why Bill Cameron hadn't phoned. His mom had never forgiven Cameron for being on his duly earned vacation when his partner was shot on duty. Her bitterness had only increased as Cameron's career had taken off and Fred's world had—in her view—shrunk to Davies Detective Agency.

"So. How can I help you?"

"I think maybe I can help you. Up until this morning, I was working for Alton Beacher."

Cameron had been absently tapping his pen on a legal pad. He stopped tapping and stared. "Working for Alton Beacher doing what?"

"He hired me to find out who was sending him death threats."

"Death threats?"

"In the form of creepy toys and puzzles."

"You've got to be kidding me." Cameron scowled. "Why the hell wouldn't he come to *us*?"

Zach said carefully, "That was my first suggestion, but part of why I was hired was to pose as Beacher's boyfriend while I conducted my investigation."

Cameron blinked. "I think my hearing is going. Did you say…?"

"I know how it sounds, and clearly it was a horrible idea, but—"

"You can say that again!"

"But Alton—Beacher—believed that if he could convince his wife he was actually gay, she'd give him a divorce without carrying out the threats against him she's made over the years."

Cameron considered this grimly for a moment before saying tersely, "Okay, kid. Start at the beginning and don't leave anything out."

Of course, Zach did leave out one or two things, but mostly he complied to the best of his ability with Cameron's request. He did not try to hide his own culpability. Or maybe *gullibility* was the better word.

"I've never heard such a load of horseshit in my entire career," Cameron summed up at the end of Zach's recital.

"I know," Zach said humbly.

"We both know what your father would have to say about this, Zee."

"I know."

"I don't get it. You're a smart kid. Why in the hell would you let yourself get dragged into something like this?"

Zach stared into Cameron's genuinely bewildered gaze, and burst out, "Because I was desperate! The retainer Beacher paid is enough to keep us afloat for the next couple of months. I figured—"

Cameron winced. "You think Beacher didn't know that? Didn't you question why someone as wealthy as Alton Beacher would hire a little hole-in-the-wall operation if he honest-to-God believed his life was in danger?"

"I knew—assumed—he thought a big company might not go along with some of the things he was asking."

"You can say that again!"

Zach did not say that again. He did not say anything. He kept his mouth shut while Cameron considered the whole sorry mess, reading over his notes and shaking his head now and then, as though he still couldn't believe what he'd heard.

Finally, Cameron said, "Tell me you kept the jack-in-the-box, the doll's head—"

"I kept everything. It's all here." Zach opened his messenger bag and removed his notes on the case as well as all the macabre items, placing them on Cameron's desk. "I don't think any attempt was made to preserve fingerprints. Alton handled everything in front of me."

"Great."

Zach couldn't help saying, "Bill, it wasn't in my power to persuade Alton to go to the police. He wasn't someone who took advice well. Or at all."

Cameron grimaced, "That I believe."

"Every time I tried to push for more information or even discuss the threats made against him, Alton brushed me off. He seemed indifferent, even bored by the subject. So much so, that I'd started questioning how genuine the threats were. Whether hiring us was just some kind of ruse."

Cameron grunted.

"*Was* Alton's accident an accident?"

"We don't know yet. What's left of the vehicle is still being examined." Cameron said grudgingly, "It's possible Beacher's death was accidental and the rest of this is moot.

But I don't like coincidences, and this is one hell of a coincidence."

"Yes."

Cameron studied Zach. His green eyes were speculative. "If Beacher was faking the threats on his life, what do you think he was hoping to gain?"

It was embarrassing to confess how very far off the track they'd been, but Zach admitted, "Flint and I thought maybe Alton's real intent was to murder his wife. She's heiress to the Kaschak amusement-park empire, which is worth almost half a billion dollars. That's a lot of motive right there."

"It is." Cameron glanced at his notes, asked, "Flint is Flint Carey, the PI across the parking lot from you?"

Somehow that casual description served to make Zach feel even more of a failure—made Flint sound like a failure, too.

"Yes."

"It's a theory, I'll give you that. But this is why it's always a good idea to check in with your friendly neighborhood law enforcement. The feds were investigating your client for tax evasion and possible money laundering."

Zach felt his mouth fall open. It took him a moment to remember how to use it.

"But..."

Cameron waited politely.

Zach pulled himself together. "Are you saying Alton could have faked his own death?"

Cameron shrugged. "Too soon to tell. The passenger, Marcus Topper hasn't regained consciousness yet. The driver's body—presumably Beacher—was too badly burned for immediate identification. Forensics will have to check dental records, etc. in order to verify just who our victim really was."

CHAPTER THIRTEEN

"It's almost a relief," Zach was saying.

Flint's, "*Is* it?" was dubious.

They were in Flint's Ford Explorer, driving the steep and windy road leading to the Beacher—well, Kaschak—estate on Mount de Sello to interview Alton's widow.

Maybe widow.

"Hell, yes, it's a relief to think maybe I *wasn't* responsible for someone's death!"

Flint, eyes on the rock-strewn road, was silent.

"Why? What are you thinking?" Zach frowned.

Flint gave a brief shake of his head.

Zach's rising spirits sank. "What's that mean?"

"It means, if Beacher faked his own death, this setup is even more dangerous than we thought. If he faked his death, we don't know where this is headed or what he has planned."

"We know he can't be planning to murder his wife. A dead man can't inherit."

"He can't be a murder suspect, that's for sure."

True. Zach thought it over, admitted, "It's possible Alton set up trusts or financial entities which *would* benefit from Zora's death. And, if he's thought this through, he probably has an accomplice who could funnel those funds to him."

"Exactly." Flint's tone was grim.

Neither had much to say after that. Zach was lost in thought, reviewing every minute he'd spent with Alton, wondering why he hadn't realized how totally off the situation—not to mention Alton—was. But that was the trouble. He *had* known the situation was off. He'd ignored his instincts, let his doubts and concerns be soothed by all that lovely money.

Honest to God, he had no one but himself to blame for the position he was now in. Even Flint had recognized—

In fact, how unfair was it that he was still thinking *even Flint*, like Flint was the half-assed amateur. Flint had not only been right about Alton and the entire ridiculous setup, he'd gone out of his way to warn Zach—and then tried to help when Zach, refusing to listen, had gotten in over his head. Flint was the boots-on-the-ground professional here. Maybe he didn't dress for success, maybe he was a little rough around the edges—well, and there again, how the hell would Zach know how rough around the edges Flint was?

He'd made all these assumptions—largely based on Ben's opinion of Flint, if he was honest. Jeez, he hadn't even noticed Flint was gay! It had never even occurred to him.

As he recalled Flint's comments about being snubbed at Jack of Hearts, Zach could have sunk through the heavy-duty WeatherTech floormat. Talk about not being able to see beyond the end of your nose!

No wonder Pop thought Zach ought to stick to accounting.

"What are you blaming yourself for now?" Flint's voice jolted Zach out of his self-recriminations.

"Huh? Me? Nothing."

Flint's mouth curved sardonically. "Come on. I'm getting to know that I-choose-to-die-in-trial-by-combat expression. What's eating you?"

Zach said bitterly, "I'm just an idiot, that's all."

Flint laughed, shook his head, and—to Zach's surprise—reached over to give Zach's knee a quick squeeze.

"You're too hard on yourself, Zachariah."

"That's not what you thought last Thursday. And you were right."

"Nah." Flint's eyes met Zach's. He said casually, "I think you're okay."

Not exactly effusive praise, and yet Zach felt instantly better.

He relaxed, accepted that for now his role was, well, not passenger, but co-captain. Okay, in the immediate *now*, in this moving vehicle, it was passenger, but that was acceptable. There was nothing to object to. Flint drove well, smoothly navigating the scattered rocks and small landslides caused by the previous night's rains, and they gained altitude quickly.

The Explorer's tires hissed on wet pavement as they wound through hills of oak trees and outcroppings of bronze-gold lichen-covered boulders. Occasionally they flashed past large, expensive homes—some in clearings next to the road, others accessible by private dirt roads leading deep into the woods.

They decelerated into another curve, accelerated past wet hillside blanketed in glistening ferns and the shiny red berries of toyon.

"There it is," Flint said abruptly. "That patch of road up ahead."

Zach snapped out of his preoccupation, scanning the empty road ahead. "The crash site?"

"Yep."

Police and emergency personnel had long since cleared the scene, but Zach could see a stretch of blackened hillside several yards ahead.

"That must be where the Porsche went over the ledge."

Flint grunted, slowed the SUV, and pulled to a bumpy stop on the muddy shoulder of the road. "Let's have a look."

Zach opened his door and stepped out. The chilly air carried the smell of rain and charred wood. He glanced over the side of the road, and his stomach gave a little flop as he absorbed how long a drop it was to the bottom. He could see a few boulders jutting out and, much farther down, treetops.

In silence, they walked up the road, boots crunching on gritty asphalt until they came to the scorched section of highway.

"There are the skid marks." Zach pointed toward the rise of road.

They studied the dark streaks in the pitted asphalt.

"If we're just going by the tire tracks, it looks like Beacher swerved, grazed the hillside—you can see where the fender took out those laurels—overcompensated, and went right over the side." Flint sounded thoughtful. "The road's pretty narrow. It could have happened like that."

"Maybe he fell asleep at the wheel?"

"Did the butler fall asleep, too?"

"Either way, it doesn't look like the accident was faked."

Flint said darkly, "There all kinds of ways to fake an accident."

"I guess so." Zach tried to read Flint's profile.

If the burned body in the Porsche wasn't Alton's, did that mean Alton had... What? Already committed murder before trying to knock off his butler as well? But why kill the butler? And who had Alton killed in order to provide himself with a body double? And how had Alton arranged to get the butler into the car with a dead body?

No, the whole scenario was crazy. It couldn't have happened that way.

They moved to the edge of the road, gazing down the fire-singed slope to a swath of burnt and broken shrubs and wind-shaped trees where the car had come to rest.

Flint said, "According to my pal at the sheriff's office, Beacher arrived home from a dinner engagement—that would have been the date with you—around ten last night. He went straight into his study, where he remained until about eleven, when he retired for the evening. He and the missus don't sleep in the same room, so this information came from the household staff."

"Right."

"Chico Martinez, the chauffeur-slash-bodyguard, received a phone call about a family emergency shortly after midnight. He took off for Santa Rosa."

"That's why Alton was driving himself." Zach stared at the drag marks where the tow truck crane had hauled the wrecked vehicle up the hillside.

"It's possible. The family emergency was genuine, though."

Zach threw Flint a quick look of surprise. "Was it?"

Flint nodded. "Yep. The call Beacher received a few hours later about a break-in at Beacher Toy Company was not."

"It was a setup?"

"The butler took a call from a man claiming to be Beacher's head of security at the toy factory. He said there'd been a break-in and that the safe in Beacher's office had been emptied. That seems to have been enough to get Beacher in his car and headed full speed down this road in the middle of a rainstorm."

"But there wasn't any break-in." Zach already knew the answer.

"Nope. No phone call originated from the Beacher facility last night."

"Why did he take the butler with him?"

"Apparently, he phoned Martinez and ordered him to meet him at the toy factory. Which I guess makes sense given that Martinez was supposed to be Beacher's bodyguard. The butler was supposed to drive Martinez's car back to the estate, and Martinez would drive Beacher home."

"So the butler just happened to be in the car."

"Exactly. The butler couldn't have been part of anyone's calculations—unless this entire scenario was cooked up by Beacher."

"Or Martinez."

Flint said after a moment, "Or Martinez."

Zach said, "If Beacher set this up, it seems like bringing the butler along would have done nothing but complicate his plans."

"Yeah, maybe."

"Someone had to have tampered with that car," Zach said.

"*Or* someone wanted it to *look* like the car had been tampered with."

That someone being Alton. Zach asked, "How long before the sheriff's—"

Flint's gaze met Zach's. "Funny you should ask. It seems there's a bit of a pissing match going on between the sheriff's office, the feds, and the Ensenada Del Sello police department regarding jurisdiction."

"Bill didn't seem to have any doubt that EDS held jurisdiction."

"Yeah, my money's on Cameron, but that doesn't mean there won't be an added delay in getting the vehicle forensics back." Flint brooded for a moment, then shrugged. "We could stand here and speculate all afternoon. Let's go have our chat with the lady of the manor, shall we?"

"I guess we shall," Zach said.

CHAPTER FOURTEEN

The enormous Gothic-style gates to the Kaschak Estate slowly slid open, and the Ford Explorer zipped through.

"It's like a private park," Zach commented as they wound their way up the wooded hillside.

Flint grunted agreement.

It took another three or four minutes to reach the clearing where the house stood surrounded by towering pines.

The Explorer rolled to a stop, and Flint whistled.

After an awed moment of silence, Zach said, "Disney wants their Haunted Mansion back."

Flint slowly shook his head. "You know how much money you'd have to spend to build a house that looks that old and decrepit?"

Once upon a time, Zach had taken an architecture course to fill a college elective requirement, and he recognized the Victorian influence of the steeply pitched gabled roof with its peaks and spires, the narrow, arched windows and all that elaborate gingerbread trim—though this fancifully cut and pierced frieze board was designed to look like cobwebs. Whatever her antecedents, this grand lady had taken a sharp turn down a dark alley. The house itself was painted indigo blue. The steps, shutters, and trim were all black. The stained-glass oriel windows were red and black and blue.

Zach said, "I've heard of keeping up with the Joneses, but keeping up with the Addams family? No wonder he thought she was capable of anything."

"It can't be healthy to bring your work home to this extent," Flint agreed.

"Granted, I don't know how active Zora was in the day-to-day operations of the Kaschak Corporation. I'm pretty sure she wouldn't have been slinging burgers or dressing up like Dracula's daughter at one of the Haunted Hollow theme parks."

Flint put the Explorer into drive. "Assume nothing. Did you not notice her outfit when she showed up to spoil your romantic tête-à-tête with Beacher?"

"Not really." The memory of the previous evening was still excruciating. From the minute Ben had popped out of the shrubbery, Zach had been trying to erase the live action play-by-play from his mental hard drive.

"Somewhere, a funeral parlor is missing their draperies. Scarlett O'Hara would be proud."

Zach laughed. He was getting to like Flint's irreverent sense of humor.

Flint parked on a large concrete pad just beyond a garage designed to look like a renovated carriage house, and cut the engine. He rested his arm along the back of Zach's seat.

"I've been thinking. It might be better if you don't come inside with me. Once she recognizes you, she's liable not to hear another word we say."

Zach protested, "But the whole idea was that I'd explain what was really going on and ask if she wanted to hire me to continue trying to—"

"Given the way things turned out, that's liable to be a hard sell."

Flint had a point, but Zach did *not* want to be left out of this interview. It wasn't even about not trusting Flint because, to his surprise, he did trust Flint. At least this far.

"We don't have to take that angle. You can introduce me as your associate. She only saw me once. She might not even recognize me."

Flint made a soft sound of derision. "She's not likely to have forgotten you, Zachariah. For one thing, the red hair's kind of a giveaway."

"I don't have red hair!"

"Red-*ish* for sure." Astonishingly, Flint's fingertips brushed the ends of Zach's hair where it curled against the back of his neck. "Chestnut, then."

Zach swallowed. Disconcertingly, he felt that feather-light touch from the roots of his red-*ish* hair to the soles of his feet.

He said weakly, "Yeah, but I want her to understand…"

"I know. I'll explain the situation. But whether she believes me or not, you sitting there right in front of her is bound to be a distraction. She saw what she saw. All the contracts in the world aren't going to change that."

Zach opened his mouth to argue, and Flint added, "Besides, she knows her husband. She knows the contract was to keep you from coming after him at a later date. Not to protect you."

"It would have been nice if you'd decided you didn't want me to take part in the interview before we drove all this way. Why am I even here?"

"Maybe I like your company?"

"Seriously."

"I know. Sorry." Flint did seem vaguely apologetic. "Why don't you take a look around the place? See what you can find out from talking to the servants?"

Zach blinked. He was thinking, *Without permission? What if I get caught? What if I—* when he recognized the look on Flint's face for what it was: half-exasperated, half-amused resignation.

Flint knew exactly what Zach was thinking.

And Zach knew exactly what Flint was thinking: *He's not cut for this.*

He said tersely, "Okay. Fine. I'll poke around and see what I can find out." He had the satisfaction of seeing a flash of surprise in Flint's green-gold eyes.

"Right. Well, keep in touch."

"I'll write home every week." Zach slipped out of the Explorer, closing the door on Flint's laugh.

He left the cement landing pad and cut across the slope to the back of the garage. The sun made a tentative appearance, throwing luminous light over the clearing. Zach paused for a moment, listening. The *buzzzz* of a saw floated in the distance. Nearby he heard the trill of a bird.

Flint got out of the Ford Explorer and started briskly toward the house. He didn't glance in Zach's direction.

Zach watched him for a moment, studying Flint's long-legged stride, the self-assured way he carried himself. It occurred to him that Flint was a guy who knew exactly who he was and what he wanted—and made no apologies.

Except Flint *did* apologize when he thought he was wrong or he thought he'd hurt you.

That probably said more about Flint's confidence, even strength of character, than anything else.

And why the heck was he standing here admiring Flint's personality traits when he was supposed to be investigating whatever he was supposed to be investigating?

Zach shook his head at himself and left the safety of his position behind the garage.

The path alongside the garage sloped steeply downward. It was covered with pine needles and pine cones from the canopy of trees overhead, which made it slippery in spots.

Flint had disappeared from view by the time Zach made his way to the bottom. He was thinking he'd try to get a look inside the garage and see if he could find any sign that the Porsche had been tampered with.

But as he came around the corner of the large building, he heard the rumble of garage doors and the Bentley pulled out, rolled a few feet, and stopped in the drive. The car door opened, and Chico, dressed in jeans and a blue San Jose University sweatshirt climbed out.

Chico went back inside the garage and came out a moment later carrying a bucket. He stopped in his tracks at the sight of Zach hovering nearby.

"What are you doing here, GQ?" His expression was dark with suspicion.

"Trying to figure out what happened to my client," Zach said.

Chico's face screwed up in contempt. "It's a little late for that, don't you think? His lawyers ought to demand a refund."

"You were his bodyguard," Zach shot back. "I was just supposed to figure out who was behind the threats."

"How's that going?"

Arguing with Chico was not useful. Zach got control of his anger. He was honest enough to recognize he was angry because he was defensive, but Chico was defensive, too. A lot of people, including Zora, were liable to think Chico as culpable as Zach in the matter.

He asked more calmly, "I take it you don't think the accident was an accident?"

Chico opened his mouth, then closed it. "How should I know? I'm not a cop."

"It seems like an awfully big coincidence."

Chico shrugged. "Coincidences happen."

They did. True enough. Chico getting called away on a family emergency the night before was an almost unbelievable coincidence, and yet it seemed to have checked out.

"Would it be okay if I looked around the garage?"

Chico stared at him in disbelief. "Why? You think the sheriffs wouldn't have noticed brake fluid on the floor or a couple of stray lug nuts?"

"No. I just thought—the sheriff's deputies already went over everything?"

"Of course."

Of course.

"It doesn't mean they couldn't have missed something."

"They didn't miss anything. *I* sure as hell wouldn't have missed anything."

"Probably not." Zach studied Chico. His anger and defensiveness were understandable after being questioned by law enforcement. "What do you think happened?"

Chico didn't unbend, didn't soften. "I'm waiting just like everyone else to hear what the law has to say."

"And if the law says it's murder?"

"You got a lot to answer for, GQ."

Zach gave a short laugh. "Hey, I don't think either of us are walking away with glowing job references."

Chico's chin jutted pugnaciously. "Why would *I* walk away? Mrs. B. has no problem with my work."

Surprise, surprise. Zach considered and discarded a couple of replies. He said, "Then you don't believe Mrs. Kaschak-Beacher had anything to do with Alton's death? Even though she's the one he—"

"No. I don't," Chico interrupted. "I also don't care if she did."

At Zach's expression, Chico laughed. It was not a pleasant sound. "Maybe you didn't notice. He wasn't a model husband."

"Yeah, I noticed. I also noticed you didn't seem to have any problem with that."

"None of my business." Chico's smile turned acrid. "You didn't have any problem, either."

"He was my client." It was true, though it wasn't much of an excuse.

"We both know that's not all he was." Chico's tone was pointed.

"What else was he?" Zach didn't understand the edge in Chico's voice.

"Come on, man. He always told me everything. I heard all about how you called him up after Spanish Bay, told him you were wearing the lace panties and begged him to give you another chance."

"*What?* That's not what happened."

"And he didn't believe you, so you sent him that video. I saw it myself." Chico snorted. "After you made such a fuss too. But you *really* got off wearing those panties. I was impressed. That was like porn-star grade performance."

"*W-What?*"

"I'm not judging. We've all got our kinks. I think you both took one hell of a risk at the restaurant, though. No wonder Mrs. B. was so worked up. Jesus."

Zach opened his mouth, but no words would come.

Chico sighed. "Like I said. He always told me everything. I know you sat on his lap all through dinner, rubbing your ass on his dick and letting him feed you crudités. He said you sucked on his fingers right there in the restaurant." Chico shook his head. "I guess that's part of what you both got off on? The risk. The excitement of messing around in public."

Zach felt hot to the bone and then ice cold. "That *never* happened. *None* of that ever happened."

"Give me a break."

"It didn't happen. Period."

"Oh, I think it did. I saw your eyes when he started naming dollar figures. I told you myself you'd give in eventually. They always do."

Zach said, "This is a total fantasy. In a crowded restaurant? Seriously? You believed that?"

"Hell, yeah, I believed it. The sheriffs did too."

"The..." Zach's voice gave out. "You told the...that bullshit to the sheriffs?"

Chico said with brutal satisfaction, "I told them everything the boss told me. That you promised you'd wear the panties, that you were sending him pics and videos, that you were doing everything you could think of, anything he wanted, if he just wouldn't fire you." He raised his shoulders. "You weren't the first one. You wouldn't have been the last. It was a lot of money. But I'm sure as hell not going to cover for you. I had to tell them everything that happened, everything that the boss said and did, and he told me that was going to be the big night. That you'd agreed to go back to the beach house after dinner and let him fuck you."

"You know damn well I didn't go to the beach house."

"No, you got cold feet. I told them. If you'd gone with him, you'd have had an extra grand for the kitty and he might still be alive."

It was like trying to argue with a crazy person. Only Chico wasn't crazy. He believed what he was saying. Alton was the crazy one.

"*None* of that happened. I don't know why Alton would make all that bullshit up or why you'd believe something so...so *preposterous*. I tossed that box away the minute I got back from Spanish Bay. It was never discussed again."

Well, sort of.

It was never directly discussed again, and Zach *had* thrown the box and lace panties in the wastepaper basket—where it had sat sandwiched between hangers from the dry cleaners and an empty Doritos bag until that morning when, despite his shock at Alton's death, some instinct warned him to get them out of the house ASAP.

Chico considered. His black gaze glinted as he said, "Maybe it did happen the way you say, GQ. Maybe you wouldn't play nice and Beacher fired you when he got home that night. I'm not sure that helps you. The way I see it, it gives you a pretty good motive for murder."

CHAPTER FIFTEEN

"**J**esus, I wish you could have been there," Flint said when he got into the Explorer. "That house really *is* like an amusement-park attraction. A skeleton in a butler's costume slides down the staircase banister anytime the front door opens."

It was about half an hour after Zach had left Chico and retreated to the safety of Flint's SUV. He had spent that half an hour trying to figure out what the hell he was going to do, while the skies overhead grew darker and gusts of wind shook the car. The occasional pine cone bounced off the windshield.

Alton's ludicrous claims about what had happened at Pinch the night before would never hold up. There had been an entire patio full of people who could vouch that Zach had not been sitting on Alton's lap, let alone the rest of it. *Flint* had been there to witness almost the entire evening. And he'd been there at Zach's request, which right there ought to prove something.

But the other stuff, the supposed video and pics? What in God's name was happening? Sure, those things could be doctored, but why would Alton *bother*? Had he planned on blackmailing Zach at some point?

Blackmailing him to do what, though?

If that video, if those pictures ever got out... Even if it was obvious that it wasn't Zach in them—and *would* it be obvious? Chico hadn't seemed to have any doubts—it was still humiliating and destructive.

It was a career killer.

Even if people accepted that it wasn't Zach in the video, the fact that Alton *wanted* it to be Zach was enough. The damage would be done. It was all people would think of when Davies Detective Agency was mentioned.

Zach Davies? Wasn't he the guy...

His face flamed, imagining it. The things people would say. The things people would think.

What did Pop used to say? *It takes twenty years to build a reputation and five minutes to ruin it.* Or for someone else to ruin it.

"It's just as well you didn't come in, though. You're pretty much all she talked about. Your ears must have been burning."

Zach realized Flint was talking—had been talking since he opened the car door. He said blankly, "What?"

"I said, it's just as well you didn't come in. As anticipated, she's blaming you for her husband's murder. The thing is, I believe her. That is, I don't believe she killed him. Assuming he didn't fake his own death."

Zach swallowed, the tiny sound audible in the sudden silence.

Flint frowned. "What?"

"I..."

Flint glanced past Zach and then out the window as though trying to find the cause for Zach's stricken expression. "What's wrong?"

"I-I spoke to Chico."

"Well done. And?"

"And..." The whole story came tumbling out of Zach in a slightly incoherent spill of words.

Flint listened, his expression changing rapidly from confused to alarmed to aghast.

"You gotta be fucking *kidding* me," he said when Zach had reached the end of his recital.

Zach shook his head. "Flint, none of that happened. You were at the restaurant last night. You know none of *that* happened."

Flint made a sound of disbelief. "Well, I should hope not! Jesus Fucking Christ, Zachariah."

"I mean, the panties happened, but not me wearing them." The panties that were now at the very bottom of his trash barrel—was that liable to look more or less incriminating if the sheriffs searched his property and found them? There was no DNA on the panties, so had it been a mistake to dispose of them?

"I don't understand why you didn't quit then and there?"

"I was hoping I wouldn't have to! If he took no for an answer, well, then it was over."

"He tried to bribe and coerce you into providing sexual favors!"

"But I said *no*, and if he was willing to accept *no*, then why would I quit?"

"Why would you— Were you born yesterday?" Flint was still staring at him like he thought Zach was insane.

"I needed the job. I thought he genuinely needed help."

Flint stared at Zach, his expression hard and unfamiliar. "If there's any truth to *any* of this, you need to tell me now."

Zach stammered, "T-There's no truth to it. I swear to God. The *only* thing that happened was he gave me those goddamned panties. I said I wouldn't wear them. When he asked to meet me for dinner, I assumed he'd accepted my answer and we were moving on."

Flint continued to regard him in that stern, steely way, and Zach said, "Flint, I get that you don't know me well, but given what you *do* know about me, how likely is it I'd be stupid enough to send porn pics and vid to someone? *Anyone.*"

Flint was unbending. "The problem is, I'd have assumed you weren't stupid enough to keep working for a creep who tried to bribe you into behaving like a two-bit rent boy. And I'd have been wrong."

Zach felt himself freezing over, limb by limb, with hurt and humiliation. He tried to summon anger, but it was a feeble, flickering thing. He couldn't help feeling Flint was partly right. Not completely right, because he knew damn well why Zach had been desperate enough to overlook Alton's attempts to seduce him with dollar signs. But enough right that Zach wanted more than anything to get out of the Explorer and far, far away from Flint. Far enough that he never had to look Flint in the eyes again.

Unfortunately, it wasn't like he could walk home or grab an Uber on Mount de Sello. He sat still and silent while Flint thought.

Finally, Flint said, "My friend at the sheriff's office didn't say a word about any of this."

"If I'm really the prime suspect, maybe they're keeping that information quiet."

"No." Flint gave a short shake of his head. "He'd tell me." His gaze met Zach's. "We're more than friends."

"*Oh*."

The voice that came out of Zach didn't sound anything like his own, but Flint didn't seem to notice.

"They must not have had that information yet." He glanced at Zach. "You should have received a call from the sheriff's by now. They're going to want to interview you as soon as possible."

Zach felt for his phone. He'd muted the ring when his plan had been to scout out the estate, and after his chat with Chico, he hadn't remembered to turn it back on. Sure enough, there was a message from Brooke as well as two other voice mails from unknown numbers.

He listened to the message from Brooke. She sounded about as rattled as he'd ever heard her.

"Yes," he said. "They want to talk to me."

Flint said flatly, "I'll bet." He started the Explorer and they bumped gingerly off the cement landing pad and onto the main drive.

Neither spoke. The only sound in all the world seemed to be the slow grind of the tires on the rain-littered pavement.

As they approached the front entrance, the stately gates slid open, and a black Subaru BRZ with tinted windows drove through, speeding past them up the drive.

"Who the hell was that?" Flint muttered, eyes on his rearview mirror.

Zach said stiffly, "Alton's brother, Ransford, I'm guessing." Though Ransford had only received a passing mention in Alton's dossier, Zach had started his own research on the younger Beacher. "Alton mentioned he was flying in last night."

Flint threw him a quick look. "Is the brother in Beacher's will?"

"I haven't been able to verify. As far as I can tell, he's Alton's only living family member, so it's likely. I can't see Alton willingly leaving anything to Zora."

"That wouldn't have been a bad thing to mention earlier."

"I hadn't ruled him out. But you wanted to focus on Zora, which I agreed with."

"What's the relationship between the brother and the widow?"

"Unknown."

Flint threw Zach another of those brief glances. He gave an unsatisfied grunt.

As they reached the main highway, Zach said, "There are two viable suspects in addition to Zora. One is Ransford. The other is Ronald Jordan, the owner of Old Timey Fun Ltd. He and Alton were college roommates. They're still friends, in theory, but they're also, at least according to Alton, business rivals." Zach related his encounter—well, Alton's encounter—with Rusty at the hotel in Spanish Bay.

"That's interesting," Flint said. "So, he was definitely Team Zora on the weekend. How far back do he and the missus go?"

"Alton met Zora in college when he and Rusty were roommates, so…"

"Hm."

"The thing of it is, Alton listed Rusty as a potential suspect. He didn't seem to consider Ransford at all, but he really was convinced Zora was behind the threats, so even his suspicion of Rusty was probably more about ticking boxes than anything."

"We need to check out Jordan's and Beacher's alibis."

"Ransford flew in this morning from Iowa. According to Alton the trip was supposed to be partly a business one."

"It shouldn't be too hard to verify when he actually arrived."

Zach said, "Right. Also, after I left you this morning, I did some checking. According to Rusty's administrative assistant, he's currently in San Diego. He received some kind of award at a children's charity banquet last night. I found photos of the event online. He was there, shaking hands and accepting his plaque. Even if he managed to get a flight at that time of night from San Diego to Monterey, which is doubtful, he'd be cutting it pretty close."

"That's good work." Flint sounded surprised, which didn't do much to make Zach feel better.

He didn't answer.

"Are you going to return those phone calls?"

No, I'm going to make a run for the border. But of course, Zach did not say that. "When I get back to the office."

Flint considered. Nodded.

The rain started again, spattering the windshield. Flint turned on the wipers, and their *squeak* and *scrub*, sounded unnaturally loud in the prolonged silence.

Finally, Flint cleared his throat. Eyes on the road, he said in a carefully neutral tone, "When I get excited, I yell. It's a bad habit. If I sounded—I'm sorry if I was rough on you. I know you weren't—didn't—fool around with Beacher. I'm worried because I'm not sure everyone is going to understand the decisions you made. *I* don't understand the decisions you made. Which is why I overreacted. Probably."

"It's fine."

"When you talk to the detectives, tell them everything. Be honest."

Zach gave Flint a look of exasperation, but he could understand why, at this point, Flint doubted his common sense. "I will."

"But don't overexplain. Don't volunteer information beyond what they're asking. Don't share your theories or guess at anyone's motives. Stick to the facts and keep the facts to a bare minimum."

Just the facts, ma'am!

"Right."

"And if they do seem to really think you're their guy, lawyer up."

Zach said, "I'll look more guilty if I lawyer up."

Flint's lip curled. "People lawyer up when they're worried. You can be worried for all kinds of reasons, including knowing that cops often get it wrong. Cops only want you to think it makes you look guilty because they hate it when people lawyer up."

This was pretty much sacrilege to the son of a former cop, but Zach swallowed his objections. He could see that Flint was genuinely trying to help.

"And you might give your godfather a call. Since the sheriff's office and the police department are already playing tug-of-war with this case, let's call in the varsity team."

"I told Bill some of what happened with Alton, but I didn't go into details."

"Did you mention lace panties?"

"Not specifically. I said Alton tried to bribe me for sexual favors, but seemed to accept no for an answer, so I continued to work for him."

Flint considered, then said, "It's good that you got on the record before it gets dragged out."

"It's the truth."

"I said I believed you. I meant it."

Zach stared out the rain-flecked window. "I didn't feel like I had a choice."

Flint said, "And at no time during your interview with *anyone* do you repeat that particular phrase. Understood?"

Zach threw him a startled glance. "Yes. Understood."

He couldn't help thinking Flint's friend at the sheriff's office would not appreciate Flint's coaching of the witness. Zach appreciated it, though. For the first time since Flint had lit into him, he felt a little warmer, a little more hopeful.

"Thanks," he said gruffly.

Flint glanced at him, gave another of those curt nods, and returned his attention to the road ahead.

CHAPTER SIXTEEN

"What's going on?" Brooke demanded before Zach was even through the front door. "Those detectives sounded like they thought *you* were a suspect! I thought Beacher's death was accidental!"

Not much rattled Brooke, but she seemed genuinely frightened, which did little to calm Zach's own fears.

"It's okay. It's got to be a-a misunderstanding. I'm going to phone them right now."

"I know cops, and those cops think you're involved somehow."

"I know, but they've got it wrong."

"Zee, if you're in trouble—"

"*Trouble?*" Zach goggled at her. "Brooke, I swear to God, I'm not in trouble. I didn't do *anything*. Anything illegal."

"I wish we'd never taken that job!"

Zach heartily concurred, but he said with an effort at calm, "Look, let me call the sheriff's office. Let me get it straightened out, and then I'll bring you up to speed."

Brooke did not look reassured.

Zach went into his office, closed the door, and phoned Lt. Bill Cameron.

Cameron, however, was unavailable, so Zach left what was probably an incoherent voice mail, and hands shaking, heart in his throat, phoned Monterey County Sheriff's Office.

Here he was in luck, sort of. The lead detectives at the sheriff's office were ready and waiting for his call. He was invited to drive up to the station to give his statement, and he assured them he was on his way.

"I'll call Uncle Bill," Brooke said when Zach filled her in on the plan.

"I've already left a message," Zach told her. "Anyway, listen. If we're really planning to run this agency, we have to be able to deal with whatever comes up ourselves. We can't go running to Bill—"

She opened her mouth, and he said firmly, "Or Flint—every time we get hit with a-a challenge."

"It's more than a challenge if you get arrested!"

Zach summoned a laugh and said with a confidence he didn't feel, "Don't worry. I'll be back before you know it. I'm not going to be arrested."

He was not entirely sure about that, of course, and he was even less sure after he arrived at the sheriff's office and was ushered into a small interview room where a couple of plainclothes officers were waiting. They didn't go so far as to lick their chops, but Zach definitely picked up a welcome-to-the-Colosseum vibe.

The detectives introduced themselves as Schneider and Barrera. Barrera was a petite no-nonsense brunette with a very large diamond engagement ring. A set of handcuffs just happened to be lying not so subtly on the clipboard in front of her.

Schneider looked like he'd just been discharged from the Marines five minutes earlier. Blond, blue-eyed, and broad-shouldered. He looked efficient and humorless.

They went quickly through the basics of who Zach was, what he did for a living, and his connection to the case. Then they got down to it.

"Why do you think Alton Beacher chose to go with a small, independent operation like Davies Detective Agency?" Barrera asked. "No offense, but you're not the most experienced investigator out there. You had to ask yourself."

"I asked Mr. Beacher that in our first meeting," Zach answered. "He felt that a small company might be more open to considering some of his eccen—idiosyncratic requests."

Barrera's gaze sharpened. "What's that mean? What were these *idiosyncratic* requests?"

They had to know, of course. They'd spoken to Chico, and however wrong he'd got the level of Zach's, er, commitment, he knew what the original job was supposed to entail.

"He told me his wife repeatedly threatened to retaliate if he attempted to divorce her. That she not only threatened to ruin him financially, but had warned him that she'd kill herself in such a way that he'd be framed for her murder. He insisted she was vengeful and obsessive. In fact, he suspected her of being behind the threats against his life, which was maybe one reason he didn't take them as seriously as he should have. But he thought, or claimed to think, that if he could convince her he was gay, it would defuse a lot of her rage. Then it would be about him and not their marriage. She'd be able to save face, that kind of thing."

Barrera looked pained.

"And he insisted that the best way to convince her he really was gay was to hire someone to pose as his boyfriend."

Schneider said incredulously, "And you thought that was a good idea?"

"I thought a fake boyfriend was a terrible idea," Zach said. "I told him I didn't think it would work. But he was offering us lot of money. Since my father passed away, our agency's struggled to retain clients. Beacher seemed to be throwing us a lifeline. The threats against him sounded genuine to me, and I believed that was going to be our focus."

"But it wasn't." Barrera wasn't asking.

"It got a little weird." Zach remembered Flint's advice to stick to the facts and not volunteer extra information. "Despite the creepy gifts and threats, Beacher didn't seem particularly fearful. Chico Martinez, his bodyguard, didn't behave the way I would have expected him to if—"

"But you don't have a lot of experience handling these kinds of cases," Schneider broke in. "So how would you know?"

"No, I don't." Zach couldn't help adding, "But I'm not sure there *are* a lot of these kinds of cases."

"Tell us about the weekend you spent with Mr. Beacher at Spanish Bay," Barrera said. She did not seem like someone who was easily distracted.

"Basically, he paid me to amuse myself for the weekend. It seemed unusual, but I used the time to find out what I could about other potential suspects. I wasn't convinced Mrs. Kaschak-Beacher was the only person who might want him out of the way. And in fact, we—he—was accosted Sunday morning at the hotel restaurant by Ronald Jordan."

This was clearly news to them. But then Chico hadn't been there when Rusty showed up at breakfast. Just as Chico hadn't been there when Zora showed up—or even when Ben popped out of the bushes. Come to think of it, if Ben were a different kind of personality, Zach might conceivably think that Ben, being jealous and angry, could've gone after Alton.

Zach wasn't going to throw Ben under the bus, though. No way had Ben sneaked onto the Beacher estate and tampered with Alton's brakes. Assuming anyone had tampered with anything and that it wasn't an accident. Or that Alton had faked his death.

Until they'd heard about Rusty Jordan, Barrera and Schneider had been zeroing in on what had gone down between Zach and Alton over the weekend, but this new information seemed to give them pause. Zach explained who Rusty was, as well as his relationship to Alton and Zora. He was asked to recall every word spoken between Alton and Rusty on Sunday. Barrera listened and occasionally made a couple of notes.

Schneider also listened, but he seemed unimpressed, kicked back in his chair, arms folded, continuing to direct a cold, unblinking stare Zach's way.

Barrera jotted down a final note, and without looking up, asked casually, "At what point over the weekend did you become sexually intimate with Mr. Beacher?"

"At no point ever," Zach said.

Barrera smiled, glanced up. "We've already spoken to Mr. Martinez. We know that you and Mr. Beacher began a sexual relationship over the course of the weekend."

Zach opened his mouth to point out that was hearsay but realized that the underlying idea was to get him to corroborate Chico's story about Alton giving Zach the panties on the drive home.

Zach shook his head. "Nope. Not a chance. Never."

Barrera continued to smile. "You expect us to believe Beacher paid you *twelve thousand dollars* just to accompany him to his golf weekend?"

"Are you saying you believe he'd pay me twelve grand just to sl—"

Schneider broke in. "How long have you known Flint Carey?"

"*Flint?*" That threw Zach. "For years, I guess. I mean, I didn't *know* him. His agency is across the mall from ours."

"Then why did you try to hire him?"

"He and my dad were cordial. Friendly rivals, I guess. My dad thought he was a decent guy and a decent investigator. We're short-handed, so I hired him to freelance on the Beacher case. He was conducting surveillance Monday night when Alton and I dined at Pinch."

"That sure was convenient," Schneider said.

Barrera threw her partner a look of impatience.

"Convenience is the point of hiring additional help." Zach couldn't help an edge of *What's your problem, man?* in his tone.

"What's your relationship with Flint outside of work?"

"Schneider," Barrera murmured.

"We don't have a relationship outside of work."

"But you'd—"

"*Schneider.*"

Was Schneider Flint's more-than-friends contact at the sheriff's office? For some reason Zach had assumed this contact would be administrative personnel. The relationship between law enforcement and professional investigators wasn't always the most amiable, and Flint seemed like someone who would rub the local constabulary the wrong way.

Which once again underscored how little Zach knew about these things. Because Schneider definitely seemed to have personal feelings where Flint was concerned.

Barrera shuffled her papers, gave Schneider a warning look, and said, "Would you like to tell us about the video you made for Mr. Beacher?"

"The one where you try to lick your nipples," Schneider put in.

"The *what?*"

Barrera leaned over and showed Zach the screen of her cell phone. She hit Play, and a man sitting on a bed, a man who looked *a lot* like Zach, began to go through the extremely time-intensive—and noisy—process of pulling on a pair of too-small white lace panties.

"That's not me," Zach said over the moans of the man in the cell phone. Forewarned was forearmed, but once he started looking closely, the resemblance *was* largely superficial.

"It sure looks like you," Barrera and Schneider said in unison.

"He's probably ten years younger than me. His hair's dyed. Look at the roots. His feet are different. Bigger. His hands don't look like mine. I think there's a tattoo on the underside of his wrist. Look at his shoulders. My shoulders are broader."

Schneider said, "No, they're not. Those are your shoulder—*ow*." He glared at Barrera.

"That's not my bed or the walls of any room I've ever been in. And if you'll notice, he *never* shows his face."

"*Ohhhhhh, Alton*," moaned the writhing man. "I need you so bad. I need you inside me. Deep inside, fucking me so good. So hard. So deep. *Please,* fuck me."

Zach cleared his throat. "That's not my voice."

The voice was sort of similar. Huskier.

"That is *absolutely* your voice," Schneider insisted. "That's *you*."

"Whatever you want," the man on the bed pleaded. "Don't be mad. I'm sorry. I'll be a good boy from now on. Let me prove it. I *want* to prove it. Please. *Please*, Alton. No more games. You're right about me. About everything. Let me show you. It's going to be how you want from now on. I just need you so much…"

Had Alton understood that when young men, like the one in the video, proclaimed *I need you so much*, it was Alton's money and not Alton they were talking about?

Mesmerized, Zach watched as the man on the bed raised his hips and thrust his hand beneath the straining lace. The lace made small tearing sounds. The man began to groan.

Over the increasingly frantic sounds, Barrera said calmly, "He was going to terminate your contract, which meant you'd be ruined. You gave in to his ultimatums. It's understandable. What's the big deal about a pair of underwear? We get it. You wore the panties. You made the tape and sent the photos." She shrugged. "We're all grown-ups here."

Schneider picked up the narrative. "But when push came to shove, you chickened out and he fired you. And you lost it. It wasn't just about Beacher pulling his account. You knew he was going to use the photos and vid to humiliate you, ruin you. You had to stop him any way you could."

Zach, still staring at the cell-phone video, shook his head. He glanced at Barrera. "You sent this to your crime lab, right?"

Barrera was frowning. Zach couldn't help thinking she didn't look nearly as convinced of his motives as Schneider sounded.

"You're damn right," Schneider cut in.

Zach shrugged. "Then it's okay. You're going to find out it's not me on this video. And that this video never came from my phone."

Barrera's eyes lit. "Since you bring up the subject, are you willing to hand your cell phone over?"

"Yes." Did he want to? No. But if they wanted his phone, they could probably get a warrant for it. The question of where the video came from made the confiscation of his cell almost a certainty.

Schneider and Barrera exchanged looks. Barrera held her hand out, and Zach handed over his phone.

"Password?"

Zach gave her his password. "Look," he said. "If you want to polygraph me, if you want to take DNA, whatever it's going to take to prove to you I didn't kill my client, I'm happy to do. I'm not the guy on the video. I didn't send photos. And Alton never threatened to fire me, by the way."

"Bullshit." Schneider sounded bored. "That's you on that video, and we all know it."

Barrera said, "Are you claiming that Beacher didn't make sexual advances?"

"Maybe technically," Zach admitted. "But the way he did it was so… It was clumsy and transactional. It didn't feel—it was just awkward. And when I turned him down, he sulked. He didn't threaten to fire me. He didn't say *anything*. But even if he had, we'd already earned—and cashed—the twelve grand. I didn't want to lose his business, but it wouldn't have been the end of the world. In fact, after Mrs. Beacher showed up at Pinch, Flint and I had begun to speculate about who the real intended victim was."

"Meaning?" Barrera said.

Schneider repeated, "You and *Flint*?"

"We thought—obviously we were wrong—but we had started to wonder if Beacher was actually planning to kill his wife. It seemed, on paper anyway, like he had more motive than she did."

There was a moment of silence while the detectives processed that.

"That's what Flint thought? That Beacher was planning to kill his wife?" That, of course, was Schneider. Barrera was still thinking.

"Yes. We ended the evening undecided as to whether we should approach Mrs. Beacher or go to the—"

"Ended the evening," Schneider echoed. "And where was this evening taking place?"

"At the office. My office. Davies Detective Agency. We were debriefing."

"Oh yeah? *Debriefing* seems to be your thing."

"*Seriously,* Schneider?" Barrera snapped.

Schneider subsided, glowering.

Barrera said, "You're claiming that last night, following the dinner at Pinch restaurant, you and Mr. Carey, *who was freelancing for you*" —she looked pointedly at Schneider— "met to go over the case. You theorized that Beacher hired you to cover his plans to murder his wife."

"Correct."

"How long were you and Carey together?"

Zach didn't dare glance at Schneider's face. "He got there late because he followed Mrs. Beacher home to make sure she arrived safely. We spoke until about eleven or so."

"So, you don't have an alibi," Schneider said. "Flint is not your alibi."

"I don't have an alibi." Flint had warned Zach not to volunteer any information, but Zach's experience with law enforcement had never been adversarial. He saw an exit sign and headed for the off ramp. "Like I said, Flint believed we should go straight to Mrs. Beacher with our suspicions. I felt we should give Alton a chance to explain himself before going to the police. We agreed to discuss the situation again in the morning."

"You suggested going to the police?" Barrera said slowly.

"Yes. I didn't feel equipped to handle the situation if Alton really was trying to get rid of his wife. But I also wasn't convinced that was what was going on. Then, after we saw the news this morning, I went to EDS PD and Flint contacted your department."

Silence.

Barrera said finally, flatly, "You went to EDS police department?"

"Yes. I turned over my files and the threatening gag gifts Al—Beacher had received, to Lt. Bill Cameron. I brought him up to speed, including our—Flint and my—suspicion that Alton had been planning to kill Mrs. Beacher."

"You gave all that evidence to Bill Cameron?" Barrera was not happy. Nor was Schneider. They exchanged speaking glances before refocusing their hard, bright stares on Zach.

"Yes. Bill said—"

"*Bill?*" Schneider said.

"Lt. Cameron informed me that Beacher was already under investigation by the feds—"

"*Jesus Christ*," Barrera swore. "It'd be nice if someone bothered to communicate with *us* once in a while. Seeing that it's *our* case."

Zach said meekly, "As far as our theory about whether Beacher was ultimately trying to get rid of his wife, Cameron didn't have much of an opinion. He seemed to think there was a question as to whether Beacher had faked his own death."

CHAPTER SEVENTEEN

He knew he should probably phone Flint. Let him know how the interview had gone.

But, despite Flint's apology, Zach couldn't forget the harsh words.

"The problem is, I'd have assumed you weren't stupid enough to keep working for a creep who tried to bribe you into behaving like a two-bit rent boy. And I'd have been wrong."

Flint was sorry about hurting Zach's feelings, but it didn't change what he thought of Zach's choices. The fact that Flint was probably right didn't help. So maybe he was being oversensitive, but Zach preferred some space between himself and Flint. At least for a while.

Anyway, let Schneider bring Flint up to speed. Unless Zach was very much mistaken, that was going to happen the minute Schneider had a chance.

Which, if Zach were honest with himself, was another reason he wanted some distance from Flint.

Why the idea that Flint might be in a relationship with Detective Schneider bothered him so much, Zach couldn't say. It really didn't make a whole lot of sense. It wasn't like he'd been thinking of Flint as anything but—well, was that *strictly* true?

But even if Zach had *maybe* started to see Flint in a slightly different light, Flint hadn't given any indication he saw Zach as anything but—well, was *that* strictly true?

Because while nothing had actually been *said*, Zach had sort of got the feeling that Flint was maybe starting to—

It didn't matter because it wasn't true. Zach had been reading between lines that didn't actually exist.

That was that. By the time he finished reassuring Brooke—who did not seem to find anything he said remotely reassuring—and then listening to Bill Cameron read him the riot act, Zach wanted nothing more than a quiet evening at home. With the shades pulled and doors and windows locked and bolted.

So much had happened that day that his final dinner with Alton felt like it had taken place years earlier rather than the previous night. Which partly explained his uncharacteristic depression. He was exhausted. Physically tired, sure, but emotionally and mentally worn out, too. He needed some time to sort his thoughts. He needed sleep. And a good stiff drink wouldn't hurt either.

The lights were still on at Carey Confidential as Zach locked up for the evening, and for a moment he hesitated. There was something sort of bracing, even reassuring, about Flint's blunt honesty and pragmatic approach to life.

But the flip side of that blunt honesty could feel like sandpaper on an open wound, so Zach headed across the parking lot and got into his car.

On the short drive back to Salinas, he stopped by Walmart to buy cat food, a ready-made meal for his own dinner, and a burner phone he could use until the sheriffs saw fit to return his cell to him. He texted Brooke his temporary number, and headed for home and hearth.

On the bright side, he was going to have a nice quiet dinner with his favorite non-human and an early night.

On the not-so-bright side... Well, he was not going to think about that stuff tonight. He would try not to, anyway. For one night, he was going to try to turn off the part of his brain that always found something in his decisions and actions to disapprove of—or, best-case scenario—belatedly remind him of better choices, better ways.

The house was dark when he got home.

That was not a surprise. He'd been rattled when he left that morning, and he'd forgotten to turn on the timers. But when he unlocked the front door and stepped inside, something felt...off.

It was very cold, for one thing. Cold and damp. For another, it was very quiet.

Empty.

Nobody home.

Zach's heart began to thump unpleasantly with instinctive dread. "Mr. B.?" he called.

No response.

That was unheard of. Never in all the years he'd had him, had Mr. Bigglesworth not showed up to greet Zach at the door.

"Mr. Bigglesworth?" Zach called sharply. "Hey, cat. Where are you?" He dropped the bag with the cat food and grilled chicken, felt for the wall light switch, flicked it, and nothing happened.

"What the hell?"

Zach moved to the nearest table, felt for the lamp, turned it on.

The front room remained shrouded in chilly moonlight.

"Kitty, kitty," Zach called. Not that Mr. B. had ever been a *kitty* kind of cat.

Zach felt his way across the room to the short hall, groped for the light switch, and once again nothing happened. It wasn't just the living room. The power was out.

But it was more than the lack of electricity. A breeze from across the hall whispered against his face, and he knew his bedroom window must be open.

"*Shit.*"

He hadn't opened any windows that morning. Someone had to have broken in while he was at work.

That was bad news, but losing every piece of electronic equipment in the house was nothing compared to the idea of losing Mr. Bigglesworth. With every step Zach took, he was terrified he was going to tread on a small, fuzzy body.

Like the day wasn't already in contention for worst of his life?

"Please," he whispered. "Mr. B. Are you here?"

He crept into the bedroom. From the doorway he could see that yes, the large window on the other side of the room was half-open. The partially raised blinds knocked against the frame in the winter breeze. The silhouettes of the trees in the backyard swayed.

Mr. B. was a cautious little cat. If someone had broken in, he might have escaped out the window.

That was not good news, but it was a more hopeful scenario than the one Zach most feared.

As he leaned out the window, calling softly for the cat, a startling idea flashed into his brain. Could *Ben* have broken in and stolen Mr. Bigglesworth?

It was hard to imagine Ben breaking into his home, but Ben might have been offended when he realized Zach had changed the hiding place for his keys. If Ben had taken Mr. B., at least Mr. B. was safe. Ben loved the cat and would never harm him, however irked he was with Zach.

Zach peered into the darkness, listening.

Was that—

A very faint sound…like a feline wail?

He stared across the small yard to the side of the garage where he stored his Mustang.

He wasn't imagining it, right?

Scrambling out through the window, Zach landed in the soggy grass, and squelched his way to the back door of the garage. He tried the handle, and the door opened with a creak of hinges. That was wrong. The garage was always kept locked, but he could hear Mr. B. yowling, and the need to rescue the cat was paramount in his brain.

He stepped inside, managing not to fall over a stack of old *National Geographic* magazines. Rain shushed against the roof, rustling the magazines and dispersing the musty garage smells of oil and old cardboard. Anemic moonlight bounced off the Mustang's hood, but everything else remained wrapped in deep shadow.

"Hey, Mr. B. Where are you?"

Meow.

The cat appeared out of the gloom to wind around his shins. Mr. B. meowed loudly, plaintively.

Thank God for small miracles. Zach stooped to pick up the cat, and just missed getting slammed in the head as something hard and solid swung over him.

Mr. B. yowled in terror, springing out of Zach's hold and vanishing once more into the darkness. Zach ducked away, crashing into the old headboard he'd bought at a yard sale with vague intentions of refinishing it one day. His glasses went flying. He half turned and got a blurry glimpse of a scene right out of a slasher movie: a tall, shiny-black faceless form with fuzzy long blond hair and a black half-mask.

Whatever he had been thinking—and he hadn't been thinking much beyond the probability his TV had been stolen—it wasn't this.

The figure brought the bat down again, and Zach, hemmed in by the Mustang, the headboard, and an assortment of cardboard boxes, barely managed to scuttle away. He groped for his glasses but couldn't find them.

"What are you doing? What do you want?" he cried. Which were legit questions given that none of this made sense. Why would a burglar lure him out to the garage? Why would a burglar—car thief?—attack him at all? Why not just take the car and flee?

His assailant swung the bat again, and Zach heard it crunch into the box next to his head. If that bat connected with his skull, it would be all over.

He scrabbled clumsily backward on his palms and soles, trying to kick boxes—anything he could—into the path of the figure in black following him with swift and terrifying deliberation. It felt like hours, but could only have been seconds, before he reached the front of the small building.

Zach scrambled up, smashed the button for the automatic door opener, and the garage door rumbled into life. The door began to rise.

Slowly.

As in just about slow motion.

Come on. Come on.

With little more than a foot of clearance, Zach dived beneath the rising door and rolled away. The tall figure followed, dropping down to duck under the door, and Zach went on the offense. He grabbed for the bat, wrestling with his attacker. The other's long, pale hair whipped against Zach's face, and then the intruder head-butted Zach.

The pain was paralyzing. For an alarming second or two Zach felt himself go completely offline—or whatever the human equivalent was to having your cord yanked out of the electrical outlet.

He stumbled back, ears ringing, and landed on his tailbone. For a few vital seconds, he saw stars. Through the whirl of lights, he saw the long-haired figure raise the bat again—only to be stopped by outraged shouts from across the street.

The intruder hurled the bat away and took off running down the sidewalk.

Zach started to rise, but sank back as pain lanced through his knee where he'd landed on it.

Jesus Christ. What just happened?

He couldn't seem to take it in.

His neighbors—and their dog, which they'd been out walking—ran across the street and joined him.

"Are you okay?" Mrs. Odlum panted. "Who was that?"

"Let me see if I can get a license-plate number." Mr. Odlum handed Sparky's leash to Mrs. Odlum, and took off down the street after the intruder.

Zach tried again to rise. Something was definitely wrong with his knee. He swore quietly and sank back.

"Oh, you're hurt!" Mrs. Odlum exclaimed.

"I twisted my knee, that's all."

Mrs. Odlum was already on her phone, calling 911.

Mr. Odlum returned a moment or two later, out of breath. "I lost her. I don't know where she went."

"That wasn't a *she*," Mrs. Odlum said. "That was a man in a wig."

"I don't think so, dear."

"I *know* so."

"We can't *know* that for a fact."

"*I* certainly do."

Mr. Odlum threw an uncomfortable look at Zach. "But dear, we don't know how she identifies herself."

Mrs. Odlum began to splutter. "That was a *man* in a terrible wig."

"Well, she—or he—didn't drive away, as far as I can tell."

"Well, no, of course not. He was here for Zach's Mustang."

"*Oh, right*! Of course."

"Not that he would have gotten far in it." Mrs. Odlum dropped her cell phone in her coat pocket and pulled Sparky, who was giving Zach a snuffling head-to-toe inspection, away. "Don't worry, Zach. The police are on the way."

"For all the good it'll do," Mr. Odlum put in.

"Now, that's not fair," Mrs. Odlum said.

The Odlums began to animatedly discuss crime statistics in Monterey County as a whole, versus Salinas specifically, and the shortcomings of local law enforcement.

"If you could just give me a hand?" Zach interrupted.

"Oh, right!" Mr. Odlum said.

"The poor boy sprained his ankle," Mrs. Odlum explained.

Zach gritted his teeth as the Odlums got on either side of him and helped him to his feet. He tested putting his weight on his injured leg, and sucked in a breath.

Mr. Odlum began to brush him off.

"I hope nothing's broken," Mrs. Odlum waved hello to the neighbors on the other side of Zach's house, who had come out to see what the commotion was. "Someone tried to steal Zach's Mustang!"

"*Why?*" cried Mrs. Daly.

The Dalys, colorfully attired in the nightwear favored by characters in '70s sitcoms, joined the enclave on Zach's driveway, Mr. Daly helpfully picking up the discarded baseball bat as he approached.

Zach opened his mouth and then closed it.

"Can you put any weight on it?" Mrs. Odlum asked.

"What? Oh. Sort of."

"Is he all right?" Mrs. Daly asked. "Was it another homeless person? Should we phone the police?"

"He's sprained his ankle. We've already called the police," Mrs. Odlum informed her.

Sure enough, the wail of sirens floated in the distance.

"Never a cop when you need them," Mrs. Daly said, which seemed a little unfair. "How's your ankle, sweetie?"

"It's actually my knee." Zach did not want to be mistaken for the heroine in a romantic suspense novel.

"This is becoming an epidemic!" Mr. Daly pushed the baseball bat into Zach's hands. "Lucky your head's still in one piece, son."

The Odlums and Dalys were still arguing whether car-theft rates were rising or falling in Salinas when the police arrived.

CHAPTER EIGHTEEN

It was well after ten when Zach poured the last of the Chivas Regal he'd once kept on hand for Pop, and hobbled into the living room. He settled on the sofa, propping his taped knee on a stack of cushions and let out an *oof* as Mr. Bigglesworth came in for a landing.

"Ohh-*kay*! Nobody needs their appendix anyway."

Mr. B. seemed to consider the validity of this, delicately inspecting Zach's face with whiskery, moon-eyed intent.

Zach smiled beneath the cat's ministrations. "The main thing is *you're* okay."

Mr. B. concurred—his *meow* held an aggrieved note—and then they both jumped, Zach narrowly missing spilling his whiskey, as the doorbell rang.

"*Now* what?" he muttered, struggling to get off the sofa. It was tempting to yell '*Go away*!' But if this wasn't yet another neighbor checking in to get the scoop, it would surely be the police back to follow-up on the report he'd just made. Like Lt. Columbo with his '*Just one more thing!*'

He set his glass on the end table, deposited Mr. B. on the stack of cushions, and limped to the front door as the doorbell *ding-donged* again.

He stared out the peephole. Flint's compact frame filled the fish-eye viewfinder.

Zach's heart skipped a beat. It was disconcerting that his instinctive response was as much pleasure as wariness. Flint, never the model of patience, stopped pressing the doorbell and instead thumped on the door. His slightly distorted expression seemed even grimmer than usual.

Zach unlocked the deadbolt and opened the door. "Jeez. You don't have to break the door down."

"*Seriously*?" Despite his irate tone, Flint's shoulders—his entire body—seemed to relax at the sight of Zach. "I have to hear from Brooke that my-my accountant was attacked in his own home!"

"I'm not your accountant!" Zach shot back. "Besides, it was my garage, not my house."

Flint cocked his head. There was the faintest suggestion of a smile on his face. "Are you going to let me in? Or are we going to shou-discuss this on the doorstep."

"I don't see why we have to discuss it all." As much as Zach wanted to hold onto his irritation, there was something about the glint in Flint's eyes, that little twist of smile, that made it impossible to turn him away. He opened the door, grousing, "Why the hell would Brooke call *you* of all people?"

"How's your knee? And what do you mean, *me of all people*? Who else would she call?"

"Why would she call anyone? I told her only this afternoon we couldn't go running to…to other people every time we have a problem at the office."

"I'm not *other people*. I have a vested interest here."

"In your dreams." Zach, trying to favor his knee without appearing to favor his knee, started for the living room. "We can talk in here."

He was startled and more than a little self-conscious when Flint caught his elbow, offering unasked-for support.

"That's okay. I'm fine."

But Flint ignored him, shortening his long stride to Zach's halting one as they crossed the hallway. His competent gentleness caught Zach off guard, made him feel—well, nothing useful or logical. Just that it would be nice to have someone in his life again he could occasionally rely on. Just a little.

"Besides," Flint was saying, "It's not like you misplaced a file. Someone tried to kill you."

Someone tried to kill you.

Yes. That.

The thing he had been trying not to focus on. The thing the police had not seemed to take seriously.

He couldn't seem to come up with an answer, and Flint said, "You filed a report with the police?"

No. What a great idea!

But Zach didn't say that. He had no energy for their usual sparring. Instead, he nodded wearily, accepting Flint's help as he lowered himself to the sofa, resettling his knee on the stack of cushions.

"Okay. I'll follow up on that. Did you get a look at your attacker?"

"Not really. I lost my glasses, so everything was kind of a blur."

"Well, that explains the tape." Flint lightly tapped the taped bridge of Zach's glasses.

It was light and affectionate and completely out of character. Or maybe it wasn't out of character. Not for the first time, Zach wondered if most of everything he'd ever thought about Flint had been not just wrong, completely unfair.

Flint, meanwhile, dragged the footstool over and seated himself, so that he and Zach were eye level.

Zach self-consciously touched his glasses. "These are an old pair. I didn't want to..." He didn't finish it because *I didn't want to go back in there* was going to sound like he'd been afraid. Mostly, he hadn't wanted to try crawling around with a wrecked knee to find his glasses. But okay, yes, also he'd been freaked out at the idea of staying in the garage longer than it took to find Mr. B. cowering behind a stack of old paint cans.

"I'll have a look," Flint said briskly, and Zach couldn't help thinking that at times like these, Flint's cool, take-charge attitude was particularly comforting. "Were you able to get an idea of size or..."

"Or?"

Flint said neutrally, "Sex."

Zach said slowly, "It's interesting you bring that up because they were wearing a shiny black raincoat and had long, blond hair."

Flint's gaze sharpened. "So, you think it *was* a woman? Zora?"

"I... No. I actually don't. I mean, I'm not sure because it was already dark and then I lost my glasses, so I couldn't see much. But I could *feel*— And I know that sounds crazy."

"No. It doesn't. You got a sense of their size from having a physical altercation."

"Yes. Right." It was a relief Flint understood so easily what he meant. "They were tall, at least my height, and thin, but strong. There was a lot of force in the way they swung that bat."

"You look like you've been through the wars, that's for sure." Once again Flint astonished Zach by gently brushing the bruise on his forehead. It was just a graze of fingertips, but Zach felt Flint's touch in the very pores of his skin.

He grimaced. That was when they head-butted me. Which, come to think of it, is why I was pretty sure they were male. That felt...male."

"I've known some pretty tough gals in my time, but I know what you mean. I realize you couldn't make out features, but did they say anything? Make any noise at all? Could you tell much from touch or sound or smell?"

Zach closed his eyes, trying to remember. "Other than when he slammed his head into mine..."

"Was he wearing aftershave?"

Zach frowned, shook his head. "I don't think so. I could smell the rubber of his raincoat. The hair felt fake, now that I think about it. Like a cheap wig. That's about it. The garage already smells like car and old furniture."

"Right."

Zach opened his eyes. "The thing of it is, that blond wig—if it was a wig—that seems like it was meant to implicate Zora."

Flint grunted. "Maybe. But presumably no one was meant to see anything. If someone hits you over the head with a baseball bat a few times, chances are you're not going to be around to report what you saw."

Zach swallowed. "True."

Flint studied him seriously. "You were lucky tonight, Zachariah."

"I guess so."

"I don't like this."

"I'm not too crazy about it either."

Flint continued to regard him in that serious, troubled way. "I don't understand why anyone would come after you. You're not as useful as a patsy if you're dead. So, unless there's something you're not telling me—"

"I've told you everything."

Their gazes locked. After a moment, Flint nodded. "I believe you. But then we're back to trying to understand why you'd be a target. As far as I can tell, you—we—don't know anything that the cops don't know."

"I agree. I think. Honestly, I'm too tired to see straight." Mostly Zach was thinking aloud, so he was a little embarrassed at the look of sympathy Flint gave him.

"I don't doubt it. It's been a long-ass day."

Flint had never struck him as overly solicitous, so the unfamiliar softness in his face both warmed and confused Zach.

Flint said, "How'd it go over at the sheriff's office?"

"Didn't your friend Detective Schneider tell you?" There was a little note in Zach's voice that probably sounded like...something he did not want to sound like. But it was kind of confusing sitting here staring into Flint's sympathetic green-gold eyes, hearing that concern in his voice. It was hard to remember that they were friendly, not friends. In fact, they were adversaries.

Except tonight, in this moment, it didn't feel like they were adversaries.

"He told me." Flint's smile was wry, but even that felt like something shared, like they were on the same team and everyone else was...not.

Which had to be further proof of how truly tired Zach was.

"Do they still think I'm a suspect?"

Flint shrugged. "Don't take it personally. At this point in the investigation, everyone's a suspect. Same with us, right? We consider everyone fair game."

That displayed a level of tact, even sensitivity on Flint's part that Zach wouldn't have expected before this evening's increasingly odd encounter.

He nodded, then admitted the thing that had been eating at him ever since they'd left the Kaschak estate. "I still can't understand why Alton did what he did."

"Which part?"

"They showed me the video. I can't understand why Alton told Chico it was me."

Flint didn't say anything for a moment. "I guess because he wanted it to be you." He added carefully, "As far as why he'd show Chico? Because Chico saw you turn him down. I'm guessing Beacher's ego couldn't take it. Not least because it didn't happen very often."

"Maybe we should try to find out who it was on that video."

Flint's brows rose. "Maybe we should."

"If he was coercing guys into making DIY pornos, what did he do with the videos? Use them to blackmail his victims into doing...what?"

"That's good." Flint sounded thoughtful. "If blackmail isn't a motive for murder, I don't know what is."

"Chico probably knows who some of those other possible victims are. He might have shared that with the police or he might have just focused on throwing me under the bus."

"When you're a bodyguard, losing clients isn't exactly a career booster. He needs a scapegoat."

"Other than wear a gun, I'm not sure I ever saw him act like a bodyguard."

Flint grimaced. "Like you, he probably got the job based on his looks."

Blunt but likely accurate. Zach was quiet.

Neither of them said anything for a minute or two. Mr. B. who had skedaddled under the chair when Flint first appeared, cautiously poked his head out, considered Flint, and leaped lightly onto the back of the sofa.

The cat meowed loudly at Flint.

Flint nodded politely. "Cat."

Zach said, "He's not pedigreed. I actually did find him going through garbage cans in a back alley. He was six weeks old."

"Of course you did."

Flint sounded resigned, and yet it kind of felt like a compliment.

Zach sighed, let his head fall against the back of the sofa. "It's weird. Even though it wasn't me on that video, I still feel…"

"You still feel?"

"Violated."

"Yeah. Of course."

"You were right. I shouldn't have taken Alton's case. I knew it was too good to be true. I had a bad feeling from the start. But I let myself be convinced by all that money."

Flint didn't say anything.

Zach lifted his head, said, "Thanks for not saying I told you so."

Flint shrugged. "You were in a tough spot. And you didn't have the advantage of knowing what a creep Alton was. I can't say for sure I wouldn't have made the same decision in your position."

Zach smiled. Flint smiled. And somehow—Zach was not exactly sure how—they leaned toward each other, leaned closer, and...kissed. It happened so naturally, so easily that Zach was conscious of Flint's warm mouth on his before he realized he'd leaned in for Flint's kiss. Like it was normal. Like it was something they did all the time.

It *felt* normal, startlingly normal, that was the thing. Flint's lips pressing against his own, the bump of Flint's nose...Zach's glasses were slipping sideways before he fully registered they were kissing.

And it was over just as fast.

Disappointingly fast.

"Whoops." Flint drew back.

"Whoops?" Zach hastily straightened his glasses.

"Well, I mean..."

Zach tilted his head in inquiry.

Flint's eyes widened. His mouth parted. "Do you—? Are you saying that was okay?"

Okay? In Zach's opinion, it had been a lot better than *okay*.

He asked uncertainly, "*Wasn't* it?"

"Well, yeah. It was with me." Flint reached forward and, astonishingly, slipped Zach's glasses from his nose. He dipped his head—Zach had a blurry view of Flint's smile coming at him—and then they did it again. They kissed.

Flint's smile landed softly, persuasively on Zach's mouth, and Zach opened to what felt like unexpected tenderness. There was no demand, no insistence. Just a warm pressure that felt almost cherishing—certainly, one of the nicest kisses Zach had ever had. Flint made a smiley sound and reluctantly raised his head.

"Gosh," Zach said.

Flint chuckled, and even his quiet amusement sounded sexy and intimate. "Just what I was going to say."

Zach laughed.

Flint traced his cheekbone, tucked a strand of Zach's hair behind his ear. "That was even nicer that I expected."

Zach had never expected to kiss Flint, so he didn't have a response.

Flint said gravely, "You've had a rough day. I don't want to take advantage."

"Oh." Zach's heart seemed to pause mid-step.

"But I don't think you should be alone tonight. I can sleep here on the sofa, if you'd prefer that."

Zach blinked. "Why would I prefer that?"

"Well, I just..." Flint abruptly seemed to lose his train of thought.

"I'm thirty not thirteen."

Flint's outline sat up straight. "Uh, I should sure as hell hope not!"

"My point is, I'm an adult. You don't need to tuck me into bed. You don't even need to stay—" Zach drew a sharp breath. "But I hope you will."

The longest three seconds in the world passed before Flint said in a funny voice, "Hell. I didn't even think you liked me."

A couple of smartass comments flitted through Zach's brain; he was so used to fencing with Flint, but there was something in Flint's tone, something surprised and genuine and maybe, just maybe even a little vulnerable. Something that called for equal honesty from Zach.

He admitted, "I didn't know you. I didn't think you liked *me*."

Flint's laugh was soft. "Yeah, I like you. I've always thought you were—" He stopped there, shrugged, and leaned in for another kiss.

CHAPTER NINETEEN

The decision—well, there was no *decision*—there were no words or discussion, but somehow, they were moving from the living room sofa to the bedroom, and the effort of rising, of walking, of thinking—as much thinking as was possible in that shimmering haze of longing and desire—threatened to burst the fragile bubble of excitement and wonder. But then they were in Zach's bedroom, standing beside Zach's neatly made bed. Flint opened his arms and Zach moved into his hold. They melted together in a long kiss, and it was instantly okay again, their hands moving caressingly, almost absently unbuttoning, unzipping, sliding shirts over shoulders, tugging jeans over hips, down legs.

Zach winced, sucked in a breath—his taped knee was very painful—and Flint murmured apology, doing his best to kiss it better. He helped Zach onto the mattress, helped him settle, gazing down at Zach in the soft light. Flint was smiling and clear-eyed.

"What do you like?" he asked.

It wasn't a difficult question, but Zach blinked because he'd only ever been with Ben. Sure, he'd read magazine articles and seen porn vids, but none of that was real. *This* was real. The possibilities of this. All the possibilities. Including some he wasn't ready to consider.

"I like *you*," Zach answered, and that was the absolute truth.

Flint's expression altered, his smile—Zach had never seen that smile before, but he couldn't help thinking he liked being able to make Flint look like that.

"We'll figure it out as we go," Flint promised—and it really did sound like a promise. He slipped Zach's glasses off—the glasses Zach didn't remember sliding back on.

It was almost shockingly easy to let go, to give into this unexpected, unlooked for…how to put a name to it? It was too chivalrous, too tender for seduction—and who was seducing whom anyway? It felt disarmingly like that Happily Ever After Alton had said only existed in fairy tales.

Flint's hard, sure hand cupped Zach's balls, and Zach squeezed his eyes tight in pleasure. He'd gotten used to—resigned to—doing without, but how lovely to have this again. To be touched with nothing expected beyond reciprocation, which Zach was more than happy to give.

At last, they were naked together beneath the blankets, the world shrinking to the slow slide of skin on skin, moist, lingering kisses, the caress of warm hands, encouraging murmurs. The hot sweetness of shared arousal, shared need, spilled all too soon between them.

*M*eow?

Zach unstuck his eyelids, blinked into the inquiring blur of Mr. B.'s aqua alien-eyes, and felt around for his glasses. He found them on his nightstand, slid them on—slid them off. His taped glasses had been replaced by the pair he'd lost in the garage.

He put the glasses back on, and studied the Flint-sized emptiness on the other side of the bed.

Did we—? Had that actually—?

But yeah. They did. That had. And he was okay with it. Surprised at himself, surprised at both of them, in the cold light of day, but okay. The surrounding circumstances had been...unique. He could blame sleep deprivation, shock, pain meds, and Chivas Regal. He could blame any number of things for his uncharacteristic behavior, but he didn't want to find blame. He didn't need an excuse. He didn't regret what had happened. Unless Flint did.

Flint was still there, though, somewhere. Zach could smell coffee brewing, could hear Flint whistling cheerily as he banged around Zach's tiny kitchen in search of...was he mining for gold? It sounded like a lot of pans involved in whatever was happening.

That was a good sign, right? That Flint had not fled into the night?

"What do you think?" Zach asked Mr. B.

Mr. B.'s *meow* definitely held a note of reserved judgment.

Zach threw back the blankets, smothering a yelp—his knee had stiffened during the night—and began to dress.

When he hobbled into the kitchen a few minutes later, Flint greeted him with a quick look and a distracted, "There you are." He held up a metal reamer. "Do you actually squeeze your own orange juice?"

Which was a little anti-climactic for sure. Zach followed Flint's cue. "I do if I have time."

"Sorry, I don't have that kind of time." Flint clattered two plates onto the table. "Eat up. We've got to get moving."

Zach studied the neatly arranged scrambled eggs, bacon, and toaster waffles. He did not usually have more than a cup of coffee for breakfast, but he said, "This looks great. Thank you."

Flint grunted, took the seat across from Zach's, and forked up a mouthful of eggs.

Zach also took a mouthful of eggs, and found them fluffy and delicious. Jesus. Flint could *cook*? He'd kind of figured Flint for a guy who lived hand-to-mouth—in the processed foods sense.

He studied Flint with new and respectful curiosity.

Flint, head bowed, seemed to have nothing more on his mind than cleaning his plate.

Oh. Kay.

Zach glanced at Mr. B., who was daintily picking his way through a plate of Smalls fresh cat food.

"Did you feed him?"

Flint raised his head, looking blank. He followed Zach's gaze, and shrugged. "I tried. He seemed to think I was trying to poison him."

"I guess he's concluded you're one of the good guys."

Flint made an unconvinced sound, and changed the subject. "Did the cops actually investigate last night? There's no fingerprint powder in the garage. There's no indication they were in there at all."

"They weren't. They didn't do more than glance inside the house either. The official opinion was that I startled a homeless person who had decided to bed down for the night in my garage."

Flint's brows pulled into a frown. "How do they explain breaking into your house?"

Zach said, "They didn't believe there *was* a break-in. They think I had to have left the window open because nothing was damaged or stolen."

"And you also left the garage door open?"

Zach nodded. "In fairness, the lock on the garage side door is mostly for show. You can get the latch to turn if you know how to wiggle the knob."

"Oh, that's terrific."

Zach shrugged. "There's nothing of value in there but my Mustang, and as you not-so-tactfully pointed out, they'd have to bring a tow truck for that."

Flint's grin was unrepentant. "You have a point."

"They basically told me this kind of thing happens during the winter. And they assured me my assailant was probably more afraid of me than I was him."

Flint returned to being unamused. "And what about the power going out?"

"These are old houses. Sometimes they blow a fuse and the power goes out. Which is true. It's one reason I wasn't that concerned when the lights didn't come on. But I know I didn't leave the window unlocked, let alone open."

Flint nodded, opened his mouth, and his cell phone rang. He glanced at it, did a quick doubletake, and rose, muttering, "Excuse me a sec."

Flint didn't just leave the kitchen, he walked down the hall and out the front door.

Zach stared after him. The fact that Flint was in his kitchen at all, was surreal. But if Zach *had* ever imagined Flint sharing his breakfast table, he'd have pictured something pretty much like this: Flint brusque and businesslike.

"Does he seem nervous to you?" Zach asked Mr. B.

Mr. B. chose not to go on the record, but Zach had already discarded that theory.

"Maybe not nervous, but... Defensive?"

That was it. Flint seemed on guard. As though he expected Zach to come at him for... What? Taking advantage of his weakened state? No way. Fearing Zach might make too much of what had happened between them? That was more like it.

Zach's happiness deflated a bit. Anyway, what was there to be so happy about?

First of all, not that much had happened. That is, nice things that felt very good had happened, but if someone wanted to get technical, the events of last evening fell more under the heading of heavy petting than actual intercourse.

Maybe Zach wasn't a-a man of the world (whatever that meant) but he did know, regardless of who had done what to whom, he and Flint were not now going steady. Zach wasn't forgetting about Detective Schneider. And for all he knew, Schneider was one of a cast of thousands.

Last night had been...

Well, it had been one of the nicest things that had happened to Zach in a long time. But he was not going to be stupid about it. Not least because he didn't want to do anything that might prevent it happening again.

The front door slammed and Flint was back in the kitchen. He said crisply, "Ensenada del Sello PD just brought Ransford Beacher in for questioning."

Why would that news bring a flush to Flint's face or put that gleam of anger in his eyes? Zach said cautiously, "That's to be expected, right?"

"They've named him a person of interest."

"A person of interest in *what*? When I spoke to Bill Cameron, they still hadn't determined whether Alton staged the accident. Or do they think Ransford helped Alton fake his death?"

"Someone died in that crash," Flint pointed out. "And the butler is still hospitalized."

"Has he recovered consciousness?"

"Conscious and apparently talking."

"That's good news. The butler has to know who was driving. The butler has to know if there was an extra person in the car."

"Yes."

Zach was still thinking. "They didn't name Ransford a suspect?"

"Person of interest," Flint repeated.

"So, they don't have enough to charge him yet. They're still gathering evidence. It could be a fishing expedition."

"Correct."

Zach asked suddenly, "What did Zora have to say when you interviewed her yesterday?" He had been so distracted after learning he had moved into the prime suspect slot—and the reason for that—he'd entirely forgotten that Flint had not simply been paying a courtesy call on the widow.

"Not as much as I'd hoped. She was half-zonked on tranquilizers, for one thing. She did say she went straight to bed after returning home from Pinch. She wasn't aware her husband came back to the house, let alone that he went out again. She said he often stayed at their beach house. But they sleep—slept—in suites on opposite sides of the house. And she takes sleeping pills. According to Zora, she had no idea Alton wasn't at work until the sheriffs arrived to notify her of the accident."

"That could all be true."

"It could. I did learn something interesting though. She and Ransford were pals before she ever met Alton."

"Were they? Ransford's quite a bit younger than her, I know."

"He worked for her at Haunted Hollow."

"The theme park? Doing what?"

"He worked there for a couple of summers. It turns out Zora was in charge of the crew responsible for maintaining and repairing the rides."

"You mean she was an administrator or a mechanic? I can't picture her in overalls, wrench in hand—"

"Then you'd be wrong," Flint cut in. "Zora's very proud of the grease beneath her nails, metamorphically speaking."

"Meta*phorically* speaking?"

"Whatever," Flint said shortly. "In my opinion, she went out of her way to point out that she's more than capable of tampering with a car engine or brakes."

"Why would she do that?"

Flint shrugged.

"Could she be trying to draw attention from Ransford?"

"Like I said, she was sedated. I don't think there was a lot of calculation going on there."

Zach thought that over.

"How does someone go from working in a theme park to being an agoraphobe?"

"Working in a theme park would turn anyone into a recluse." Flint was probably kidding, but his expression remained hard to read. Some instinct made Zach ask, "Was that Detective Schneider on the phone?"

"Yep."

"Did he—"

Flint cut him off with a crisp, "He's fine."

Not what Zach had been wondering, but okay. Did Schneider's call explain things or no? Because something was definitely up with Flint. Presumably, he regretted what had happened with Zach. Which hurt. A bit. Maybe more than a bit. But Zach was not going to complicate either of their lives by being difficult.

He said, "Does the fact that Ransford was brought in for questioning mean I'm off the hook?"

Flint gave a funny laugh. "Wellll…"

"*Wellll* what? I explained everything!"

"I know. But they have to verify. They can't take your word. You know how it works."

Zach nodded curtly. He knew how a lot of things worked.

Flint considered him for a moment, said, "I don't think you're the sole focus of the sheriff's office investigation, but you won't actually be cleared until they get the mobile forensics. As far as Ransford's concerned, I guess they'll wait and see what EDS comes up with."

Zach considered the implications of that.

"I don't understand how the police and the sheriffs are both still claiming jurisdiction."

"I do. This is the biggest case to come along in two decades. In fact, the sheriffs may have a stronger claim. The Kaschak estate is outside city limits and the accident took place on a county road. But the DA favors the case going to EDS PD for a lot of reasons, including the fact Beacher initiated the investigation by coming to you."

"Did Schneider have any idea why Ransford is suddenly the focus of the police investigation?"

Flint's smile was cynical. "It turns out Ransford lied about when he flew in. He ended up catching an earlier flight."

Zach whistled. "He doesn't have an alibi."

"Bingo."

Not conclusive, but damning for sure. "I wonder what Alton and Ransford were planning to meet about."

"*I* wonder what Alton's will looks like," Flint said.

"That, too."

They exchanged looks.

Ransford had not even been on Zach's radar. But then Ransford hadn't been on Alton's radar, either. This new information put Alton's brother in the hot seat, for sure. Maybe, for once, the least likely suspect actually *was* guilty.

But how did any of this tie in with last night's attack? Was it possible there *wasn't* a connection? It wasn't like Zach was juggling a bunch of cases or had a lot of enemies. The assumption that the attack on him was somehow connected to the Beacher case had seemed, not just reasonable, inevitable.

But maybe he had it wrong.

Maybe he and Flint both had it wrong.

"Okay, well, where do we go from here?" Zach asked. "Or do we?"

Flint frowned. "What do you mean *or do we*?"

"Are we still pursuing this? It seems like a surplus of investigators as it is."

"Which is why it's going to be so satisfying when *we* bust this case right open."

Zach opened his mouth—and closed it.

Flint hesitated, said shortly, "Unless you've changed your mind. You want out?"

Zach didn't have to think about it. "No. I don't want out."

Flint nodded approvingly. "Good. Then let's go see what Jeeves has to say for himself."

CHAPTER TWENTY

The hospital parking lot was still mostly empty when they arrived in separate cars at Monterey Memorial shortly after nine o'clock.

"How's your knee?" Flint asked as they passed through the sliding glass doors and entered the hospital lobby.

"It's okay," Zach replied. "Just a little stiff."

Flint nodded, headed straight for the building directory next to the elevators.

"How do we know what floor Topper is on?" Zach asked, joining him.

"Third floor," Flint punched the button for the elevator.

Okay, then.

The doors instantly slid open. The elevator was empty. Zach followed Flint inside. Flint pressed the Close button, leaned back against the wall of the car. The doors slid shut.

Zach glanced at Flint's granite profile. Flint's attention seemed glued to the button panel.

"Everything okay?" Zach couldn't help asking.

Flint considered him, considered the question, nodded. "You?"

"Me? Yeah. Great." Zach smiled.

Flint blinked as if all the window shades in the world had suddenly snapped up.

He said finally, neutrally, "Well, good."

The sound of a television could be heard several yards down the hall from Topper the butler's private room.

An empty chair was positioned beneath the room number. The door stood open. Flint rapped on the door frame. Zach stuck his head inside.

The room's only occupant was an elderly man in navy pajamas sitting upright in bed. He was watching TV.

"May we have a quick word, Mr. Topper?" Flint called over the blast of a local weather report.

Topper looked around wildly as though he thought the weather lady had sneaked into his room. "Who's there?" he asked querulously, adjusting his spectacles.

Flint glanced pointedly at Zach. Was Zach supposed to take lead on this?

He stepped inside the room, saying, "Glad to see you're feeling better, sir. I'm Zach Davies from Davies Detective Agency. I was working for Mr. Beacher at the time of his death."

"What's that?"

Zach raised his voice. "Zach Davies, Davies Detective Agency."

Topper picked up the remote and muted the television. "What are you supposed to be, another insurance investigator?"

Flint and Zach exchanged quick looks. Zach advanced into the room. "No. I was working for Mr. Beacher."

"Since when?" Topper asked skeptically. "I don't remember you."

"For the last week. Mr. Beacher hired me to find out who was threatening him."

Topper stared. "How's that coming along?" he asked sourly.

"Everybody's a wiseass," Flint remarked.

"What's that?" Topper demanded. "Who's there with you?"

"This is my associate, Mr. Carey."

"Why's he skulking in the doorway?"

Zach ignored that, removing his ID and moving to the bed to hand it to Topper. He could see the older man was badly bruised. There were tiny cuts over his face and hands. But his injuries didn't look life-threatening. Zach had expected more medical equipment at the very least.

Topper took Zach's ID, stared at it, handed it back.

"Mr. Beacher was a man with a lot of secrets," he said cryptically.

"What kind of secrets?" Flint asked.

Topper looked at him like he was an idiot. "How should I know? They were secrets."

Zach swallowed a laugh and intervened. "You look like you've had a rough time, Mr. Topper. Can you tell us about the accident?"

"I slept through most of it."

"You *slept* through it?"

Topper raised his chin. "Of course I did. Dragging a man of my age out in the middle of the night. I work hard. I was exhausted."

"How did you—?" Zach began.

"The cops think I was thrown from the car before it went over the edge."

Flint said, "You weren't wearing a seatbelt?"

Topper gave a sharp, short shake of his head. "Never wear 'em. More people are trapped in cars and burned alive than get killed in head-on collisions."

"That's not even remotely true," Flint said.

"Sure, it is. I saw it on YouTube."

Zach made a point of not looking at Flint. "Can you tell us anything about the phone call Mr. Beacher received?"

"I didn't take the phone call. He did. It was on his private line."

"Did he say anything about it?"

"He said he had to get down to his office right away. He said someone had broken into the safe in his office."

"Did he say who phoned him?"

"I don't remember. I don't think so."

"Did he have any idea about who might have broken into his office?"

"Someone working for Mr. Jordan."

Flint said, "The owner of Old Timey Fun, Ltd.?"

Topper nodded. "Mr. Beacher and Mr. Jordan were friends but they were also business rivals."

"The kind of business rivals who break into each other's offices?"

"Are there any other?" Topper seemed to think the question was rhetorical.

Zach said, "So Alton—Mr. Beacher—had no doubts the call he received was legitimate."

"He didn't seem to. He couldn't get to the office fast enough. That was my impression."

"And it was just the two of you in the car?"

Topper looked at Zach as though he were an idiot. "Who else would be in the car?"

"We're asking you," Flint said.

"Chico?" Zach suggested.

Topper said impatiently, "If Chico had been available, why would Mr. Beacher have dragged me out of bed?"

Flint asked, "How soon after you got in the car did you fall asleep?"

Topper seemed to cast his mind back. "I remember we passed through the gates. Mr. Beacher had put some music on. Kreisler's *Liebesleid*." He shrugged. "The next time I opened my eyes, Mr. Beacher was struggling to control the car."

"Did he say anything?" Flint asked.

"Not that I can repeat in public. He was swearing. Understandably. He tried to run us onto the hillside, to slow us down, I suppose. We nearly turned over. Maybe it would have been better for us if we had. As it was, the car continued to pick up speed. Mr. Beacher tried to use the handbrake, but we hit another curve. I'm not sure if Mr. Beacher clipped the hillside, but he seemed to lose control completely and we headed for the cliff." He shuddered. "The next thing I knew, I woke up lying in this bed."

"He didn't say anything about the condition of the car?" Flint persisted.

Topper looked at him in disbelief. "What do you imagine he would have said? The car was always perfectly maintained."

"Something like... The brakes aren't working?"

"That was self-evident."

Zach said, "You were very lucky, Mr. Topper."

Topper sniffed. "Yes. Poor Mr. Beacher."

When Zach and Flint left Topper's room, they discovered a young uniformed EDS officer, settling herself in the chair next to the doorway. She was so startled to see them, she nearly dropped her coffee cup.

"Who are you?" she demanded.

"Sorry we startled you," Flint said. "I'm Flint Carey. This is Zach Davies. We're private investigators Mr. Beacher hired shortly before his death."

The officer took their IDs automatically, frowning down at the pieces of plastic. "How did you get in here?"

"The usual way," Flint said. "We didn't realize Mr. Topper was supposed to be under guard."

She turned red, handed their IDs back, and said defensively, "It's just a precaution. Mr. Topper is witness to a homicide."

"Not really," Flint said, and she looked more confused.

Zach sighed. "Sorry if we overstepped. We just needed to verify a couple of things before I check in with Lt. Cameron."

The officer relaxed. "Lt. Cameron knows you're here?"

Zach opened his mouth, but Flint said, "Yep. I guess we'll leave you to it, officer." He didn't exactly drag Zach away, but that hand under Zach's elbow wasn't about Zach's stiff knee.

As the elevator doors closed behind them, Zach said, "Alton was driving."

"It sounds like it."

"So, he is dead."

"Probably. Yes."

Zach expelled a long shaky breath.

Flint glanced at him, said briskly, "That was always the most likely scenario."

"I guess so."

Probably. But Zach had been hoping hard for the alternative.

Flint was not one for allowing time to wallow. "Look, the more we learn, the less likely it seems to me that Beacher really believed he was in serious danger."

"But if Alton was manufacturing the threats—"

"I'm not saying that. Given how things turned out, I think we can assume the threats were real and that Alton's reasons for coming to you were, all things being relative, legit. But I also think he quickly dismissed them as anything more than threats. I'm guessing he probably convinced himself Rusty Jordan sent them."

"How do you figure that?"

"The fact that he jumped to the conclusion that Jordan tried to break into his safe. It seems like he did believe that the break-in was real. He didn't wait for the bodyguard. He didn't phone the police. He didn't even phone you. He didn't suspect a trap. And yet that was an obvious, *obvious* set up."

"But—"

"As far you're concerned, I think he got distracted from his original reason for hiring you. I think he decided you could serve a better purpose, and he set about trying to seduce you. He wasn't honest with you, which is a big part of why you weren't able to do the job he originally hired you for."

Zach said slowly, "Do you really believe that?"

"One hundred percent." Flint's smile was sardonic. "You must know me well enough by now to realize I'm not going to tell you what I think you want to hear, unless I believe it's the truth."

Fair enough. Zach was pretty sure Flint was not the type to soothe people with comfortable lies. Which he was grateful for. Flint really believed everything he was saying, and he made a convincing argument. Zach still felt guilty about Alton, but maybe not as guilty as he'd felt the day before.

When they reached the parking lot and their separate cars, Flint said, "I've got some things to check on. Let's meet back at your office around noon. We can have lunch and determine where we are with the investigation."

"Uh… Okay." Zach had assumed they would go back to the office and figure out their next move. It seemed Flint already had a next move. That was a bit disappointing. Not that Zach needed direction from Flint, but it was kind of nice working with a partner. "What are you checking on?"

Flint said vaguely, "I'll let you know, if it pans out."

"That's a little mysterious."

Flint grinned. "I'm a mysterious kind of guy, Zachariah."

"Huh." Zach was openly skeptical, and Flint grinned again.

"See you shortly. Don't do anything I wouldn't."

"So, no limits?"

Flint touched his finger to his temple in a *here's-looking-at-you-kid*, climbed into his SUV, and started the engine.

Brooke was in the office at her computer, typing away at who-knows-what—a Facebook post?—when Zach pushed open the glass door.

"Hey," Zach began. "Could you—" He broke off at Brooke's pointedly sideways look.

Zach glanced at the lobby chairs as a tall, handsome, blond man rose. The man looked familiar, but Zach couldn't quite place him.

"Zachery Davies?"

"Zachariah. Yes?" Zach's initial curiosity gave way to wariness as he took in the other's flushed face and too-bright eyes. Whoever this guy was, he was mad as hell. "Can I help you?"

The man's mouth opened in what looked like a snarl.

Brooke cut in quickly, "Zee, this is Ransford Beacher."

"Mr. Beacher?" Zach was startled. "I'm so sorry for your loss." Now that he knew what to look for, the family resemblance was noticeable. Ransford was taller, thinner, and younger than Alton, but he had the same chilly good looks.

Ransford spat out, "Not half as sorry as you're going to be, if you don't stop harassing Zora!"

"W-what? I haven't had any contact with your sister-in-law since the night Alton—your brother—"

"Don't give me that bullshit! Your partner was up at the house yesterday interrogating her while you were trying to question the household staff. Martinez came straight to Zora the minute you left. In fact, I saw you myself on your way out the gate."

"Your brother hired me to find out who was threatening him. I have an obli—"

"And we all know how that turned out. Anyway, you can cut the pretense, Slick. I know all about Alton's side interests."

Slick? That was a new one.

"Regardless of what you think you know, my relationship with your brother was strictly professional. Rightly or wrongly, he thought your sister-in-law might be behind the threats he received."

"And who the hell would blame her? When I think of what Zora's had to put up with through the years. The humiliation. The disrespect. The way he used her and her money. I wouldn't blame her if she did kill him. Which she didn't. Never in a million years."

"That's why we talk to people," Zach said. "So we can eliminate them from our inquiry."

"You think I never saw a cop show? You don't question people to *eliminate* them. You question them to trap them into admitting their guilt. And you questioned Zora knowing full well she'd been sedated and was in total shock."

"First of all, I'm not a cop. Secondly, no one was trying to trap your sister-in-law. Our assumption was she knew

Alton better than anyone else. She might have some ideas, some insight into who wanted Alton dead."

"If anyone killed my brother, it was Rusty Jordan. Period. End of story."

"Rusty Jordan has an alibi."

"Rusty Jordan destroyed my business just to get back at my brother."

This was a new, and in Zach's opinion, unlikely angle on the acquisition and ultimate dissolution of Pacific Playhouse.

"How would destroying *your* business get back at your brother?"

Ransford didn't seem to have an answer for that. He said instead, "There was no reason to dissolve the company. We had plans to reorganize after the bankruptcy. It was nothing but spite on Rusty's part."

"But after all, your company was still in bankruptcy at the time of the acquisition. I can't see what part Jordan could have played in that."

"I didn't say he forced us into bankruptcy. But he pretended the acquisition was a chance for a vertical or horizontal integration with Old Timey Fun, Ltd., when the truth is, it was just a financial ploy to take over and liquidate our assets."

It was possible, of course. It was also possible that Jordan had attempted to bail out the brother of his college roommate, but determined there was no salvaging Ransford's company. Zach would have to see the financials to be able to determine either way. No doubt as to what Ransford believed, though. And if anyone was holding a grudge, it was he.

Zach tuned back in to hear Ransford still building his case against Jordan. "He's been jealous of Alton ever since they were college roommates. Everything Alton had, Rusty had to have. Alton was a toymaker, so Rusty became a toymaker. He even married a woman who looked like Zora."

Zach considered that. "Did Rusty have feelings for Zora?"

"Maybe."

"Did they date or anything?"

"No. *We* dated."

"Who? You and Rusty?"

Ransford goggled at him. "*What*? Of course not. Me and Zora!"

"You and Zora dated before she married Alton?"

Ransford said bitterly, "I introduced them. Like an idiot."

Zora was nearly ten years older than Alton, so there was an even greater age gap with Ransford. Zach couldn't help thinking she had to have changed a lot through the years.

"I can see there are hard feelings, but I'm not sure how any of this makes Rusty Jordan look guilty. If anyone—

Zach stopped, but not in time.

Ransford's already red face turned puce. "*Me*? You think *I* had something to do with Alton's death? You're even stupider than the police!" Ransford brushed past Zach on his way to the door.

"Mr. Beacher—"

Halfway out the door, Ransford stopped and turned. "Come near Zora again, Slick, and you'll find out whether I'm capable of murder."

CHAPTER TWENTY-ONE

As the glass door *voomped* shut on Ransford's heels, Brooke said, "That went well, Slick."

"Not so much," Zach replied.

"I hate to press you, but it would be nice—as a shareholding member of the company—if you'd occasionally fill me in what the heck is going on."

"We don't have stock or a mutual fund. So."

Brooke shot him a look that could've dropped a bear at eighteen paces.

"Okay, okay. But really. There's *nothing* to worry about," Zach assured her. "Everything is under control."

"You know what? Every time you say there's nothing to worry about, I get more worried."

"I'm serious. Flint and I interviewed Alton's butler just a little while ago. Now Flint's following up a lead on his own—"

"What lead?"

Zach shook his head. "He didn't say. I'm going to phone Bill and let him know everything we've learned so far."

"Which is what?"

"That Alton was coercing men for sexual favors—he may have even been blackmailing them."

"Holy shi—"

Zach hadn't meant to share that bit of information lest it lead to his own tangential involvement in Alton's kinky affairs. He was desperately hoping to keep Alton's attempts to seduce him from Brooke. He forged on, "That Alton stole his brother's girlfriend."

Brooke was instantly distracted. "*Hello*? A girlfriend is not an inanimate object. She usually has some say in the matter."

"You know what I mean."

"No one knows what you mean, Zee. Which is probably best."

Zach ignored that. "I want to see what he has to say about Rusty Jordan. I want to update him on my interview with the sheriff's office and talk to him about the break-in last night."

"It's a start," Brooke said grudgingly. "What does Flint say?"

"About what?"

"All of it. Especially the break-in. Does Flint think it was a homeless person who attacked you?"

"It's adorable you put so much importance on what Flint thinks." Zach answered automatically. He was thinking of Flint's *'someone tried to kill you'*.

No way could he share that with Brooke.

Brooke said seriously, "He's got a lot more experience than we do, Zee. Besides, I think he really…"

She had a funny expression on her face.

"You think he really what?"

Brooke vaguely, "I think he...likes us and feels like he should look out for us a little."

"Yeah, that's probably true."

She was still giving him that peculiar look. "He was definitely concerned when I told him what happened last night."

"Okay, well since you bring it up, why would you call Flint and tell him that? Especially, after we had that talk about not running to Bill or...anyone else when we've got a problem."

That expression was easy to read. *That* expression was pure sisterly exasperation.

"First off, I didn't phone Flint. He phoned me because when he tried to phone you, he got the sheriff's office. He was worried about you."

"Oh." Zach's face warmed.

"He was especially worried because I guess you guys had a fight and he was feeling like he maybe came down on you too hard." Brooke was as painstaking as if she were trying to explain something in a foreign language.

"He— Really?" Zach was flustered, slightly confused, and not even sure why. "I mean, it wasn't a *fight* fight. He... disagreed with some of my choices." To put it mildly.

"Don't we all. Anyway, he's under the delusion that you're a lot more sensitive than you are. And because you'd just called to tell me what had happened, I told him."

"I see. I guess that makes sense."

"*And* he was really worried. Even after I told him you were perfectly fine." Brooke stared at him with gimlet-eyed intensity.

Zach blinked. "Right. Got it." He added, "I don't know what that look's for."

"He. Was. Really. Worried. About. *You*. Zee. Because he *likes* you. A lot."

Zach gave a nervous laugh. "No, I don't think..." He swallowed. "I don't think it's like *that*." He asked uncertainly, "Do you?"

"*Yes*. What do you think I'm doing here? I'm trying to clue you in before you blow it."

"B-b-blow it? What are you talking about? How am I blowing anything?" A very unseemly but unexpectedly exciting picture flashed into Zach's mind. He felt himself change color—mostly out of fear Brooke might read his mind. "I have no clue what you're talking about."

"You don't have to tell me." Brooke sighed. "Zee, did you never wonder why Flint was always dropping by when you were in the office and Pop was out?"

"I don't recall Flint dropping by a lot."

"It was a lot for someone who had no reason to drop by! Why do you think Ben disliked Flint so much?"

Zach frowned. He *had* wondered about that. Ben had always been so critical and suspicious of Flint, with seemingly little reason. Granted, Zach hadn't had the highest opinion of Flint either. Back then, he'd considered Flint a blunt and abrasive Magnum PI knockoff. Partly, that had been defensiveness borne of his suspicion that Flint thought he was nothing more than a bean counter in a nice suit. Partly, he'd let Ben's feelings color his own perception.

It turned out they'd both been wrong.

But, taking into account Detective Schneider, Brooke probably had it wrong, too.

"Anyway, I'm fine. Everything's fine. I'll just talk to Bill and then I'm going to do some deep diving into Alton's financial records."

"Do we have Alton's financial records?"

"We have what Alton wanted us to see. So, not everything, no. I'm working on it." Alton's reluctance to share crucial information about his business and finances should have been a red flag, but there had been so *many* red flags with Alton, Zach had quickly of lost track.

"What can I do?" Brooke asked.

Zach opened his mouth to give her the usual spiel, but it suddenly, belatedly dawned on him that not only was Brooke sincere, she was smart, capable, and resourceful—a valuable asset in other words—that he continually overlooked and dismissed. Yes, she was his kid sister. Yes, he wanted her to reach her full potential. But by ignoring, discounting Brooke's wishes, was he maybe making the same mistakes with her that Pop had made with him?

Pop had wanted what was best for Zach and Zach wanted what was best for Brooke.

But Zach had ultimately rebelled against Pop's plans for him, and Brooke was already starting to balk at Zach's ambitions for her.

"*Hellooo?*" Brooke peered into Zach's face. "Did you forget to charge your battery pack again?"

"Yes. I mean, no, and yes, you can help."

"You're kidding."

"Were you not serious?"

"Yes, I'm serious! But you always—never mind. What do you want me to do?"

"If you could head over to the county courthouse and see what you can find out as far as pending lawsuits, criminal actions, or judgements against our client, either personally or professionally. *And* our client's wife."

Brooke brightened. "Really?"

"Really. The more I learn about Alton, the more likely it seems someone along the way would surely have filed a criminal complaint."

Brooke was already getting her purse out of the desk drawer. "Do you want me to turn the answering machine on?"

"No. I'll cover the phones. I'm going to start checking through the NAIC database."

Brooke's brows shot up. "The National Association of Insurance Commissioners?"

"I can use the life insurance policy locator service to check for policies or annuity contracts. I want to see for myself what Ransford and Zora have to gain by Alton's death."

"You're so cynical, Zee. I like it!" Brooke headed for the door. "I'll let you know what I—"

She stepped back hastily, as someone threw open the glass door. "*Oh!* H-hey, Ben!"

Ben, looking wild-eyed and as close to disheveled as Zach had ever seen, charged past Brooke—it was doubtful he even saw her—and confronted Zach.

"HOW DARE YOU?"

Zach, blinking in the face of that ferocity, protested, "How dare I *what*?"

"How dare you accuse me of breaking into your house and assaulting you?"

"I don't know what you're talking about. I never—"

Brooke interjected nervously, "Zach, do you need me to—"

Ben swung on her. "*Really*, Brooke? *Seriously?*"

"It's okay," Zach said quickly. "We're fine here."

Brooke did not look reassured. She looked worried. But, with many glances over her shoulder, she reluctantly pushed through the glass door.

"Look, I didn't accuse you of anything," Zach said. "I know it wasn't you in the garage."

"No! You didn't even have the decency to confront me yourself. You sent Flint. *Flint*, of *all* people."

Realization dawned—and it was not a pleasant one.

"Flint accused you of attacking me?"

"That's what I said!" Ben added bitterly, "You said you weren't involved with him."

"We're working together."

"On *what*? You can't drum up enough business for one agency, let alone two."

Zach let that pass. Ben subscribed to the *New York Times*. He did not read the local paper or watch local news, so it was very possible he knew nothing about Alton Beacher's death or Zach's involvement in the case.

"Flint didn't discuss questioning you with me. I didn't know anything about it. I'm sorry—"

"He didn't just question me, he *accused* me. He accused me of being a stalker. He accused me of attacking you. He made *me* sound—" Ben's mouth worked. "He made *me* sound like I was some kind of...of *psycho*."

Zach winced. "Ben..."

"As if any of this is *my* fault! As if you didn't bring *all* of this on yourself!"

What the hell was it about Ben that could drive Zach from remorseful to resentful in zero to sixty?

"Ben, Flint decided to question you without discussing it with me. If he'd checked with me first, I would, of course, have told him it wasn't you in the garage. And when I see him, I'll make it clear to him—"

"Don't bother," Ben broke in. "I'm filing a restraining order against both of you."

Zach started to reply, then stopped. Maybe this was the best solution. It didn't seem to have occurred to Ben that a restraining order worked both ways.

And while Zach was genuinely sorry Flint had gone after Ben—they were going to have that out just as soon as Zach could get hold of him—he couldn't help noticing that Ben had zero concern or even sympathy that Zach had been attacked. This was entirely about Ben's experience, Ben's feelings.

Which, frankly, was kind of how it had always been.

Why had it taken him this long to realize that?

Ben was saying, "When I think of how much of my life I wasted on you."

"Why was it a waste?" Zach broke in. "We loved each other and we were happy for a long time. Why doesn't that count?"

Ben glared. "Because it was all leading to this. It was all for *nothing*."

"Ben—"

Ben did a *talk to the hand!*

"I don't want to hear it. I don't want to hear anything you have to say, Zachariah. Now or ever. It's *over*. I'm *done*." He turned and shoved open the glass door, pausing to throw back a scathing, "I'm so glad it's Flint. You're going to get back everything you did to me times ten." He stepped out into the bright sunlight.

The heavy glass door *shoomped* shut on air-conditioned silence.

CHAPTER TWENTY-TWO

"**D**id it not occur to you to tell me what you were planning before you called on Ben?"

The minute Ben left the office, Zach was on his cell phone to Flint. He was shocked and angry that Flint had not bothered to consult him before approaching, no, *accusing* Ben.

He had been even more flabbergasted when Flint answered with a cool, "What's up?"

And when Zach said what was up, Flint replied, "Sure, it occurred to me. I knew you'd be against the idea. But it's important for us to be able to rule Franken out. That attack on you seemed to fly out of left field, so if it isn't part of the larger pattern, we need to—"

"I'd be against the idea because I know it wasn't Ben!"

Flint said patiently, "It's understandable you'd feel that way."

"No, you don't get it, Flint. I'm not being sentimental. I lived with the guy for years. Do you seriously think I wouldn't know if I was wrestling around with *Ben*?"

The hesitation on the other end was more telling than words.

"His size, his shape, his smell... Even the way he breathed. That was *not* Ben. I'd have spoken up if I thought Ben attacked me."

"Would you? Or would you think you could talk to him on your own?"

Okay, Flint wasn't wrong about that. On that one single, solitary point, he was right. Zach would probably have tried to talk to Ben. And, yes, that probably would have been a mistake. But it was all beside the fact, because his attacker had not been Ben.

"I'm not an idiot."

"I don't think you're an idiot. I think you're inexperienced. And too soft-hearted."

"And I don't appreciate being treated like the junior partner when this is my case."

"Okay, well, it started out as your case, but it's our case now." Before Zach's outrage found voice, Flint clarified, "We're partners on this."

"If we're partners, then treat me like a partner and tell me what the hell you're planning *before* you go in with guns blazing."

After a pause, Flint said mildly, "No guns were drawn, let alone blazing. I asked a couple of basic questions, Franken lost his mind—he wasn't very convincing in his denials, let me tell you that—and I left."

"It doesn't matter whether you're convinced or not. He told you the truth. Which you'd have known, if you talked to me first."

"I get it, I get it. I should have communicated with you." Flint did not sound bored, exactly, but he did sound like it was a complaint he had received many times before—which did little to relieve Zach's concerns.

"If you don't want to keep working together, then say so—"

"Hold on. When did I say I didn't want to work together?" Flint seemed genuinely startled. "You made your point, Zachariah. I'll…confer with you first the next time I decide to deviate from the flight pattern." Before Zach could respond, Flint added, "*Before* I decide."

Frankly, that was way more of a concession than Zach had expected. In fact, he hadn't expected any concession.

Into his silence, Flint asked, "Okay?"

Zach said lamely, "Okay." He added, "Thank you."

"You're not being unreasonable," Flint conceded magnanimously.

Zach rolled his eyes. Still, a concession was a concession.

Flint cut into his thoughts. "Are we good? Because I need to go. Schneider wants a lunch meeting."

"I thought we were—"

That was disappointing. So disappointing, Zach didn't want to examine his reaction too closely. He amended briskly, "Okay. I'm going to try to see Rusty Jordan."

"Jordan? I thought we'd ruled him out. He has an alibi."

"We did. Kind of. And he does. Kind of. But he could have hired someone to kill Alton."

Flint considered, said, "That's true. And it doesn't hurt to remember, so could Ben."

Rusty Jordan's administrative assistant was a sleek blue-eyed blonde who looked a lot like a Barbie doll knock-off.

But then that was the Old Timey Fun Ltd. business model: cheap, mass-produced replicas of expensive, high-end toys and games. Whatever their public mission statement might be, it was pretty clear the underlying corporate philosophy was something like *the more they break, the more they buy.*

Zach had not phoned ahead to try and set up an interview with Jordan. He'd been pretty sure any such request would be denied. Instead, he'd opted for driving the two hours from Ensenada del Sello to Jordan's manufacturing plant and administrative offices in downtown Oakland. His hope was that if he showed up, live and in person, Jordan might think Zach had information on the investigation into Alton's death. He was bound to be curious.

While he had not yet been granted an audience, he hadn't been turned away, either. He'd spent the last hour sitting in a large, empty waiting room, watching the Barbie doll receptionist guard the gates of the citadel with ruthless efficiency.

Ruthless efficiency seemed to be the rule. Old Timey Fun Ltd. was located in a large, unprepossessing building seemingly made out of gray cinderblocks and crushed Christmas wishes. There were a lot of security guards and very few windows.

As a matter of fact, Jordan was meeting with his head of security that very minute. Hopefully, that was a coincidence and nothing to do with Zach showing up without an appointment. In fairness, corporate espionage and counterfeiting were a major problem in the toy industry. That was something Zach had learned from Alton.

Alton's view of "competitors" like his old school chum Rusty, seemed mostly dismissive. Rightly or wrongly, Alton believed Old Timey Fun did not pose any real competition, that the beautifully crafted toys and games his company produced couldn't truly be replicated through short cuts and cheap materials. And maybe he was right.

Sitting in that chilly waiting room gave Zach plenty of time to think. It was hard to see what motive Rusty Jordan might have in wanting Alton out of the way. Yes, they were both in the toy business, but it seemed more and more likely Alton's assessment had been right. Old Timey Fun and the Beacher Toy Company were pursuing different market shares.

But the weird threats had come via Old Timey Fun products. And Rusty had accosted Alton at the Inn at Spanish Bay. More, he had seemed incensed on Zora's behalf. So maybe there was a non-business-related angle there? Rusty had been the only name Alton seemed able to come up with when pressed for possible suspects.

True, Alton hadn't seriously considered Rusty a threat, but surely, he'd had some reason—maybe subconscious?—for offering his name up.

The door to Jordan's office opened and a tall, thin man in a black uniform with lots of made-up braid and insignia—much like the costume a toy security guard (or storm trooper) would wear—stepped out.

Barbie nodded to the man in uniform. The man nodded curtly to her. He threw Zach a measuring look and clearly dismissed him as a possible threat. He left the office.

Barbie went back to clicking away on her desktop.

After another ten minutes, the intercom on Barbie's desk buzzed. She clicked, listened to the voice in her headset, and said to Zach, "Mr. Jordan will see you now."

Zach rose and went into an office the size of a small warehouse. Or maybe a showroom. There were the usual accoutrements: a wet bar, a life-sized oil painting of the founder himself—looking uncannily like the titular character in "The Princess and the Frog"—and a curio cabinet with vintage toys. Like the things the Beacher Toy Company produced? The carpet was plush enough to lose your shoes in. On one side of the room, giant picture windows offered a view of the bustling city and, beyond, the Oakland Bay Bridge and the rolling golden hills of Berkeley. The opposite wall was lined with tall walnut shelves displaying Old Timey Fun Ltd.'s greatest hits: plastic snow globes, plastic musical instruments, plushy alien creatures in garish colors, good luck charms, and you name it.

Jordan, strategically positioned behind a megalith-sized desk beneath the spotlight of recessed lighting, did not rise. As Zach approached, he pointed what appeared to be a pink fairy wand with a plastic gold star on the end to the chair in front of his bulwark.

"This is a surprise," he said. "But then you're full of surprises, Mr. Davies."

"Thank you for agreeing to see me on such late notice, sir."

Jordan grimaced. "How could I resist? I've never been questioned by a PI before. I have to say, you don't look anything like I imagined a private investigator would look."

"It's very helpful in my line of work." Zach sat down in the chair Jordan indicated and was treated to the unmelodic sounds of a whoopee cushion deflating fast.

Jordan bellowed with laughter as Zach shot off of the chair.

"What the—?"

"Oh my God. *Your face*," howled Jordan. "That's priceless!"

Zach collected himself, managed a lofty, "I guess we're both having our expectations realigned."

"HAR HAR HAR," roared Jordan, wiping his eyes. "You're so *dignified*. Oh my God."

Zach snatched up the whoopee cushion and tossed it into the chair next to his. He sat gingerly down again. "I'm trying to be polite."

Jordan tossed his fairy wand on the desk. "Don't bother. My feelings toward you aren't polite."

"Okay, I realize you're a friend of Zora Kaschak-Beacher. And I know Alton has—had—an unsavory reputation. But my relationship with him was entirely professional. He hired me to find out who was sending him death threats. That's it. There was no...no..."

"Yeah, yeah," Jordan drawled. "Don't get your panties in a twist, kid. I knew Alton a *long* time."

Zach stared. It wasn't just the words; it was the way Jordan delivered the words. Pointedly.

Or was Zach being paranoid?

He met Jordan's protuberant gray eyes. Jordan's expression was hard to define, but he knew something. Zach was sure of it.

"Right. You were college roommates."

"Yep. I got a close-up view of how Alton operates, early on."

That had probably been an education in itself.

Zach said neutrally, "But you stayed friends."

Jordan shrugged. "Frenemies. Isn't that what your generation calls it? We had more in common back in college. He had a sense of humor. He could be entertaining. He was always a cold fish, though. I was sorry for Zora when she got involved with him. She was a great girl before he sucked all the life out of her."

"If she was unhappy, why wouldn't she leave him?"

It wasn't entirely rhetorical. Zach knew from personal experience, people who stopped loving each other had many reasons for staying together. His parents were typical of a lot of couples of their generation. But Alton and Zora didn't have children to consider. And they both had financial resources a lot of people didn't.

"I used to wonder about that. I guess she was still getting something out of it. Power? Control? Or maybe it's not even that complicated. Zora doesn't like change."

"Yeah, but…"

"Nobody knows what happens in a marriage. I can tell you that."

"Are you married?"

Jordan's gaze went automatically to the large gold-framed photo facing him. He smiled at the photo. "I sure am. We'll be celebrating our twentieth anniversary next month. I won the marriage lottery. I can tell you that."

Zach had seen a few internet pics of Mrs. Jordan appearing at charity functions with her husband, and not only was she attractive, she always looked like she was genuinely having a good time. In fact, despite a vague physical resemblance to Zora, she couldn't have seemed more different.

Jordan was still talking. "Alton might have been more successful in business. But he was a sick, sad fuck. So who's the *real* success?"

As Zach listened, he couldn't help thinking Jordan was casually knocking down each of his potential theories as to why he might want his old friend out of the way. It had crossed Zach's mind that Jordan might still have feelings for Zora, and he seemed fond of her, but unless he was a very good actor, there was no murderous passion lurking in his heart. That instinctive smile for the woman in the photo had been one-hundred-percent genuine.

Nor did he come across as a particularly bitter business rival.

Hell, he hadn't even asked if Zach knew how the police investigation was going.

"Would you say you and Mr. Beacher—"

"Kid, I don't know why you're bothering with the formalities. I watched the two of you at Spanish Bay. You weren't calling him *Mr. Beacher* behind closed doors."

Zach said calmly, "Well, no. The idea was to convince Mrs. Kaschak-Beacher that Alton was involved in a gay relationship. He hoped that might make her more agreeable to the idea of a divorce."

"And you were okay with that?"

"I told Alton that I thought his ruse was a bad idea. But he was my client. It was his decision to make."

Jordan's pale eyes bulged ever farther. "Like Zora didn't already know he was gay?"

"I'd never met Alton Beacher before he hired me. I had to assume he was telling me the truth. The truth would have been in his best interests."

"It would have been against his nature, too."

That seemed more and more likely. Zach attempted to redirect the conversation.

"Would you say that you and Alton were business competitors?"

"Maybe in a broad sense," Jordan conceded after a moment's consideration. "We were both operating in the toys and games market. The Beacher Toy Company targets a completely different audience segment than Old Timey Fun, Ltd. People who don't mind paying through the nose for toys that went out of fashion fifty years ago. People who lap up that claptrap about buying *heirloom works of art* versus toys kids might get some use out of. We have probably six times the market share Alton does. Did."

"I see." He was beginning to.

"Frankly, I don't think Alton was a particularly shrewd businessman. That was *his* narrative. Not the toy industry narrative. Zora had to bail him out repeatedly over the years."

"Maybe she got tired of bailing him out."

"I'm sure she did. Which is why she eventually stopped writing checks. She wouldn't kill him. Not over that."

"Can you think of anyone else who might have wanted Alton dead?"

"To know him was to hate him." Jordan laughed heartily. "Nah. The people who would have wanted him dead weren't anybody I'd have known. As I'm sure you're aware, Alton kept a good chunk of his life secret. That's where you want to look."

"Do you have a name or—"

Jordan's face screwed up in contempt. "Hell, no. I don't know. I didn't want to know. But if you really are a detective, it shouldn't be hard to figure out. Those people probably hang out the same places you do."

"Probably not."

Jordan's expression changed, brightened. "Actually, I do remember a name. Part of a name. Galileo."

"Galileo? Like the astronomer?"

"I doubt that. I don't know if that was his first name or his last name, but Alton was obsessed with him for a while."

"When was this?"

"Six months ago? When it ended, I mean. They never lasted long. Alton's little friends. But that one, Galileo, I think he stuck for a time. When it ended, Alton was pretty angry."

"Angry? Not afraid or—?"

Jordan snorted. "Alton didn't know enough about people to understand when he should be afraid."

CHAPTER TWENTY-THREE

Flint's SUV was in its usual place toward the back of the shopping center parking lot.

Zach parked beside it, got out, and headed across the lot to Davies Detective Agency. What he *wanted* to do was talk to Flint, but he couldn't help thinking that ever since that morning, Flint had been transmitting very mixed messages.

Well, no. Actually, until Brooke had chimed in with her theories of what Flint might or might not be feeling, Zach had felt he understood perfectly what was going on with Flint. Flint was hoping Zach wouldn't make too much of what had happened between them the night before. Clearly, Flint was a guy who enjoyed playing the field and, just as clearly, he had recognized that Zach…was not.

And Zach made no apologies for that. It was true. His problems with Ben hadn't stemmed from boredom with monogamy or domesticity. He liked regular companionship and reliable sex. He liked having someone to share the fun and help shoulder the worries. He liked teamwork and partnership and private jokes and shared memories. His problems with Ben had ultimately been Ben.

That said, it wasn't like Zach was so naïve or so desperate that he mistook one night of sex for the start of something permanent. Or the start of anything at all.

True, he wouldn't have minded if it had been the start of something. He had woken up, literally, to the idea of seeing what might happen. The night before had been kind of a revelation. Flint had been so funny and tender in bed, so, well, generous, that Zach couldn't help seeing him in a new light.

Well, even that wasn't completely accurate, because he had already started to see Flint in a new light from the minute he had, albeit reluctantly, agreed to provide Zach with backup the night Zach dined with Alton at Pinch.

There was something refreshing, even relaxing, about Flint's honesty and directness. Flint was not a guy who played games. And after years of Ben's (probably unconscious but real all the same) emotional manipulation, it was a relief to be around a guy who said what he meant and meant what he said.

Flint had allowed himself to be vulnerable the night before—they both had—so Zach had been disappointed, maybe a little hurt, but not surprised by Flint's retreat the next morning. He'd understood that Flint maybe wanted a little breathing room. He had figured if he showed Flint he was more than okay with taking things one step at a time, Flint would work through his wariness.

But then Brooke had chipped in with all that talk about Flint maybe having been interested in Zach for a long time.

What did that really mean?

And if Brooke was right—a very big if, going by prior experience—that cast a different light on Flint's retreat.

Maybe it turned out that Flint enjoyed the chase more than the, er, capture. Maybe the reality of a night with Zach hadn't lived up to expectation. Maybe Flint's interest didn't stretch beyond a very occasional tumble in the hay (or whatever bedding he preferred). He seemed pretty involved with Detective Schneider, so...

Part of what drew Zach to Flint was how forthright Flint was, but now Flint was suddenly, uncharacteristically reserved, and Zach was confused and unsure about how to proceed.

It seemed best to leave it up to Flint as to whether they proceeded at all.

As far as the case went, they were supposedly still working it together, but he hadn't heard a word from Flint since that morning. After Flint had canceled their lunch in order to have lunch with Detective Schneider, he had gone radio silent.

It was great having Flint's experience to rely on, but Zach was making progress without that extra help. He felt confident he was going to solve this thing, with or without Flint.

That's what he told himself anyway as he strode across the parking lot. Thin, half-hearted sunshine barely took the chill off the afternoon. The rain had stopped the night before, but pond-sized puddles dotted the asphalt, offering watery reflections of the tall palm trees and darkening clouds. Another storm was coming, following on the heels of the last.

He reached the office, pushed open the door, and halted in the doorway.

Flint was right there, standing in the reception area, laughing with Brooke.

Having just delivered a long lecture to himself on how much he didn't need Flint in either a personal or professional capacity, the shock of delight at finding Flint waiting for him felt a little out of proportion.

Flint grinned in welcome. "Hey there, Slick!"

Zach turned a withering gaze on Brooke, but Brooke, per usual, remained unwithered. "Flint and I agree. Ransford is not our guy."

Off-balance, Zach picked up on the one thing he was sure of. "*Our* guy?"

Brooke's chin shot up in defiance. "That's right, Zee. *Ours*. This business is half mine."

This unexpected rebellion caught him off-guard.

"I know that. I never said—"

Technically, the company was one third Brooke's. Their mother was also one-third owner of Davies Detective Agency, but their mother wanted nothing to do with the business. She had been pushing Zach to sell since Pop had passed.

"Furthermore, I'm going to be twenty-four in another week. I'm an adult, technically, legally, and…totally."

"Well, yes, but—" Zach threw Flint a slightly harassed look. Why was Brooke choosing now of all times?

"Which means I get a say on what I do with my life." Brooke gave him a surprisingly stern look. "And on what we do with the agency."

"What we do with the agency?"

The last piece of puzzle fell into place. Zach's previous delight gave way to confusion and then alarm. His heart felt like it dropped to the pit of his stomach. His knees actually went weak. He half-stammered, "You're s-selling the business to Flint?"

If Flint had managed to convince Brooke, then it was game over. Their mother would certainly back that plan.

Brooke glanced at Flint. Flint was watching Zach. His expression was unreadable.

"I have a new proposal," Flint said.

Zach turned his back on Flint. "I don't want to sell." Zach was speaking to Brooke. Pleading with Brooke. Up until now, she'd been one hundred percent on board with not selling. He couldn't help feeling this reversal was a total betrayal—and he blamed Flint for it.

"Just hear him out, Zee."

"I don't care what his proposal is," Zach swung back on Flint. "You know how I feel."

"I know." Flint sounded unfairly calm, unfairly reasonable. "And I respect that. I'm talking about a partnership."

Zach stopped, blinking uncertainly.

"A—"

"A three-way partnership," Brooke put in.

"Yes," Flint said. "A merger."

Some of Zach's panic subsided. Was he hearing this right? A merger between Davies Detective Agency and Carey Confidential? He folded onto the nearest chair. Both Brooke and Flint were watching him so seriously.

"You don't like the idea?" Flint asked.

"I—" He was still trying to take it in.

Brooke said, "Instead of buying *us* out, Flint will buy out Mom's share of DDA. Then we don't have to worry about her investment *or* her leveraging her interest to force us to sell."

"But if we're selling to Flint—"

"Zee, you're not listening. We're not *selling*. We're partnering up."

Flint sat down in the chair next to Zach's. He gripped Zach's knee. "We're combining our separate businesses to form a brand-new single operation. I know what a merger means."

Zach looked at Flint's tanned, capable hand resting on his thigh. Flint was not a particularly touchy-feely guy. Did he realize how casually intimate that gesture was? He stared into Flint's green-gold eyes. Flint looked kind—and concerned.

Zach unstuck his dry lips. "I don't want to be your accountant, Flint." It wasn't easy to say because the idea of partnering up with Flint was surprisingly, startlingly, appealing.

Flint's grin was lopsided. "Believe me, you've made that very clear."

Was this really a possibility? Partnership? Hope tentatively, cautiously bloomed.

"A partnership of equals." Brooke added, "Which means *I* get equal say."

Zach frowned, opened his mouth, but was forestalled by Flint's firm, "Yes. Brooke gets equal say."

Brooke beamed at them. "I'll be the tie-breaker when you two can't agree."

The look Flint gave Zach was rueful. "I have to hope she'll occasionally caucus with the opposition party."

"No fear of that," Zach muttered. "I let her do one simple background check and she sold the business out from under me." He was kidding, mostly, but he couldn't help feeling like he'd left town for a couple of hours and returned to a different planet.

And yet… As the idea of this possible business merger slowly took root, he was not unhappy. He was actually, cautiously, kind of…thrilled.

To not have the weight of everything on him all the time? Just the hope of it was a relief. And together, they did have the combination of skills and experience and resources for success. Together… Well, together was kind of a nice combination all on its own.

Flint was saying, "Plus, I know you well enough to know no way are you going to leave our finances in the hands of a stranger, so I—our company—will be getting an investigator *and* an accountant for the price of one."

"Ha."

But yeah, probably.

Flint was smiling at him and Zach smiled uncertainly back.

"You *do* see things the way I do." Flint seemed surprised and happy.

Was this really going to happen? Because there had been nothing in the way the day started to indicate this was on the horizon.

Wellll, okay, well, yes, there had been *one* thing. Flint waking up in Zach's bed. But Zach hadn't wanted to place too much importance on that because Flint didn't seem to.

Brooke said, "Okay, let's not get carried away. Zach doesn't see anything the way other—"

Zach, still holding Flint's gaze, interrupted, "I see Flint."

Flint's eyes flickered, his mouth softened, he leaned toward—

Brooke said loudly, "I see dead people. Like our former client. *Hello?*"

Flint drew back. Zach sat up straight.

"I mean, we can't merge anything if we don't still have a company, right?"

"When she's right, she's right." Flint gave Zach's knee a final squeeze and rose. He was smiling ruefully down at Zach, and Zach smiled back, although he was half-convinced he was dreaming. He was certainly short enough on sleep.

Brooke, meanwhile, was flipping through a manila folder stuffed full of photocopies and pages of yellow legal paper.

"So. I did what you said. I checked for pending lawsuits, criminal actions, or judgements against Alton. There's nothing."

"Nothing?" Zach echoed.

Brooke shook her head. "Nope. I checked everything I could think of. I thought maybe somewhere along the line charges might have been filed and then dropped, but his record is spotless."

"Suspiciously spotless?" Flint asked.

"How would I know?"

Zach said, "It's a rhetorical question."

"Not really," Flint said. "There's no way a guy like Alton didn't cross a few lines, morally, ethically, legally…"

"I agree. But Alton was really fastidious. In all ways."

"Meaning what?" Brooke asked.

Zach hesitated. Flint said, "She's twenty-four, Zachariah."

Brooke laughed. "*Zachariah*? Oh my God. He *hates* that."

Flint looked startled. "Do you?"

Well, yes. Zach had always hated being called Zachariah. It sounded too much like Jedediah, his least favorite character on the 1970s PI show, *Barnaby Jones*. But somehow over the past few days he'd gone from detesting Zachariah to kind of liking it. When Flint said it, anyway.

"I don't mind," he told Flint.

Brooke did a doubletake. "*Okaaaay*. Anyway, from everything I could find out, Alton was purer than the driven snow."

"I'd say he had a strong sense of self-preservation," Zach said, "but clearly not strong enough."

"He was too arrogant to believe anyone would really come after him." That was Flint.

Yeah, arrogance had probably been a factor in Alton's demise. Being rich provided a certain amount of insulation, and Alton had clearly mistaken insulation for Kevlar.

"Chico knows plenty, you can bet on that. But he'd probably have to be subpoenaed and dragged into court to talk. It sounded to me like he had every intention of staying on at the Beacher estate."

"He's got his eye on the rich widow," Brooke remarked.

Zach was startled. "How do you figure that?"

"I saw his photo in the paper. He's hot. And he knows it. Were you aware he graduated from San Jose University with a degree in business?"

"Uh, no," Flint said.

Zach said, "Who are you and what have you done with my kid sister?"

"If Chico knows where the bodies are buried, he also knows enough to keep his mouth shut."

Flint said to Zach, "We'll be lucky if we don't end up working for her."

"I tried to warn you."

Brooke checked her notes. "The same is also true of Zora. There are no pending lawsuits, criminal actions, or judgements against her, either personally or professionally. Which, in her case, makes sense because she almost never leaves the compound. I think the agoraphobia is for real."

"It'd be a weird thing to make up," Zach said.

"People do weird things when they're motivated by hate and anger." Flint looked thoughtful. "So, no divorce proceedings filed by either of our principals at any time?"

"Nope."

Flint shot Zach a look of commiseration. "All those promises he made you." He shook his head sadly.

"Not funny," Zach said.

Flint laughed. So did Brooke.

Zach thought it over, sighed. "Okay. We'll just have to keep digging."

"And that's exactly what I did," Brooke said with triumph. "When I couldn't find anything on Alton or Zora, I started going down our list."

"Our list? I didn't give you a list."

"Good job," Flint told Brooke.

Which, yes, that show of initiative was unexpected and...good.

Zach said, "Ransford lives out of state, so we're not going to—"

"I'm not talking about Ransford," Brooke interrupted. "Ransford isn't our guy. But guess what? I found a slew of liens against Ronald Jordan."

Flint stared at her. "The college roommate? The CEO of Old Timey Fun, Ltd.?"

"Exactly. It looks to me like Jordan is in serious financial trouble."

"Jordan or his company?" Zach asked.

"I don't know about his company, but there's a tax lien against his home in Carmel and another on his luxury condo in Oakland. Plus, Jordan's accumulated over half a million in unsecured personal debt. That's almost double his annual income."

"How do you know his annual income?"

"I Googled it. By the way, did you know one of the biggest sales drivers in the toys and games industry is kidults?"

"Kidults?"

"Adults buying toys for themselves."

Flint said, "I'd say half a million in personal debt is a good reason to take a closer look at Jordan."

"Is it?" Zach asked. "Because I'm not seeing how this gives Jordan a motive. How does Alton's death help Rusty Jordan out of the financial hole he's in?"

"He must be in Alton's will," Brooke said.

"We don't know that."

Flint said, "Maybe he plans on marrying the rich widow."

Zach shook his head. "He's already married."

"There are a couple of remedies for that."

True enough. Murder could be habit forming. But thinking back to that little smile Jordan had given the photo of his wife? Zach didn't buy it.

Then again, if that smile was as genuine as it seemed, if Rusty was truly, madly, deeply about his missus, those liens were against *her* home too. Rusty's financial peril was inevitably shared by his spouse. And love was every bit as motivating as hate when it came to crime.

Flint was still thinking. "Then maybe he *is* in Beacher's will."

"Maybe. It didn't seem like they were on those terms, but who knows how old Alton's will is."

Brooke suggested, "Maybe Jordan plans on taking over Beacher's company."

"I guess it's possible." It would give Jordan access to a customer base not currently available to him. But surely there were less violent and risky paths to entering the high-end toy market.

"We've got to verify the details of Beacher's will, one way or the other," Flint said.

"That's easier said than done," Zach said. "The contents of a will don't become public record until after the probate proceeding has concluded."

"There's got to be some way to find out before that," Brooke said.

Flint nodded. "There is. The police can get a subpoena if there's reason to believe the contents of the will are material to their investigation. The executor has fourteen days to comply, but in most cases, they're going to cooperate with law enforcement right away. Why don't you contact Bill Cameron, tell him what we've found out so far, and see if he can get hold of Beacher's executor."

Zach tried to imagine a world in which Lt. Bill Cameron jumped to provide him with evidence in a police investigation. "I'm pretty sure Bill is already trying to get his hands on that will. Especially since the Ensenada del Sello PD seems to have focused on Ransford."

"Ransford sure thinks so," Brooke said. "He was freaking out this morning."

Flint thought it over, said to Zach, "You met Jordan. What do you think?"

Zach considered his brief meeting with Jordan. While Jordan hadn't been openly antagonistic, their conversation had an odd undertone of hostility, no question. In fairness, not everyone welcomed visits from law enforcement, let alone private investigators. But had something else been going on? Had there been an undercurrent that had nothing to do with intruding on someone's privacy, maybe nothing to do with Zach at all?

Rusty Jordan had known Alton Beacher half his life. He probably knew him about as well as anyone could outside the Beacher family circle. And Rusty did not like Alton. Did not pretend to like him.

So, who's the real *success?*

Rusty detested Alton, of that, Zach had no doubt. But dislike, even hatred wouldn't be enough to convince a pragmatist like Rusty to risk everything by committing murder.

"He could be our guy," Zach admitted. "But I think we need a lot more than we have now before we go to the police. I'm still wondering about Chico. He certainly had opportunity. Who had better access to Alton's car? And he'd be in position to clean up all the evidence. His alibi is awfully convenient. And, depending on his relationship with Zora, maybe he does have a strong motive."

Brooke looked thoughtful. "True."

"Okay." Flint grinned. "The day is young, partners. Let's go find our proof."

CHAPTER TWENTY-FOUR

In fact, the day was *not* young.

The afternoon was fading fast and so were a lot of the county and state officials who they tried to reach. After hitting one *has-left-for-the-day* after another, Flint lost patience and departed to go work the "Galileo" angle. Brooke turned to her banking contacts, i.e., Mary Ann Spenser at Del Sello Savings and Loan, while Zach followed the long and winding road through the National Association of Insurance Commissioners database.

In crime fiction and mystery films, the emphasis was usually on a victim's last will and testament, but in Zach's experience, insurance money was an equally big incentivizer.

Founded in 1871, the National Association of Insurance Commissioners "provided expertise, data, and analysis for insurance commissioners to effectively regulate the industry and protect consumers." For the average consumer, the NAIC provided information on different types of insurance, claims processes, tracking complaints, and so on.

It could also be used by potential beneficiaries to find unclaimed insurance policies or locate a copy of missing paperwork.

Neither of those was likely to apply in this case. Zach was working a hunch that someone might have taken out a policy on Alton without Alton's knowledge. That was illegal, of course, but there were ways around it. Forgery was easier to prove. Once someone was dead, it was harder to make the case that they hadn't understood what they were signing.

But Alton hadn't been old or doddery. Zach had watched him in action at Spanish Bay, and Alton had gone over every contract, every report, hell, every *menu* put in front of him with a fine-toothed comb. No way had he been conned or tricked into signing anything he didn't intend to sign.

So maybe not a policy Alton hadn't knowingly signed. Maybe a policy Alton had forgotten about? Or a policy he believed to be canceled?

Something like that. Zach was sure of it.

Except…there didn't seem to be anything out of the ordinary.

Both Alton and Zora had life insurance policies naming the other as their sole beneficiary. Alton was insured for 1.3 million and Zora was insured for 2.9. If Zora had killed Alton, it hadn't been for the money.

Since Ransford wasn't listed on Alton's insurance policy, it gave him one less possible motive, but if he figured prominently in Alton's will, that might be enough to convince investigators he was their guy.

What am I missing?

"Two dicks and a dame," Brooke called from her desk in the front office.

"Say what?"

"Our new company name. Two dicks and a dame."

"Pop would roll over in his grave."

It occurred to Zach that for the first time ever, he could think of Pop without a pang of fear that he was failing to live up to his father's expectations. Things weren't working out the way Pop had expected, but all Pop had really wanted was for his kids to be happy, healthy, and doing well.

"What's your idea then?" Brooke answered.

Zach said at random, "Davies, Davies, and Carey."

"It sounds like a personal injury law firm."

Zach started to reply, but the idea of personal injury claims started him thinking.

Jordan was unlikely to pop up in Alton's will or have any share in his life insurance, but what if there was something else? The two men had known each other since college. They had even gone into the same industry.

In fact, hadn't Alton mentioned in passing that at one time he and Rusty had considered going into business together?

Zach rose and went to the doorway of his office. "When you were at the county clerk's office, did you come across anything related to Rusty Jordan and Alton starting up a business together?"

Brooke nodded. "Fifteen years ago, they filed a Business Certificate for Partners."

Zach felt a flash of excitement. "So—"

"It was a dead end. Two months later they filed a Certificate of Dissolution and Certificate of Cancellation."

Zach's elation faded. "They were never actually business partners?"

"Nope. They couldn't get the financing. At the time, Alton's company was underwater financially. I guess Zora wasn't in the mood to bail him out again, though it seems like she came around in the end."

"They tried to get financing..." Zach was thinking out loud.

"Right. But they couldn't." She added, "What's that look for?"

He said slowly, "I think I have an idea."

"You think you have an idea about what?"

"About a possible motive for Rusty Jordan killing Alton Beacher."

"What possible motive?"

Zach said, "I've got to verify a couple of things first."

"*Argh*. Zach—"

Zach ducked back in his office and sat down at his computer once more.

Thirty minutes later, Flint rapped on the doorframe of Zach's office.

"Hey. What'd you find out?"

Zach snapped out of his preoccupation. "What?"

"Brooke said you think you found Rusty Jordan's motive. Did you?" Flint studied Zach; his eyes widened. "Holy hell. You did!"

Zach leaned back in his chair and grinned. "It's not for sure, but yeah. I think there are people who might believe twelve million dollars is worth committing murder over."

"Twelve *million* dollars?"

Zach grinned, nodded.

Brooke joined Flint in the doorway. "You got it?"

"Maybe. When Alton and Rusty were trying to get financing for their joint venture, the banks stipulated that the company take out a key person policy on Alton."

"What's a key person policy?" Flint asked.

"Basically, it's a life insurance that a company takes out on an employee or employees considered indispensable to the success of the business. A lot of times it's the founder or owner or CEO."

Flint began, "How's that different from—"

"Because the *business* pays the premiums and is the beneficiary. The business owns the policy. In this case, that business ultimately became Old Timey Fun, Ltd."

"Beacher was insured for twelve million?" Flint asked.

"Yep."

"I don't understand," Brooke said. "Rusty and Alton didn't go into business together. They dissolved their partnership."

"That's true. But Rusty didn't cancel the insurance policy. He—Old Timey Fun, Ltd.—has been faithfully paying those premiums for the last fifteen years."

"Can he do that?"

"He can. It could probably be challenged in court because Alton is not, and has never been, a key figure in Old Timey Fun Ltd.'s operations, but the premiums have been paid and it's possible Rusty or someone in his employ has altered employee records to make it appear like Alton was acting as an advisor or consultant or silent partner."

"But wouldn't Beacher know about this insurance policy?" Flint objected.

"He'd certainly have known when the policy was drawn up. But he'd reasonably assume the policy was canceled when the partnership with Rusty fell through. Rusty might even have told him it *was* canceled."

"Great. How do we prove it?" Brooke asked, looking from Zach to Flint.

Flint grimaced. His gaze met Zach's. "We don't. Do we?"

Zach shook his head. "We have to hand this over to the EDS PD."

Brook's face fell. Flint looked noncommittal. Zach amended, "Or the sheriff's office, I guess." Depending on whose good graces they most wanted to stay in.

Flint studied him for a moment. He said briskly, "EDS PD, it is."

Zach relaxed, just managed not to beam at him, but that was his preference for sure.

Brooke was not taking it nearly as well. "Wait. We're handing *everything* over to the police?"

Though Zach shared her disappointment, he said firmly, "We have to. We've taken this as far as we can. We don't even have a client."

"Well, that sucks."

"I agree," Flint said. "But that's the name of the game. We can't legally withhold evidence from law enforcement. Not if we want to hang onto our PI licenses. Plus, the sheriff's office still considers your brother a viable suspect. We want to take him off the board as soon as possible."

"Oh." Brooke said. She looked thoughtful. "I *suppose* we need him..."

"I appreciate that," Zach said.

Brooke's grin was unrepentant. Flint's, exaggeratedly wolfish as he said, "I'm counting on it—your appreciation, that is."

"Two dicks and a dame is right," Brooke murmured.

"Huh?" Flint threw her a startled glance.

"I'll explain it to you later," said Zach, but he was surprised and maybe even nonplussed at Flint's open flirtation.

For a second or two no one said anything. It was definitely an anticlimactic end to their first case as a partnership. Still, Zach was reasonably confident they were on the right trail, and it was to their advantage to get in good with EDS PD.

Finally, Brooke sighed, seeming to shake off her disappointment. "Okay, well, if that's that, I'm taking off." She turned away, throwing over her shoulder, "You two have fun storming the castle or whatever you get up to. I've got a date."

Zach opened his mouth to ask—but Flint shook his head. Zach grimaced and subsided.

"Let's go make Bill Cameron's day," Flint said.

Two hours later they stood in the parking lot in front of Del Selmo Police Department, beneath the buzzing power lines and flickering parking lot lights.

Flint was saying, "Oh well, it never hurts to keep in with the cops. Cameron's a useful guy to have on our side."

No lie. After they'd handed over everything they had to a very surprised and cautiously optimistic Lt. Bill Cameron, Cameron had gone so far as to bring them up to speed on some of the details of the police investigation, including the prior-to-their-visit imminent arrest of Ransford Beacher, who did indeed figure prominently in his brother's will.

"Realistically, I don't think we had another choice," Zach replied. "We'd be spending a lot of non-billable hours tracking down records and documents the police can get in a fraction of that time. And who knows what would happen within that window?"

"True."

He couldn't help feeling like they were making conversation, because they'd already had this conversation before they'd met with Bill. It was like they were both stalling. Like neither of them were sure where they went from here.

He asked, "What do you think was in Alton's safe?"

Flint said grimly, "I think we both know what was in Alton's safe—and why the very idea of it falling into anyone else's hands was enough to get him in his car and race down that mountainside in the middle of the night."

Cameron had informed them the police had retrieved the contents of Alton's safe. He hadn't revealed what those contents were, but his stony distaste was a pretty good indicator. How the hell many "Galileos" had there been through the years? Zach felt queasy just thinking about it.

"Do you think Alton really was planning to kill Zora?"

"Yeah. I do." In the yellowish haze of the towering parking lot lights, Flint's expression was hard and uncompromising.

"So the threats were all manufactured by Alton?"

Flint pondered, said slowly, "That, I can't say for sure. From what you've described, I think he believed he knew where the threats came from."

"I agree. It's why he wasn't nearly as concerned as he should have been."

"He might have assumed Zora was behind the scary gifts. In which case, he'd figure that threat would soon be neutralized. Even if he suspected the gifts came from Jordan, I don't think he'd take it that seriously."

"No way could Rusty Jordan have crawled beneath that Porsche to tamper with the brake lines. I mean, not only does he have a solid alibi, he's physically not built for sabotage."

"Yeah, Cameron says the alibi is solid." Flint said thoughtfully, "He'd have had to have help with that."

"Zora?"

Flint shrugged. "If so, I don't know that I blame the lady. Especially, if she knew what he was planning."

Zach couldn't agree. "If she thought her husband was planning to kill her, she should have gone to the police."

Flint said peaceably, "We're just speculating. We have no proof. Even if Zora had the know-how, she's probably not dumb enough to do job herself."

"Chico?"

"He's got an awfully convenient alibi."

"It checked out, according to the police."

"Yep."

Zach bit his lip, considering Chico's attitude when he'd confronted him the morning after Alton's death. Chico had been pretty cocky for a bodyguard whose client had been killed on his watch. So maybe Flint was onto something.

Either way, not their problem. Their part in the investigation was, per Bill Cameron, over.

"Anyway," Zach said. A brilliant conversational opening if there ever was one.

At the same time, Flint said, "Speaking of billable hours..."

They both stopped. Zach laughed. It sounded nervous to his own ears—and maybe to Flint's too, because he offered a quizzical smile.

"What are you doing tonight?"

"Not a clue," Zach said.

Flint's smile grew crooked. "No clue at all?"

"Well, I mean... I *hope*—"

The rest of it was smothered in Flint's kiss as Flint closed the distance between them. Flint's mouth was warm, his lips were soft and persuasive, and Zach opened without hesitation to that silent question, losing himself for seconds that felt like lifetimes. It was expected and unexpected all at the same time, and over before Zach had time to fully realize it was happening.

"I hope so too," Flint said. He wasn't smiling. He looked very serious. "In fact, I haven't been this hopeful in a long time."

"Where do we go from here?"

Flint seemed to take him literally. "Your place or mine?"

They ended up at Zach's.

As much as Zach wanted to see where Flint lived, Mr. Bigglesworth would be waiting for his dinner. After the events of the night before, Zach was a little uneasy about what was liable to happen in his absence. He'd been relying on nosy neighbors and the fact that he didn't own much of value, but the previous night's break-in had shattered his sense of security.

As much as Zach wanted to believe his attacker had only been after the Mustang, he couldn't quite convince himself. But it was equally hard to believe someone wanted him dead, had staged the break-in to cover up intended murder.

What possible reason could anyone have for killing him?

Even if they were right about Rusty Jordan arranging for Alton's fatal accident, it hadn't been Rusty who Zach wrestled around with in the garage. Never mind that unshakeable alibi, Rusty was at least three inches shorter than Zach and a whole lot wider.

And what would be the point of going after Zach? Getting rid of Zach wouldn't stop the investigation into Alton's murder.

Rusty could have hired someone, of course. Someone like Chico? Zach didn't think Chico had been his assailant, but he wasn't sure, would not have wanted to swear to it either way.

Anyway, Zach's it was. And they did not waste any time on drinks or dinner or even much conversation. They literally tumbled into Zach's bed, grabbing and groping and fumbling with their clothes, laughing and breathless, like it was their first time—until they reached the serious business of hot velvet naked skin rubbing hot naked velvet skin. They were lost in the sensation of twining legs and hungry, searching hands.

"I've been thinking of this all day," Flint muttered between love bites.

Zach gulped, "Me, too."

His mouth locked onto Flint's nipple and Flint groaned.

His stroking hands were bringing Zach closer and closer to the edge. Zach bucked against Flint, and Flint's muscular thighs clamped around Zach's hips, gripping him in heat and friction, they banged and rocked and finally slid into exquisite rhythm, every stroke and thrust sending jolts of electrifying pleasure across seemingly raw nerve-endings, almost too good to bear.

Orgasm rolled up and crashed over them in a relentless, sweeping tide of sticky, salty, sweet release. First Zach, then Flint with a half-laugh/half-shout. Or maybe Flint and then Zach? Too close to call. Not a competition. Teamwork. Both of them taking home the prize.

Flint was still laughing as Zach collapsed in his arms. It was the nicest, happiest sound in the world. It made Zach smile, lightened his heart. He couldn't remember ever feeling that relaxed, that content. But wrapped in Flint's muscular arms, it felt like there was a very real possibility of happiness becoming a regular thing.

Flint kissed his ear, said, "That was even better than last night."

Zach gave a little laugh, but yeah. Last night had been sweet and surprising. Tonight was a revelation.

He couldn't help asking, "What's Detective Schneider going to say about this?"

He felt rather than saw Flint's grimace. "I'm not sure there's anything he hasn't already said."

Zach considered that. Considered the implications for himself. He would be smart not to get too used to this.

Flint seemed to read his mind. "There have been a lot of Schneiders over the years. I've always been honest with people I'm with, and I'll be honest with you, too. I didn't suggest we go into business together because I see you as a one-night stand."

"It's two nights now."

"I'm serious."

Zach had dropped his glasses early in the proceedings, so Flint's face was a pale and unsmiling blur. He blinked up and Flint's mouth covered his. Flint whispered, "I'm serious about you, Zachariah. Serious about giving this a chance."

"You don't really know me."

"Sometimes you know without knowing."

When Flint said it, it didn't sound like a line. It felt like the truth. Maybe because it was how Zach felt, too. He felt like he'd come to know Flint better in the past week than he'd known Ben in all the years they were together.

"I'd like—"

His cell phone rang.

Flint's groan was comically heartfelt, but Zach didn't laugh. His heart stopped. He used that "circuit" ringtone for one person and only one person: Alton.

He bolted upright, leaning over the bed and grabbing his jeans off the floor. He groped through his pockets until he found his phone. He showed the screen to Flint.

"What am I looking at?" Flint sounded puzzled.

Zach snatched his phone back and pressed Accept. "Hello? Who's speaking?"

"Mr. Davies? Is that you?"

Not Alton. But still confusing. The voice was strange. High and sing-songy. Female? Zora?

"This is Zach."

"It's me. Zora Kaschak. I'm in terrible, terrible trouble. Chico Martinez tried to kidnap me!"

"What?"

"What's going on?" Flint demanded.

Zach shook his head. "Where are you?"

The voice said breathily, "I managed to get away. But he's looking for me. I think he's going to kill me. He's going to try to make it look like I killed Alton and then killed myself."

Flint said, "What the hell's going on?"

Zach ignored him. "Where are you? Do you know?"

"I'm at Haunted Hollow."

"Where?"

"Haunted Hollow."

Where the—?

His brain finally kicked in. "The theme park?"

"Yes! Yes! He tried to drag me to the top of Mount Doom. He was going to throw me off. But I got away. I'm hiding in Malice Mansion." Her voice dropped even lower. "But he's looking for me. He's going to find me. I know he is. It's only a matter of time."

"Okay. I—"

"Help me," Zora wailed. "Oh, help me, Mr. Davies!"

She disconnected.

Flint was already out of bed and getting dressed.

Zach, in the process of phoning Bill Cameron, stared at him. "It's a trap, Flint. It has to be."

"Of course, it's a trap." Flint dragged his shirt on. "Are you phoning Cameron?"

"Yes."

"Good." Flint buckled his belt. "You wait for Cameron outside the park. I'll—"

"You'll what?" Zach snatched up his glasses, scrambled off the mattress. "What are you doing?"

"A little bit of recon."

"It's a trap!"

"It's not a trap when you know it's a trap." Flint was already through the doorway.

"What are you *talking* about?" Zach, half-hopping as he dragged his jeans on, followed. "Flint, this is for the police to handle."

"We're ten minutes away. That's about seven minutes closer than EDS PD. Let's suppose it *isn't* a trap and Zora really is fighting for her life."

"Suppose she's *not*."

Flint shrugged into his brown leather jacket. "Are you really willing to take that chance?" His eyes were dark and serious. He thought that was a rhetorical question.

"Wait." Zach immediately disconnected, speed-scrolled for Alton's contact info, and pressed the number for the Kaschak estate. *"Wait."* He grabbed Flint's arm as he listened to the ring.

Flint halted, waited. He was practically vibrating with impatience.

After two rings, the phone picked up. A woman's soothing voice came on the line. "Beacher residence."

Zach blurted, "This is Zach Davies. May I speak to Mrs. Kaschak-Beacher? It's urgent."

"Mrs. Beacher isn't here at the moment."

Zach protested, "She *has* to be!"

The housekeeper sounded surprised. "I'm sorry. She's out for a drive. I'm sure she'll be home soon, if you'd like to leave your number."

"Is Chico Martinez driving her?"

Sounding increasingly leery of the nut on the other end of the line, Mrs. Honeybun replied, "Mr. Martinez is driving Mrs. Beacher, yes. May I ask what this is in regard to?"

"I don't believe this," Zach said to Flint.

"Hello?" Mrs. Honeybun's faraway voice called. "Hello? Mr. Davies?"

"Hang up and call EDS PD." Flint shook off Zach's hand and strode toward the front door. "I'll see you over there."

"*Flint.* Can you just…" Zach ended the call and redialed the police department. The phone began to ring.

"Zach."

Distractedly, Zach looked up to meet Flint's level gaze.

"Wait for the cops. Do *not* enter that park on your own."

"That goes for you too, Flint. You're not in the Marines now."

Flint was unmoved. "You heard me. Wait for the cops."

The door closed quietly behind him.

CHAPTER TWENTY-FIVE

The October moon seemed frozen in place.

Much like Zach.

He turned up his jacket collar and tried to warm his hands in his pockets. He was parked next to Flint's SUV, in the middle of the empty car park, still waiting for the police. He'd been waiting for what felt like hours, though he'd only arrived five minutes earlier.

Ahead of him, the area of the amusement park was a black mass of silence, a paper cut-out of mysterious angles and curves silhouetted against a giant white honeycomb moon. Moonlight revealed rutted, fallow fields and leafless apple orchards stretching on either side of Haunted Hollow. A single lonely lamp illuminated the vacant parking area and Flint's abandoned vehicle. A distant string of street lights pinpointed the motionless highway beyond.

Were the police coming?

Lt. Bill Cameron had already left for the night when Zach phoned the Ensenada del Sello police station, but had not yet reached home. So, strike two. Zach had tried explaining current events to the sergeant on duty, but he wasn't convinced he'd managed to convey the urgency of the situation. The sergeant seemed inclined to think someone was pulling Zach's leg.

There had been a time, not so long ago, when Zach would also have assumed he was being pranked.

Still, the sergeant had promised to send a patrol car to check out the situation, which was better than nothing.

Zach resisted the temptation to phone Bill Cameron again. Mrs. Cameron had taken his message, and she was not the kind of police officer's wife to forget to deliver an urgent request for help.

Five more minutes, he told himself.

It was already twenty past nine. Five more minutes, and Zach was going in after Flint. He couldn't leave Flint to deal with whatever this was on his own.

None of this made sense though. Off season or not, Haunted Hollow had to be protected by all kinds of security personnel and equipment. There would be sensors, cameras, half-trained college students with guns. Flint could very well be sitting in a security guard's office, trying to explain his way out of being arrested for trespassing, at that very moment.

Or not.

Besides, if Chico really was trying to get rid of Zora, there were easier ways to do it.

What would his motive be?

Unless Chico was working for Rusty and Rusty had decided they needed a patsy?

If Chico had Zora, well, Zora certainly had the authority and knowledge to bypass the park's security systems.

The same was true if Zora was behind this. Zach couldn't say for sure it *hadn't* been Zora on the phone. He didn't think so, but...

He spent the last five minutes alternating between staring into his rearview mirror at the deserted highway behind him and refreshing his phone screen. He was hoping against hope the cops would arrive before he had to do something he was almost certainly going to regret.

The night remained stubbornly silent and still.

At last, the white numerals of his cell clicked onto 9:25.

Zach sucked in a harsh breath. "Okay, that's it."

He picked the up the Glock 43, which he'd only ever fired on the shooting range, from the passenger seat, shoved it into his waistband, and got out of the car. His heart was thumping unpleasantly and his legs felt a little wobbly. It was aggravating, but no use pretending he wasn't afraid. Frankly, he was scared shitless. But he was even more scared for Flint.

His breath misted in the damp autumn night. It was so damned quiet out here. The sound of his careful closing of the car door sounded like a shot.

Was that all-encompassing hush a good sign or not? Certainly, the absence of shots or screaming had to be a positive.

He loped across the car park to the enormous iron entrance gates. The words *Haunted Hollow* were spelled out in wobbly, whimsical letters.

The gates were locked. No surprise there. But the ten-foot forbidding fence consisted of solid iron bars, rather than netting, so Zach was able to scale it with relative ease. He landed on the ground on the other side, trying to ignore the throbbing in his injured knee, and limped awkwardly on.

Almost at once he came upon a small security kiosk, closed and shuttered.

Okay. But there still had to be some kind of security presence on the grounds. Right? A central office somewhere? He gazed up at the black screen of an overhead camera. At the very least, wouldn't someone be monitoring the cameras?

If so, would that someone be friend or foe?

He'd thought to upload the visitor's map for Haunted Hollow, and he took a moment to double-check his location. His first and only visit to the theme park had been years earlier and a lot had changed. Malice Mansion was supposed to be dead center in the middle of the park, right between the Ferris wheel and Doom Mountain.

This is a really bad idea. This is such a terrible idea.

The jaunty refrain kept time with the pound of his feet as he jogged down the cobbled streets, watching for security cameras, sticking to the shadows as much as possible.

Maybe the phone call *was* a prank. Because as far as Zach could tell, he was the only person in the entire amusement park.

But no, Flint was here somewhere.

Now that he was moving, Zach felt a little less shaky, a little more focused. He was still fearful, but waiting and wondering had been worse.

In two weeks, on Halloween night, the park would open for twenty-four hours before completely closing down for the rest of the season. But tonight, it was a ghost town. Sheeted figures and grinning skeletons were posed along the way, peeking out of doorways or around corners. Zach cut down a narrow alley and came out on a grassy village square designed to accommodate an enormous pumpkin merry-go-round with skeleton horses.

From where he stood, he could see the tippy top of the pointed roofs of Malice Mansion behind the rows of crooked, thatched roof shops and cafés lining Goblin Street. He ducked down another alley and came out a bit to the west of the two-story building with its purple fish scale-shingled roof and arched windows.

For a minute or two he waited beside a life-sized—presumably life-sized—plastic goblin, trying to catch his breath and sizing up the situation.

A massive pair of fiberglass troll sculptures guarded the closed and barred entrance to the mansion. Clearly, no one had entered the building that way.

Had anyone entered the building at all? Because, as far as Zach could tell, it was completely dark and utterly silent.

Should he try phoning Flint?

But if he called Flint, was he liable to reveal Flint's location to whoever had lured them here? Zach had put his phone on vibrate, and he assumed Flint had done the same, but was that a chance he wanted to take?

Where the hell were cops?

Zach gnawed his lip and tried to decide what to do.

Malice Mansion was the site of whatever was supposed to happen, so he needed to get inside that building. The caller's assumption would probably be that he'd try to sneak in through the back. Right?

Instead, Zach would try to get in through the side as close to the front entrance as he could manage.

He nerved himself for the sprint across the cobblestone lane, and took off, rubber soles soundless on the cobblestones, landing without incident in a small hedge of what turned out to be real and very prickly bushes. Above the hedge was a row of hollow windows covered by plastic that was painted to look like dusty glass and cobwebs.

He waited, heart pounding, for signs he'd been spotted.

The only sounds were dead leaves scraping along the pavement, the creaking of signs in the night breeze.

Zach crept quietly along the building and quickly realized that the structure wasn't actually two-stories. In fact, behind the façade of pointed rooftops was a long utilitarian building with a flat roof. That simplified the situation.

Or did it just make it more dangerous?

He used his penknife to slit the "glass" of one of the fake windows, climbed onto the sill, and leaned his full weight against the plastic and fiber webbing until it gave and he half-fell, half-jumped into near-total darkness.

Zach picked himself up, righted the pistol in his waistband. As his eyes adjusted, he could make out the sickly glimmer of scattered emergency lights and the outline of tracks and electrical equipment. It felt like he was standing in a large warehouse. The air was cold and quiet and smelled strongly of plastic, wood, and dust. In fact, it was so quiet, he felt sure he could have heard a spider spinning its web.

Cautiously, Zach picked his way through an obstacle course of gears and shafts, passing the blinking lights of metal boxes storing electronic equipment and a long row of still and silent animatron skeleton horses harnessed to a small train of half-shell pumpkin carriages.

At last, Zach came to a wide doorway and pushed through strands of fake cobweb. He found himself in a long dining room with artistically curling wallpaper and still more cobwebs hanging from an ornate chandelier. Rubber tarantulas and mechanical red-eyed rats were frozen motionless on the dining table and velvet-upholstered chairs. Fake flames, surrounding a grinning demon face, filled the faux fireplace at the end of the room.

He stepped forward and, disconcertingly, the floor beneath his tennis shoes seemed to turn soft and mushy, as though he were sinking into quicksand. The pallid glow of the emergency lights was reflected time after time in the row of mirrors that alternated with the creepy portraits lining the wall. As Zach crept past the mirrors, he could see flashes of himself, stretched to an unnatural length one moment, as wide as a sumo wrestler the next.

His footsteps slowed. He came to a stop in the middle of the narrow room.

Where the hell was he going? What the hell was he doing? Where was Flint? Where were the cops?

Had he made a serious miscalculation by coming—

Bang! Bang! Bang!

The eerie atmosphere was shattered by the sound of gunshots fired in quick succession. One. Two. Three. Instinctively, Zach dropped to the floor and realized the carpet was actually covering what felt like a thick layer of bean bags.

He listened tensely.

Those shots had come from outside the building.

But even as he made that determination, another gunshot followed—someone returning fire—and that shot seemed to echo inside the mansion.

"Fuck." One of those shooters was almost certainly Flint. But which one?

Heart in mouth, Zach began to traverse the length of sinking floor, commando style. He had no idea what he was going to do—he wasn't even clear where he was going—he just knew he had to get to Flint as quickly as possible.

The shots stopped as abruptly as they'd begun.

Zach was afraid to consider what that might mean.

He made it across the dining room, threw a quick, cautious look around the doorway, and dived into the next room. His thought was to get back to the outermost hall of the mansion which should, in theory, give him straight access to the main exits, but that was liable to place him directly in the path of whoever had set this trap.

He scrambled to the relative safety of the nearest corner, drew his pistol, and wondered if he'd be able to hit anything, the way his hands were shaking.

What was so wrong with being an accountant, anyway?

A loud click-and-switch sound came from overhead, and every light inside the structure flared into dazzling life. Zach was left blinking and bewildered as all around him the attractions came alive.

A witch's shrieking cackle rippled through the speakers high above, bouncing off the papier-mâché beams and boulders of the mansion's secret passage. A deafening and disorienting cacophony of sound followed: booming ghostly laughter, demonic wailing, a loud and disembodied owl's *'Who? Who?'* And underneath it all tinkled the discordant melody of a broken music box.

"Welcome to the Malice Mansion. We hope you have a terrible stay!" cried a mechanical voice from the rafters. Manic chortles followed.

Zach flattened himself against the wall as the skeleton horses and pumpkin carriages pushed through the floating cobwebs and rolled slowly toward him.

The first three cars had passed when an idea occurred. Zach vaulted into the nearest carriage, crouching down in the well and peering over the sill of the carriage door. His view from inside the carriage was surprisingly different; the ticket-holder's perspective was designed to conceal the illusion-destroying rails and ropes, nuts and bolts of what amounted to an elaborate wagon ride across an elaborately decorated stage.

As the skeleton horses rounded the corner into another shadowy tunnel, Zach spotted movement ahead. He peered through the gloom. His scalp prickled as realized the figure in front of him was human, not mechanical.

In fact, he was looking at two figures.

Both human.

One was straight out of Zach's waking nightmare from the evening before: tall and scarecrow-thin, dressed in a shiny black raincoat. He—it—had long, flowing blonde hair—and no face. The faceless one was struggling to drag the other, inert, figure onto the tracks.

Even before he recognized the fallen man's leather jacket and jeans, before he saw his face in the red glow of the skeleton horses' eyes, Zach knew who the victim had to be.

Horror gave way to desperation. If Flint wasn't already dead, he soon would be.

Zach jumped up, aiming his pistol. "*Stop!*" he shouted.

He definitely had the advantage of surprise. The faceless figure dropped Flint and looked around wildly, as if expecting to see one of the animatronics come to life. But the shock didn't last long. Spotting Zach, the figure snatched their own weapon from beneath the raincoat.

Zach gasped. He fired.

And missed.

CHAPTER TWENTY-SIX

Fuck.

Zach ducked down as the other opened fire. The bullets sang overhead and *thunked* into the walls of the metal cars.

Almost instantly, Zach lost count of how many bullets had been fired. Too many, for damned sure. If he stayed where he was, he was going to pass right in front of this maniac, and the other could just reach over the side of the pumpkin car and shoot him point-blank.

Of course, Zach could return the favor, and they could both go out in a blaze of Hong Kong cinematic glory. He'd prefer to survive the night, though.

Scooting to the other side of the car, Zach sidled up and spilled over, landing mere inches from the track and the remorseless grind of the car wheels. He'd lost his glasses when he'd slipped out of the car, but his frantic groping was rewarded. His fingers closed on the frames; he pushed his glasses on.

The other person was still firing round after round at the pumpkin carriage. From where Zach landed, he could see the shooter's legs as he paced back and forth, trying to see where Zach was hiding.

Zach steadied his pistol with both hands, aimed—then had to wait for the nearest set of wheels to pass—and fired.

A man's scream of pain and outrage seemed to coincide with that deafening *bang*. The man in the raincoat crumpled to the ground, still firing wildly. A ricochet pinged off the side of a carriage, whined overhead.

Zach prayed silently.

The shooter's pistol began clicking harmlessly on an empty chamber. But did he have Flint's weapon?

"You shattered my shin, you mother fucking little cock sucker…"

From beneath the carriage, Zach could see the man trying to crawl away. He made it a foot or two, but gave it up, moaning. He began to swear. "I'm going to kill you, you little bastard!"

Zach waited, panting, sick and shaking with adrenaline, until the last of the line of pumpkin shell cars trundled past. He pushed up, and saw to his abject relief that Flint was not dead.

In fact, Flint was not only conscious, he was on his feet.

Zach launched himself across the tracks, closing the distance between them, landing in Flint's arms, which closed tightly around him.

"Jesus Christ. Flint…"

Flint gulped, "You okay?" Gory rivulets of blood streamed down his face. He seemed to be clutching Zach as much for support as offering comfort.

"Did he shoot you?"

Flint raised one hand, wincing as he touched his head. "That asshole couldn't hit the side of a barn. One of his ricochets knocked a wall torch loose and *that* hit me."

"A *wall torch* hit you?"

"I don't want to talk about it. Are *you* okay?"

Flint's heart was banging like a locomotive against Zach's. He was bruised, bloody, but alive, and Zach had never seen anything more wonderful.

"Great. Never better."

Flint snorted, rested his face against Zach's. "I told you to wait for the cops. Didn't I tell you to wait?"

Zach said shakily, "I couldn't leave you to face all those flying wall torches alone."

Flint gave a husky laugh, raised his head and then scowled, pushing Zach aside to go after the man in the raincoat, who was trying to crawl across the tracks to where Zach had dropped his weapon.

The man raised an arm in defense. Flint knocked his arm aside, grabbed him by the front of the raincoat and pulled him upright. The fuzzy wig fell off. The man screamed in pain. "My leg! You crazy bastard. I'm *shot*!"

"If you don't want to be shot again, talk. Where's Zora?"

The man shook his head.

Flint bit out, "Last chance. Where. Is. Zora?"

"She's not here! That was me on the phone."

"And who the fuck are you?"

"R-Roger Simmons."

Who the hell was Roger Simmons?

"Why were you trying to kill us?"

"I don't even know who you are." Simmons pointed at Zach. "I was trying to take *him* out!"

"Why?"

"Do I even know you?" Zach protested.

Flint reached down and dragged off the sheer gray stocking Simmons wore over his head. The weirdly smooshed features rearranged themselves into a completely unfamiliar face.

"*Do* you know him?" Flint demanded.

Zach stared.

Simmons scowled back at him.

Zach slowly shook his head, but then a small but key piece of memory clicked into place.

"Wait a sec. Yes. I do. You're the head of security for Old Timey Fun, Ltd!"

"I'm not saying another word," Simmons said quickly. "I want a lawyer."

"No? Sure about that?" Flint gave Simmons another of those teeth-rattling shakes. Simmons cried out in pain. And, despite the fact that he'd been willing to shoot the guy a few minutes earlier, Zach couldn't help a wince of sympathy.

Flint demanded, "Why were you trying to kill Davies?"

The man moaned. "I'm *dying* here, you bastard."

"Not from that little hole in your leg."

"The asshole blew half my fucking leg off!"

"*Talk.*"

Simmons babbled, "Once the cops got suspicious about Beacher's accident, Mr. Jordan knew he'd eventually come under suspicion. He came up with the idea to make it look like one of Beacher's kinky playmates murdered him out of jealousy. But to make that idea stick, we figured your friend had to be attacked, too. That way it would look like some crazy queer was after both of them."

"There never was any Galileo." Zach had suspected as much. Not that it mattered. There had been plenty of other Galileos.

"Nah. Mr. Jordan came up with that on the spur of the moment." Simmons sounded a little proud of Rusty's initiative.

Flint was not impressed. "How do you dumbasses not know the police are already onto your boss?"

"That's why he panicked." Simmons nodded at Zach. "After *he* showed up asking questions, Mr. Jordan knew we had to commence phase two. He figured if Davies was dead, the police would *have* to take the idea of a jealous boyfriend seriously. We knew it had to happen tonight before they dragged him in for questioning tomor—" He broke off, listening.

Zach heard it, too.

The entire structure seemed to shake beneath that heavy, rhythmic pound.

A police battering ram?

Flint met his gaze, said calmly, "That's our cue."

Simmons began to shout, "Help! Help! Police!"

"Attention! Inside the building!" Bill Cameron's voice, magnified by a bullhorn, reached them. "Come out with your hands up!"

As abruptly as it had come to life, Malice Mansion went dark. The animatronics stopped mid-antic. The music and sound effects died. The lights blinked off.

Outside the building, Lt. Cameron was still exhorting them to exit the building with their hands locked behind their heads.

"Help!" Simmons yelled. "He—*oww*."

"Sorry," Flint's shadow spoke solicitously. "Let me help you."

"Stay away from me!" Simmons stumbled forward as flashes of blue and red light sliced through the cracks as the doorway in the grand entrance hall noisily gave way.

"Zach?"

"Right here."

Flint's arm wrapped warmly around his shoulders. Zach's arm circled Flint's waist, offering support.

"Ready or not," Flint muttered. "Here we come."

"Next time, wait for the police," Lt. Bill Cameron said. Again.

It was his parting shot before departing to arrest Ronald "Rusty" Jordan.

Flint, his head bandaged and his knuckles taped, was sitting on a wrought iron bench outside Malice Mansion. "See," he said to Zach. "I told you to wait for the police."

"He meant you." Zach, standing beside the bench, was watching EDS PD pack up their gear and load everything into their vehicles. Roger Simmons had been carted off in an ambulance nearly two hours earlier, but Flint's injuries were determined to be superficial, and he and Zach had been explaining and re-explaining their actions for what felt like most of the night.

"Nah."

Cameron, apparently still within earshot, called back, "I meant *you*, Carey."

Zach laughed.

"I'm winning him over," Flint said. "He just doesn't know it yet."

"Sure you are." Zach offered his hand to Flint. "I don't want to get locked in here, so if you've had enough fun for one night, maybe we should go."

Flint sighed. "Yeah, I guess so." He gripped Zach's hand, rose, and pulled Zach into his arms for a quick but thorough kiss.

Zach closed his eyes, leaning into Flint's embrace, and kissed him back.

When they finally drew apart, they were getting some funny looks from the remaining police officers.

"They're just jealous," Flint assured Zach, and Zach smiled.

Life would not be boring with Flint. That was for sure. Flint would make him laugh. He'd probably also make Zach want to strangle him. Maybe every day wouldn't be an actual adventure, but he was pretty sure they would never run out of things to talk about.

The night was fading to carnival shades of pink and blue, the sun cautiously poking its head over the horizon as they made their way down the cobblestone streets toward the main gate.

"What day is it?" Flint said suddenly. "Tell me it's Friday."

"Wednesday."

Flint laughed, but wasn't kidding when he said, "The publicity from this case isn't going to do us any harm. I'd be surprised if we didn't get some business from it."

"I hope so."

Flint threw him a quick look. "You okay?"

"Just tired."

He was surprised when Flint reached out, bringing him to a stop.

"Zach?"

"Hm?"

"You were great last night. I mean that. Your dad would be proud of you—even more proud than he already was." Flint's gaze was serious. His words sincere.

Zach's face warmed. "Thanks."

"I mean it. You saved my ass last night."

Zach cleared his throat. "It's a nice ass."

Flint blinked, then grinned. "Thanks." He looped his arm around Zach's shoulders, drew him in for a quick kiss on his temple. "Do you think I'm going to be able to win over that snooty cat of yours?"

Zach considered. "Maybe. How hard are you willing to work at it?"

"I'm willing to do whatever it takes."

Zach said gravely, "Then I'm betting you'll be successful."

Flint said, "And am I going to be able to win you over?"

Zach's said slowly, "How hard are you willing to work at it?"

Flint said softly, "Whatever it takes, Zachariah."

Zach leaned in for Flint's kiss. He whispered, "I think you know the answer to that one."

AUTHOR'S NOTE

Dear Reader,

Puzzle for Two was originally written for my Patreon subscribers.

What is Patreon?

Patreon is a membership platform that connects content creators with fans and supporters. Crucially, it offers financial tools that let supporters subscribe to projects that give creators a predictable income stream as they continue to create content.

The life and fortunes of a freelance artist is a precarious one. There is no paid leave, no company paid health coverage, no investment savings, no retirement plan. There is no "fixed income." There is nothing but what the artist can earn in any given month. Depending on both the life of the artist and whatever is happening in the publishing world, some months are great. Some months are disastrous. For me, Patreon is a safety net. Patreon is a little bit of semi-steady income each month. Sometimes that income gets rolled right back into making cool, often exclusive stuff for Patreon: audio, art, etc. Sometimes it's the difference between paying all my bills that month.

Whether you subscribe for a month or a year, every single contribution makes a difference to the life and work of an artist.

I am forever grateful to each and every one of my patrons.

ABOUT THE AUTHOR

Author of 100+ titles of Gay Mystery and M/M Romance, Josh Lanyon has built a literary legacy on twisty mystery, kickass adventure, and unapologetic man-on-man romance.

Her work has been translated into twelve languages. The FBI thriller *Fair Game* was the first Male/Male title to be published by Italy's Harlequin Mondadori and *Stranger on the Shore* (Harper Collins Italia) was the first M/M title to be published in print. In 2016 *Fatal Shadows* placed #5 in Japan's annual Boy Love novel list (the first and only title by a foreign author to place on the list). The Adrien English series was awarded the All-Time Favorite Couple by the Goodreads M/M Romance Group. In 2019, *Fatal Shadows* became the first LGBTQ mobile game created by *Moments: Choose Your Story*.

Josh is an EPIC Award winner, a four-time Lambda Literary Award finalist (twice for Gay Mystery), an Edgar nominee, and the first ever recipient of the Goodreads All Time Favorite M/M Author award.

Josh is married and lives in Southern California with her irascible husband, two adorable dogs, a small garden, and an ever-expanding library of vintage mystery destined to eventually crush them all beneath its weight.

Find other Josh Lanyon titles at www.joshlanyon.com

Follow Josh on Twitter, Facebook, Goodreads, Instagram and Tumblr.

ALSO BY JOSH LANYON

NOVELS

The ADRIEN ENGLISH Mysteries
*Fatal Shadows • A Dangerous Thing • The Hell You Say
Death of a Pirate King • The Dark Tide
Stranger Things Have Happened • So This is Christmas •*

The HOLMES & MORIARITY Mysteries
*Somebody Killed His Editor • All She Wrote
The Boy with the Painful Tattoo • In Other Words...Murder
The 12.2-Per Cent Solution*

The ALL'S FAIR Series
Fair Game • Fair Play • Fair Chance

The ART OF MURDER Series
*The Mermaid Murders •The Monet Murders
The Magician Murders • The Monuments Men Murders
The Movie-Town Murders*

BEDKNOBS AND BROOMSTICKS
*Mainly by Moonlight • I Buried a Witch
Bell, Book and Scandal*

The SECRETS AND SCRABBLE Series
*Murder at Pirate's Cove • Secret at Skull House
Mystery at the Masquerade • Scandal at the Salty Dog
Body at Buccaneer's Bay • Lament at Loon Landing
Death at the Deep Dive • Corpse at the Captain's Seat*

OTHER NOVELS

*This Rough Magic • The Ghost Wore Yellow Socks
Mexican Heat (with Laura Baumbach) • Strange Fortune
Come Unto These Yellow Sands • Stranger on the Shore
Winter Kill • Jefferson Blythe, Esquire
Murder in Pastel • The Curse of the Blue Scarab
The Ghost Had an Early Check-out
Murder Takes the High Road • Séance on a Summer's Night
Hide and Seek • Puzzle for Two*

NOVELLAS

The DANGEROUS GROUND Series
*Dangerous Ground • Old Poison • Blood Heat
Dead Run • Kick Start • Blind Side*

OTHER NOVELLAS

*Cards on the Table • The Dark Farewell • The Dark Horse
The Darkling Thrush • The Dickens with Love
I Spy Something Bloody • I Spy Something Wicked
I Spy Something Christmas • In a Dark Wood
The Parting Glass • Snowball in Hell • Mummy Dearest
Don't Look Back • A Ghost of a Chance
Lovers and Other Strangers • Out of the Blue
A Vintage Affair • Lone Star (in Men Under the Mistletoe)
Green Glass Beads (in Irregulars) • Blood Red Butterfly
Everything I Know • Baby, It's Cold (in Comfort and Joy)
A Case of Christmas • Murder Between the Pages
Slay Ride • Stranger in the House • 44.1644° North*

SHORT STORIES

A Limited Engagement • The French Have a Word for It
In Sunshine or In Shadow • Until We Meet Once More
Icecapade (in His for the Holidays) • Perfect Day
Heart Trouble • Other People's Weddings (Petit Mort)
Slings and Arrows (Petit Mort)
Sort of Stranger Than Fiction (Petit Mort)
Critic's Choice (Petit Mort) • Just Desserts (Petit Mort)
In Plain Sight • Wedding Favors • Wizard's Moon
Fade to Black • Night Watch • Plenty of Fish
Halloween is Murder • The Boy Next Door
Requiem for Mr. Busybody

COLLECTIONS

Short Stories (Vol. 1)
Sweet Spot (the Petit Morts)
Merry Christmas, Darling (Holiday Codas)
Christmas Waltz (Holiday Codas 2)
I Spy...Three Novellas
Dangerous Ground The Complete Series
Dark Horse, White Knight (Two Novellas)
The Adrien English Mysteries Box Set
The Adrien English Mysteries Box Set 2
Male/Male Mystery & Suspense Box Set
Partners in Crime (Three Classic Gay Mystery Novels)
All's Fair Complete Collection
Shadows Left Behind

SPECIAL EDITIONS

Fatal Shadows: The Collector's Edition

Printed in Great Britain
by Amazon